GONE

JAMES PATTERSON

& MICHAEL LEDWIDGE

Random House Group Limited supports the Forest Stewardship Council® (FSC®), the leading international forest-certification organisation. Our books carrying the FSC label are printed on FSC®-certified paper. FSC is the only forest-certification scheme supported by the leading environmental organisations, including Greenpeace. Our paper procurement policy can be found at www.randomhouse.co.uk/environment

arrow books

Typeset by SX Composing DTP, Rayleigh, Essex
Printed and bound by CPI Group (UK) Ltd, Croydon, CR0 4YY

Published by Arrow Books in 2014

5 7 9 10 8 6 4

First published in Great Britain in 2013 by Century

Arrow Books
Random House, 20 Vauxhall Bridge Road,
London SW1V 2SA

www.randomhouse.co.uk

Addresses for companies within The Random House Group Limited can be
found at: www.randomhouse.co.uk/offices.htm

The Random House Group Limited Reg. No. 954009

A CIP catalogue record for this book
is available from the British Library

ISBN 9780099574026
ISBN 9780099574033 (export edition)

The R
Co
org
FSC
sup
G

Prir

Prologue

FATHER AND SON

One

IT WAS THREE A.M. on the button when the unmarked white box truck turned onto the steep slope of Sweetwater Mesa Road and began to climb up into the exclusive Serra Retreat neighborhood of Malibu, California.

Majestic mountain peaks rising to the left, thought Vida Gomez as she looked out from the truck's passenger seat. *Nothing but moonlit ocean to the right.* No wonder so many movie stars lived here.

As if the sights matter, Vida thought, tearing her eyes off the million-dollar view and putting them back on the screen of the iPhone in her lap. What was up with her? She never got distracted on a job. She took a calming breath. She seriously needed to buckle down. Taking her eye off the ball here would not be prudent. Not tonight.

She was in the midst of typing a text when out of the corner of her eye she noticed the driver trying to look down her shirt again. No wonder she was a little off her game, she thought with a muffled sigh. The new, pudgy driver that the cartel had sent at the last minute was incompetence walking on two legs. That was just like them to send her some fat-assed chump for "training" at the last minute. All he had to do was drive, and apparently, he couldn't get even that done.

The next time the oaf let his eyes wander, Vida made a command leadership decision. She calmly lifted the MGP-84 machine pistol in her lap and placed the long, suppressed barrel to one of his stubbled chins.

"Do you think we're on a hot date here tonight? On the way to the prom, maybe? By all means, give me your best line, Romeo. If it's good enough, maybe we'll skip first and go straight to second base," she said.

"I'm sorry," the suddenly sweating driver said after a long, tense beat. "I made a mistake."

"No, that was your parents," Vida said, digging the gun in hard under his fleshy chin. "Now, here's the deal. You can either (a) keep your eyes on the road, or (b) I can splatter what little brains you possess all over it instead. Which do you prefer?"

"*A*," the driver said, nodding rapidly after a moment. "I choose *a*. Please, señorita."

"Excellent," Vida said, finally lowering the chunky black metal pistol. "I'm so glad we had this little talk."

The truck killed its lights before they pulled into the darkened driveway of 223 Sweetwater Mesa Road ten minutes later. She was about to retext the alarm company tech they'd bribed when he finally texted back. It was a one-word message, but it was enough.

Disabled, it said.

She wheeled around and slid open the small window that separated the rear of the truck from the cab. The eight cartel soldiers crouched there were wearing black balaclavas over their faces, black fatigues, black combat boots.

"*Ándele*," she barked rabidly at them. "It's time. What are you waiting for?"

The truck's rear double doors opened silently, and the black-clad men issued forth onto the shadowed driveway and began gearing up. They strapped themselves into military-grade personal protective equipment, black nuclear-biological-chemical suits. Each suit had a self-contained breathing apparatus and was made of rubber over reinforced nylon and charcoal-impregnated felt.

Vida joined her men, slowly and carefully fitting the positive-pressure mask over her face before meticulously checking the suit's material for any slits or gaps, as per her extensive training. When she was done, she bit her lip as she stared up at the seven-thousand-square-foot mission-style house behind the wrought iron gate. She let out a tense breath and closed her eyes, wondering if she was going to throw up the flock of butterflies swirling in her stomach.

She felt stage fright every time right before a job, but this was ridiculous. It was the uncertainty of what they were about to try. What they were about to do was . . . something new, something so volatile, so incredibly dangerous.

I really don't want to do this, Vida thought for the hundredth time.

Who was she kidding? As if she had a choice after accepting her latest promotion. The path before her was excessively simple. Either go through with what the cartel had ordered or blow her own brains out right here and now.

She stared at the machine pistol in her heavy rubber-gloved hand, weighing her options. Then, after another moment, she did what she always did. She pulled herself the hell together and nodded to her right-hand man, Estefan. Two muffled coughing sounds ripped the warm quiet as he blew off the hinge bolts of the iron walkway gate beside the driveway with a suppressed shotgun.

"Remember, now. No guns unless completely necessary," Vida said through the face mask's built-in microphone as one of the men handed her a small video camera. "You all know why we are here. We are here to leave a message."

One by one, the men nodded. The only sound now was that of their breathing from the interior speakers, an amplified metallic, metronomic hiss. Vida turned on the camera and pointed it at the men as they poured through the open gate and converged on the darkened house.

Two

THREE THOUSAND MILES EAST of balmy Serra Retreat, it was cold and raining along the still-dark shore of southwestern Connecticut. Downstairs, in his basement workout room, Michael Licata, recently appointed don of the Bonanno crime family, was covered in sweat and grunting like a Eurotrash tennis pro as he did his Tuesday kettlebell workout.

As he felt the burn, Licata thought it was sort of ironic that out of all the rooms in his new, $8.8 million mansion on the water in moneyed Westport, Connecticut, he liked this unfinished basement the best. The exposed studs, the sweat stains on the cement, his weights and beat-up heavy bag. Pushing himself to the limit every morning in this unheated, raw room was his way of never forgetting who he was and always would be: the hardest, most ruthless son of a bitch who had ever clawed his way up from the gutter of Sheepshead Bay, Brooklyn.

The short and stocky fifty-year-old dropped the forty-pound kettle bell to the concrete floor with a loud crack as he heard the intercom buzz on the basement phone. It was his wife, he knew from bitter experience. Not even six-thirty a.m. and already she was on his case, wanting some bullshit or other, probably for him to pick up their perpetually late housekeeper, Rita, from the train station again.

And he'd imagined that by working from home instead of from his Arthur Avenue social club in the Bronx, he could get more done. *Screw her,* he thought, lifting the bell back up. The man of the house wasn't taking calls at the moment. He was freaking busy.

He was stretched out on the floor, about to do an ass-cracking exercise called the Turkish get-up, when he looked up and saw his wife. She wasn't alone. Standing there in the doorway with her was his capo and personal bodyguard, Ray "The Psycho" Siconolfi.

Licata literally couldn't believe his eyes.

Because how could it be possible that his stupid wife would bring Ray here, into his sanctuary, to see him shirtless and sweating like a hairy pig in just his bicycle shorts?

"You're kidding me, right?" Licata said, red-faced, glaring at his wife as he stood.

"It's *my* fault?!" Karen shrieked back at him, like his very own silk-pajama-clad witch. "You don't answer the frigging phone!"

That was it. Licata turned like a shot-putter and slung the kettle bell at her. Before she could move, the forty-pound hunk of iron sailed an inch past her ear and went right through the Sheetrock, into the finished part of the basement, popping a stud out of the frame on the way. She moved then, boy. Like a scalded squirrel.

"This better—" Licata said, staring death up into his six-foot five-inch bodyguard's eyes, "and, Ray, I mean *better*—be fucking good."

Ray, ever expressionless, held up a legal-sized yellow envelope.

"Somebody just left this on the gatehouse doorstep," Ray said, handing it to him. "I heard a truck or something, but when I came out, it was gone."

"What the—? Is it ticking?" Licata said, shaking his head at him.

"C'mon, boss. Like you pay me to be stupid?" Ray said, hurt. "I fluoroscoped, as usual. It looks like a laptop or something. Also, see, it's addressed to you, and the return address says it's from Michael Jr. I wouldn't have bothered you except I called Mikey's phone, and there's no answer. Not on his cell. Not on his house phone."

"Michael Jr.?" Licata said, turning the envelope in his large hand. His eldest son, Michael, lived in Cali now, where he ran the film unions for the family. Teamsters, cameramen, the whole nine. What the heck was this?

He tore open the envelope. Inside was, of all things, an iPad. It was already turned on, too. On the screen was a video, all set up and ready to go, the Play arrow superimposed over a palm-tree-bookended house that was lit funny. There was a green tinge to it that Licata thought might have been from some kind of night-vision camera.

The green-tinged house was his son's, he realized, when he peered at the terra-cotta roof. It was Michael Jr.'s new mansion in Malibu. *Someone's surveilling Mikey's house? The feds, maybe?* he thought.

"What is this shit?" Licata said, tapping the screen.

Three

THE FILM BEGAN WITH the shaky footage of a handheld camera. Someone wasn't just filming Mikey's house, either—they were actually past his gate, rushing over his front lawn! After a moment, sound kicked in, an oxygen-tank sound, as if the unseen cameraman might have been a scuba diver or Darth Vader.

Licata let out a gasp as the camera panned right and what looked like a team of ninjas in astronaut suits came around the infinity pool and went up the darkened front steps of Mikey's house. One of the sons of bitches knelt at the lock, and then, in a flash, his son's thick wood-and-iron mission-style door was swinging inward.

Licata's free hand clapped over his gaping mouth as he noticed the guns they were carrying.

It was some kind of hit! He was watching his worst nightmare come true. Someone was gunning for his son.

"Call Mikey! Call him again!" Licata cried at his bodyguard.

When he looked back down at the screen of the tablet, the unthinkable was happening. The double doors to his son's upstairs master bedroom were opening. Licata felt his lungs lock as the camera entered the room. He seriously felt like he was going to vomit. He'd never felt so afraid and vulnerable in his entire life.

The camera swung around crazily for a second, and when it steadied, the scuba-masked hit team was holding Mikey Jr., who was struggling and yelling facedown on the mattress. Two of them had also grabbed Mikey's hugely pregnant wife, Carla. She started screaming as they pinned her by her wrists and ankles to the four-poster bed.

There was a sharp popping sound, and then the screen showed a strange metal cylinder, a canister of some kind. Billowing clouds of white smoke began hissing out as it was tossed onto the bed between his son and daughter-in-law.

Tear gas? Licata thought woodenly. They were tear-gassing them? He couldn't put it together. It made zero sense. What the fuck was this? Some kind of home invasion!? He felt like he was in a dream. He wondered idly if he was going into shock.

Mikey Jr. started convulsing first. The astronaut-suited bastards let him go as he started shaking like he was being electrocuted. After a moment, he started puking violently, with a truly horrendous retching sound. Then Carla started the same horror-movie shit, shaking and shivering like bacon in a pan as snot and puke loudly geysered out of her like they did from the girl in *The Exorcist*. The whole time, the camera was panning in and out as a hand moved blankets and sheets out of the way to make sure to get up-close, meticulous footage.

Ten, maybe fifteen seconds into the truly bizarre and hellish spasming, they both stopped moving.

Licata stood there, staring at the screen, unable to speak, unable to think.

His son Michael, the pride of his life, had just been killed right before his eyes.

"Oh, shit, boss! Boss, boss! Look out!" Ray suddenly called.

Licata looked up from the screen.

And dropped the electronic tablet to the cement with a clatter.

The mobster didn't think his eyes could go any wider, but he was wrong. Out of nowhere, two guys were suddenly standing in the doorway of his workout room, holding shotguns. They were Hispanic—one Doberman lean, the other one squat. They were wearing mechanic's coveralls and Yankees ball caps, and had bandannas over their faces.

Without warning, without a nod or a word, the shorter guy with the acne shot Ray in the stomach. Licata closed his eyes and jumped back at the deafening sound of the blast. When he opened his eyes again, there was blood all over the small room—on the heavy bag, on the raw concrete walls, even on Licata's bare chest. Incredibly, Ray, with his bloody belly full of buckshot, kept his feet for a moment. Then the big man walked over toward the weight bench like he was tired and needed to sit down.

He didn't make it. He fell about a foot before the bench, facedown, cracking his forehead loudly on one of Licata's dumbbells.

Licata slowly looked from his dead bodyguard to the two silent intruders.

"Why?" Licata said, licking his suddenly dry lips. "You killed my son. Now Ray. Why? Who are you? Why are you doing this? Who sent you?"

There was no response from either of them. They just stared back, their doll's eyes as flat and dark as the bores of the shotguns trained on his face. They looked like immigrants. Mexicans or Central Americans. They didn't speak English, Licata realized.

Suddenly, without warning, two sounds came in quick succession from upstairs: a woman's piercing scream, followed quickly by the boom of a shotgun.

Karen! Licata thought as he screamed himself, rushing forward. But the Doberman guy was waiting for him. With a practiced movement, he smashed the hardened plastic of the shotgun's butt into Licata's face, knocking him out as he simultaneously caved in his front teeth.

Four

IT WAS TEN OR so minutes later when Licata came to on the floor of the basement's tiny utility closet. After spitting his two front teeth from his ruined mouth, the first thing he noticed was that he was cuffed to the water pipe.

Then he noticed the terrible whooshing sound and the rank stench of sulfur.

He glanced through the half-open closet door and saw a severed yellow hose dangling between two of the tiles in the drop ceiling. It was the gas line, Licata realized in horror. *Oh, God, no.*

Licata went even more nuts when he saw what was sitting on the coffee table halfway across the long room. It was a large, white bath candle.

A large, *lit* white bath candle.

"Mr. Licata? Yoo-hoo? Are you there? Hello?"

said a French-accented voice beside the doorway.

Licata kicked the closet door open all the way, expecting someone to be there. Instead, sitting on a tripod just outside the closet was a massive plasma TV with a whole bunch of cords and some kind of video camera attached to the top of it.

And on the TV screen itself, in super high definition, waved the Mexican drug-cartel kingpin Manuel Perrine.

Licata sat and stared, mesmerized, at the screen. The handsome, light-skinned black man was wearing a white silk shirt, seersucker shorts, a pair of Cartier aviator sunglasses. He was sitting Indian-style on a rattan chaise longue, drinking what looked like a mojito. There was a long, lean woman in a white bikini on the chaise beside him, but Licata couldn't see her face, just the tan, oiled line of her leg and hip, the toss of white-blond hair on her cinnamon shoulder. They were both barefoot. It looked like they were on a boat.

Licata groaned as his scrambling thoughts began catching traction. About a year ago, Licata had met Perrine in the fed lockup in Lower Manhattan, and for the princely sum of $10 million cash, he had helped the Mexican cartel head escape from federal custody. *But does he go away and leave me alone?* Licata thought. *Of course not.* The multilingual maniac calls him up a mere two months after his world-famous escape and insists on working together. Like he needed that kind of heat.

As Licata watched, a beautiful four- or five-year-old dusky girl with light-blue eyes filled the screen. Her corn-rowed hair was wet, the sequins of her bright-teal bathing suit twinkling.

"Who's the funny man, Daddy?" the little girl said as she squatted, peering curiously at Licata.

"Back in the pool now, Bianca. I want you to do two laps of backstroke now," Perrine said lovingly from behind her. "Daddy's just watching a grown-up show."

Licata watched the girl shrug and walk offscreen.

"What do you think of this TV setup? Amazing clarity, yes?" Perrine said, removing his sunglasses to show his sparkling light-blue eyes. "It's called TelePresence, the latest thing from Cisco Systems. It's costing me a small fortune, but I couldn't help myself. I couldn't pass up the opportunity to see and speak with you one last time."

Licata opened his mouth to say something, then suddenly found himself weeping.

"Tears, Mr. Licata? Seriously? You of all people know perfectly well that men in this world fall into two categories, tools or enemies. You refused to work with me. What did you think was going to happen?"

Perrine took a sip of his drink and wiped his lips daintily with a napkin before he continued.

"It's not like I didn't give you a chance. I offered friendship, remember?" he said. "A mutually beneficial partnership. I explained to you how the world was changing. How I could help you and the American Mafia to weather that transition. In earnest I said these things.

"Do you remember what you said before you hung up on me? It was rather humorous. You said that instead of working with your organization, my Mexican friends and I ought to, and I quote, 'go back and do what you're good at: washing dishes and cutting grass.'"

He brushed an imaginary speck from the shoulder of his pristine silk shirt.

"Mr. Licata, as you see now, my people aren't the type that do dishes, and instead of grass, the only things we cut are heads."

"You're right," Licata said, blood from his wrecked mouth flecking the cement floor. "I was wrong, Manuel. Way, way off base to disrespect you like that. I see how serious a player you are. We can help each other. I can help you. We can work it out."

Perrine laughed as he slipped his shades on and leaned back.

"'We can work it out'?" he said as he put his hands behind his head. "You mean like the famous Beatles song, Mr. Licata? That's precisely the problem. There's no time, my friend."

"But—" Licata said as the downward-flowing gas finally touched the candle flame.

Then Licata, his basement, and most of his obnoxious Connecticut McMansion were instantly vaporized as five thousand cubic feet of natural gas went up all at once in a ripping, reverberating, ground-shuddering blast.

Part One

DON'T FENCE ME IN

Chapter 1

AWAKE AT FIVE O'CLOCK in the morning and unable to sleep with all the incessant peace and quiet, I pushed out through the creaky screen door onto the darkened porch, clutching my morning's first coffee.

Dr. Seuss was right on the money, I thought with a frown as I sat myself beside a rusting tractor hay rake.

"Oh, the places you'll go," I mumbled to the tumbleweeds.

The porch rail I put my feet up on was connected to a ramshackle Victorian farmhouse a few miles south of Susanville, California. Susanville, as absolutely no one knows, is the county seat of Northern California's Lassen County. The county itself is named after Peter Lassen, a famous frontiersman and Indian fighter, who, I'd learned from my daughter Jane, was murdered under mysterious circumstances in 1859.

As a New York cop forced into exile out here in the exact middle of nowhere for the past eight months, I was seriously thinking about asking someone if I could take a crack at solving Lassen's cold case. That should give you some indication of how bored I was.

But what are you going to do?

Bored is better than dead, all things considered.

I was sitting on an old wooden chair that we called an Adirondack chair when I was a kid, but that I guess out here was called a Sierra chair, since I could actually see the northern, snow-tipped rim of the Sierra Nevada from my porch. It was cold, and I was sporting, of all things, a Carhartt work coat, worn jeans, and a pair of Wellington boots.

The wellies, knee-high green rubber boots, were perfectly ridiculous-looking but quite necessary. We were living on a cattle ranch now, and no matter how hard you tried not to, you often stepped in things that needed hosing off.

Yeah, I'd stepped in it, all right.

Mere months ago, I'd been your typical happy-go-lucky Irish American NYPD detective with ten adopted kids. Then I arrested Manuel Perrine, a Mexican drug-cartel head. Which would have been fine. Putting drug-dealing murderers into cages, where they belonged, happened to be an avid hobby of mine.

The problem was, the billionaire scumbag escaped custody and put a multimillion-dollar hit out on me and my family.

So there you have it. The feds put us in witness protection, and I'd gone from *NYPD Blue* to *Little House on the Prairie* in no time flat. I'd always suspected that "luck of the Irish" was a sarcastic phrase.

If I said I was settling in, I'd be lying. If anything, I was more amazed now at our bizarre new surroundings than on the day we arrived.

When people think of California, they think of surfboards, the Beach Boys, Valley girls. That's certainly what I and the rest of the Bennett clan all thought we were in for when the feds told us that was where we were headed.

But what we actually ended up getting from the witness protection folks was the other California, the one no one ever talks about. The northern, high-desert boondocks California, with log cabins left behind by settlers turned cannibals, and cow pies left behind by our new, bovine neighbors.

But it wasn't all bad. The eight-hundred-acre ranch we were now living on was surrounded by devastatingly majestic mountains. And our landlord, Aaron Cody, fifth-generation cattle rancher, couldn't have been nicer to us. He raised grass-fed cattle and organic you-name-it: eggs, milk, veggies, which he constantly left on our doorstep like some rangy, seventy-five-year-old cowboy Santa Claus. We'd never eaten better.

From my kids' perspective, there was a definite mix of emotions. The older guys were depressed, still missing their friends and former Facebook profiles. With the younger crowd, it was the opposite. They had fallen in love with farm life and all the animals. And, boy, were there a lot of them. Cody had a veritable zoo half a mile back off the road: horses, dogs, goats, llamas, pigs, chickens.

Our nanny, Mary Catherine, who had grown up on a cattle farm back in Ireland, had hit the ground running. She was in her element, always busy either with the children or helping out our landlord. Cody, a widower, who was obviously head over heels in love with Mary Catherine, said he'd never had a better or prettier hired hand.

And we were safe up here. One thing it's hard to

do to someone who lives half a mile off a main road in the middle of the wilderness is sneak up on them.

At times, I probably could have committed a felony for a real slice of pizza or a bagel, but I was trying to look on the bright side: though the nineteenth-century lifestyle certainly took some getting used to, at least when the dollar collapsed, we'd be good.

So here I was, up early, out on the porch drinking coffee like your classic western men of yore, looking around for my horse so I could ride the range. Actually, I didn't have a horse or know what "the range" was, so I decided to just read the news on my iPhone.

Beavis and Butt-Head were coming back, I read on the Yahoo! news page. Wasn't that nice? It was a real comfort to know that the world out beyond the confines of my eight-hundred-acre sanctuary was still going to hell in a gasoline-filled recyclable shopping bag.

It was what I spotted when I thumbed over to the *Drudge Report* that made me sit up and spill coffee all over my wellies.

MOB WAR!!? 20-Plus Dead! Manuel Perrine Suspected in Multiple Bloodbaths!

Chapter 2

IT TOOK ME ABOUT half an hour of reading through the just-breaking news reports to wrap my blown mind around what was happening.

There had been seven attacks in all. Three in the New York area, and one each in Providence, Detroit, Philly, and Los Angeles. Reports were preliminary, but it was looking like the heads of all five Mafia families involved had been among those massacred in their homes last night by unknown assailants.

Wives were dead, it said. Children. A mobster's house in Westport, Connecticut, had actually been blown to smithereens.

"'Twenty-three bodies and counting,'" I read out loud off the *Los Angeles Times* website.

Twenty-three dead wasn't a crime, I thought in

utter disbelief. Twenty-three dead was the body count of a land war.

The scope and sophistication of the attacks were daunting. Alarms had been disabled, security tapes removed. It was still early, but there didn't seem to be any witnesses. In the space of seven hours, several mobsters and their families had been quickly and quietly wiped off the face of the earth.

An unmentioned source tipped off law enforcement that it might be Perrine. The anonymous tipster said that Perrine had offered the American Mafia some sort of partnership a few months back, a deal that was turned down. Not only that, but the article was saying that today was actually Perrine's forty-fifth birthday.

It definitely could have been Perrine, I knew. The attacks actually made sense when you realized how the cartels worked. The cartels' brutally simple and efficient negotiating tactic was called *plata o plomo* on the street. Silver or lead. Take the money or a bullet. Do business with us or die.

It was one thing to strong-arm a bodega owner, I thought, shaking my head. But Perrine apparently had just done it to the entire Mob!

You would need how many men for something

like that? I wondered. Fifty? Probably closer to a hundred. I thought about that, about Perrine, out there somewhere, free as a bird, coordinating a hundred highly trained hit men in five cities, like markers on a board. Then I stopped thinking about it. It was way too depressing.

Because it really was an unprecedented power play. The American Mafia had been running the underworld show since—when? Prohibition? Perrine, obviously, was out to change that. He was upping his cartel's influence and operation, branching out from Mexico and into the good ol' US of A.

It was truly very scary news that Perrine was on the scene again. Coming from a penniless ghetto in French Guiana, he'd somehow made his way to France, where he joined the army and worked his way into the French special forces. His fellow squad members in the French naval commandos described him as incredibly intelligent and competent, extremely competitive yet witty at times, a talented, natural leader.

What Perrine decided to do with his charismatic talent and elite commando military experience was to return to South America and hire himself out as a mercenary and military consultant to the highest-bidding criminal enterprises he could find. Two bloody decades later, he had risen to become the billionaire head of the largest and most violent cartel in Mexico.

You would have thought that his career was over when I bagged him in New York about a year ago. It wasn't. He'd had the judge at his own trial murdered and actually managed to escape from the fourteenth floor of the Foley Square Federal Courthouse via helicopter. I should know, because I was there at the time and actually emptied my Glock into the chopper to no avail as it whirlybirded elegant, intelligent Manuel Perrine away.

So you can see why I was concerned as I sat there. Wanted international fugitives usually try to spend their time hiding, not expanding their criminal enterprises. Reports were saying that in the past few months, he had actually joined together his cartel with that of one of his rivals. Los Salvajes, they were calling this new supercartel. The Wild Ones.

And Perrine, at its head, was fast becoming a popular folk hero. Which was a head-scratcher for me, since this Robin Hood, instead of robbing the rich and giving to the poor, smuggled drugs in metric-ton loads and decapitated people.

I began to get extremely pissed off after a bit more reading. So much so that I turned off my phone and just sat there, fuming.

It wasn't the loss of five Mafia kingpins that I cared so much about. Despite the sweeping, romantic Francis Ford Coppola and HBO portrayals, real mobsters were truly evil, bullying individuals who, when they weren't ripping everybody off, loved nothing more than to demean and destroy people at every opportunity.

For example, I knew that one of the dearly departed godfathers, Michael Licata, had once pistol-whipped a Bronxville restaurant waiter into a coma for not bringing his mussels marinara fast enough. The fact that last night Licata had been blown up in his own house was something I could learn to live with.

What was really driving me nuts was that Perrine had done it. It was completely unacceptable that Perrine was still free, let alone operational. American law enforcement had never looked so pathetic. I mean, who was on this case?

Not me, that was for sure. After Perrine's escape, I'd been blackballed. Then, to add insult to injury, after Perrine had left a truck bomb out in front of my West End Avenue building, the feds had put me into witness protection. I'd basically been mothballed.

I love my family, but I can't describe how upset I was as I sat there, taking in the helpless, hopeless situation.

Perrine was the one who should have been hiding, I thought, wanting to punch something.

Chapter 3

I QUICKLY TUCKED MY smartphone away as I heard the screen door creak open behind me.

Mary Catherine, dressed in worn jeans, Columbia University hoodie, and her own pair of trusty wellies, came out with the coffeepot. Her blond hair was in a ponytail, and she looked great, which was pretty much par for the course for my kids' nanny, even this early in the morning.

I hated this farm about as much as Mary Catherine loved it. I'd thought she was going to be devastated when she was forced into hiding along with the rest of us. It turned out the opposite was true. Even a cartel contract couldn't keep my young Irish nanny down.

"Howdy, partner," she said in her Irish accent as she gave me a refill.

"Hey, cowgirl," I said.

"You're up early," she said.

"I thought I saw some rustlers out yonder," I said with a gravelly voice.

I squinted to enhance my Clint Eastwood spaghetti Western impression.

"Turned out it was a couple of outlaw chickens. They started making trouble, so I had to wing one of them. Which actually worked out. I put a little hot sauce on it, and it was delicious."

Mary Catherine laughed.

"Well, just don't tell Chrissy. You know how much she loves our fine feathered friends."

"How could I forget?" I said, laughing myself.

Chrissy, the baby of our massive brood, had taken a liking to one of our landlord's chickens, whom she immediately named Homer, for some inexplicable reason. She'd even sworn off chicken nuggets after one of her ever-helpful older brothers informed her she was probably dipping a member of Homer's family into the sweet-and-sour sauce.

"So, what's on the agenda today?" she said.

"Well," I said, "I say we grab the paper and some bagels down at Murray's, then hop a Two train down to MoMA for the latest installation. Afterward, we could go to John's on Bleecker for lunch. I'm thinking a large, with everything on it, and some gelato for dessert. No, wait—we could go to Carnegie for a Bible-thick pastrami sandwich. It's like butta."

Mary Catherine shook her head at me.

"MoMA?" she said. "Really?"

"Sure, why not? You're not the only one interested in culture around here."

"You never went to MoMA in your life. You told me yourself you hate modern art. And the Two train! Of course. I love taking the kids on the subway. It's so much fun. Look, Mike, I love—and miss—the Big Apple as well, but don't you think you're laying it on a tad thick? Why do you continue to torture yourself?"

I gestured out at the endless space and sky all around us.

"Isn't it obvious?" I said. "There's nothing else to do."

"That's it," my nanny said. "Less moping, more roping, as Mr. Cody likes to say. You're coming with us this morning. No more excuses."

"No, that's OK," I said when I realized where she wanted me to go. "I have plenty to do. I have to go over today's lesson plan."

Due to the truly insane circumstances, we had

decided to homeschool the kids. I was handling the English and history, Mary Catherine the math and science, while my grandfather-priest, Seamus —big surprise—tackled religion. I had never taught before, and I was actually getting into it. I wasn't smarter than a fifth-grader yet, but I was getting there.

"Nonsense, Mike. You don't think I know you have your lessons planned at least two weeks ahead? You need to give in to it, Mike. I know you don't like being here on a farm, but face facts. You are. Besides, you haven't even given it a chance. When in Rome, you have to do as the Romans do."

"I would if we were in Rome, Mary Catherine," I said. "The Romans have pizza."

"No excuses. Now, you can warm up the cars or wake the kids. Your choice."

"The cars, I guess," I mumbled as she turned to head back inside. "If I have to."

"You have to," my iron-willed nanny said, pointing toward the shed at the side of the house as she creaked open the screen door.

Chapter 4

TWENTY MINUTES LATER, WE were rolling up the road toward our landlord's farm.

Seamus, Brian, Eddie, and the twins took our new Jeep, while Mary Catherine and I piled the rest of the kids into the vintage station wagon that Cody insisted on loaning us. Cody's awesome wagon was an old Pontiac Tempest muscle car that reminded me of my childhood in the seventies, when seat belts were optional, the cigarette lighter was for firing up Marlboro reds, and even station wagons could haul it off the line.

I was truly impressed with Mary Catherine when I saw all the teens up and about so early. The kids were even talking and joking with each other instead of fighting. Which was saying something, since no one had eaten breakfast yet.

"What's up with everybody? They seem excited," I said to Mary Catherine as we rolled up the half mile of dirt road for Cody's farm. "Seamus hasn't even insulted me once. What gives?"

"They don't *seem* excited. They *are* excited," Mary Catherine said. "They love this, Mike. So will you. Watch."

Cody was already outside his huge modern barn. He was waiting for us by his old green Ford tractor. Behind the tractor was a hay-bale-littered trailer that the kids immediately started piling into after we parked.

"Howdy, Mike. I see you decided to join us this morning," Cody said, smiling as he shook my hand.

I liked Cody. His son was the special agent in charge at the FBI's Chicago office, so he knew and respected our whole situation with Perrine. He had actually offered his secluded ranch as a witness protection sanctuary a few times before. We really couldn't have asked for someone better to hide us and watch our backs than the friendly former marine sergeant and decorated Vietnam vet.

"We can always use another cowpoke in the gang, isn't that right, kids?" Cody said, squaring his Colorado Rockies baseball cap. "But, of course, we'll have to see how you do. We like to take on hands on a day-by-day basis around these here parts. How does that suit you?"

"Sounds fair, Aaron," I said, as everyone laughed at Daddy. "I'll try not to let you down."

"Enough yappin' to the greenhorn, Cody," Seamus said, smacking the hood of the old tractor. "Time to saddle 'em up and move 'em out."

We all piled into the trailer, along with Cody's three black-and-white border collies. I watched as my kids and the super-friendly dogs couldn't get enough of each other. Mary Catherine was right. The kids really couldn't have been happier as we rolled out over the fields, bouncing around like a bunch of jumping beans.

We saw the cattle ten minutes later. There were about sixty head of them, milling along an irrigation ditch.

"See, Dad? Those over there are cows," my seven-year-old son, Trent, said, showing me the ropes as Cody opened the cattle gate. "They're girl cattle, big but actually kind of nice. You can control 'em. Also, see that wire running along the other end of the field? That's electric, Dad. Don't touch it. It's for keeping the cows in."

I smiled at Trent's contagious energy. Back in

New York, at this hour, he would have been—where? Stuck in class? And yet here, he was outside, learning about the world and loving every minute of it.

As Cody got us going again, Trent suddenly pointed to a pen we'd passed that had a couple of truly enormous red-and-white bulls in it. They looked like oil tanks with fur.

"Those guys there are bulls, Dad. Boy cows. They're, um . . . what did you call the bulls, Mr. Cody?" Trent called up to the farmer.

"Orn-ry," Cody called back.

"Exactly. Bulls are orn-ry, Dad. Real mean-like. You gotta stay away from them. You can't even be in the same field as them. Once they see you come over the fence, you have to get back over it real quick, before they come runnin' like crazy to mow you down!"

"Why do I think this information comes from personal experience, Trent?" I asked.

"Eddie's the one who does it the most, Dad," Trent whispered confidentially. "Ricky, too. I just did it once. Cross my heart."

The trailer stopped. Cody climbed down from the tractor. The border collies, whose names were Flopsy, Mopsy, and Desiree, immediately jumped over the rim of the trailer as Cody whistled.

"Check this out, Dad," my eldest son, Brian, said, putting his arm over my shoulder.

"Yeah," said Jane, as the dogs made a beeline for the cattle. "Step back and watch. This is the coolest."

My kids weren't kidding. The cattle turned to watch as the three dogs ran in a straight line along the opposite side of the large field. Before the cows knew what was happening, the collies had followed the field's perimeter and were behind them, with an occasional bark or nip at their hooves to urge them along.

Cody, approaching the side of the slowly driven herd, whistled occasionally to his dogs as they weaved back and forth behind the none-too-happy-looking cows. In minutes, the cows were trotting past the tractor and trailer, jogging through the gate into the lane we had just come up, on their way to the milking barn.

"How did you teach them to do that?" I said, staring at the dogs in awe as Cody came back to the tractor.

"It's not me," Cody said, petting the happy, energetic dogs. "It's in their blood. Border collies are the best herding dogs in the world, Mike. They never stop moving and circling; plus, they always look the cattle in the eye to show them who's boss."

As it turned out, I wasn't done being shocked that morning. Back at the milking barn, Mary Catherine blew me away as she guided the bawling cows into the separate stalls like a farm-girl traffic cop. Then she put on a smock and gloves and hopped down into the sunken gutter between the stalls and started hooking up the cows to the milking equipment. She worked the octopuslike snarl of tubes and pumps like a pro, attaching things to their proper . . . attachments. It was beyond incredible.

"Hey, Mike," Mary Catherine said, stepping up into the stall, holding a bucket. "Thirsty?" she asked, showing me some milk fresh from the cow.

I leaped back as I almost blew chow. Unlike the cold, white stuff we picked up in cartons from the cooler at the 7-Eleven, this had steam coming off it and was yellow and chunky.

"Come on, Mike. I know you're thirsty," Mary Catherine said, smiling, as she sensed my discomfort. She waved the bucket menacingly at me. "Straight up or on the rocks?"

"How about pasteurized and homogenized?" I said, backing away.

"EAT LESS CHICKEN!" Chrissy suddenly yelled to everyone as a clucking chicken landed on the windowsill of the barn.

"And drink less milk," I said to Mary Catherine.

Chapter 5

AFTER THE MILKING WAS done and the cows were put back to pasture, the older girls went with Shawna and Chrissy to the henhouse to collect eggs.

The girls returned shortly, and Cody insisted that everyone have breakfast at his house.

"You want to keep the hands happy, you got to keep their bellies full," he said.

We filled our bellies, all right. After we hosed off the wellies, we were greeted by Cody's short and stout sweetheart of a housekeeper, Rosa, who cooked us up a feast of steak and biscuits and scrambled-egg tortillas with lots of homemade salsa. As Rosa busted out the churros, I even put a drop of the superorganic milk Mary Catherine had brought in from the barn into my coffee.

"Who says country living is boring?" I said to Mary Catherine, with a wink. "My horizons are expanding at warp speed."

It really was a great morning. Looking at my kids, hunched around the two tables Rosa had pushed together, eating and talking and laughing, I couldn't stop smiling. We may have been dislodged from our lives back in New York, but they were actually making the best of it. We were together and safe, and that was all that really mattered when it came down to it. Team Bennett had gotten knocked down, but we were getting back up again.

As the kids went outside to kick a soccer ball around the dusty yard with the dogs, I sat with Cody and Seamus, sipping a second cup of coffee.

"You got things pretty good out here, Aaron. The view is amazing, you grow all your own food, have fresh water. I mean, you pay for—what? Electricity? You could probably get along without that."

"And have," Cody said.

"You love this life, don't you?" I said.

"*Love*'s a strong word," the weather-beaten farmer said. "I don't love when the cattle get themselves stuck in a ditch at three a.m., or when feed prices skyrocket, as they do from time to time, but it's a life, Mike. Don't suit everyone. You have to like being alone a lot. All in all, there's something to be said for it. It's simple enough, I guess."

"I like simple," I said, clinking coffee cups with the farmer.

"You are simple," Seamus said.

Chapter 6

CREEL, MEXICO

IT WAS THE BEST moment of Teodoro Salinas's life.

His daughter, Magdalena, had been a preemie when she was born. As if it were yesterday, he could remember her impossibly tiny hand clutching his finger for dear life among the cords in the hospital ICU. But now, suddenly, magically, her cool hand was resting in his sweating palm and the guitars and horns were playing and all the people were clapping as they danced the first dance of her *quinceañera*.

The whole event was like a dream. From the solemn Mass they had attended this morning, to the formal entry, to the first toast, and, now, to the first dance. His wife had told him he was crazy to hold the celebration up here at their remote vacation ranch, but Salinas had put his foot down. For his beautiful daughter's coming-of-age, they would fly everyone in and put them up, no matter what the expense.

Teodoro reluctantly released his daughter's hand as the waltz ended. She was crying. He was crying. His wife was crying. It had been worth every penny.

Salinas hugged his daughter, careful not to wrinkle the beautiful pale-pink tulle of her dress. He could feel the eyes of all the guests upon them, feel their tender emotions, their envy. Salinas was a tall man, a dapper dresser, and, even at fifty-five, still quite handsome. But he couldn't hold a candle to his daughter, Magdalena, who was model thin and statuesque and exceedingly beautiful.

"I love you, Daddy," his angel whispered in his ear.

He squeezed her bare shoulder.

"Enough being with your old father. Go with your friends now," he said. "Enjoy yourself. You are a young woman now. This is your day."

Salinas watched his daughter walk away, then headed toward his ranch manager, standing at the edge of the dance floor. His name was Tomás, and, like all the staff on the ranch, he was a local Tarahumara Indian. Tomás and the entire staff, from the security to the waiters to the members of the three mariachi bands, were wearing bright-white linen uniforms purchased solely for the occasion. No expense had been spared today.

"Please inform my partners that they are to join me in the billiards room, won't you, Tomás? Tell them to come alone. No security. This is my daughter's day, and this meeting is to be as quick and discreet as possible."

Tomás nodded and smiled, his crooked teeth very white in his dark-brown, lean face.

"Just as you say, sir," Tomás said. It was what his loyal employee always said. "Would you like a drink first?"

"No, please," Salinas said. "With all this ceremony, I've needed to take a piss for about an hour. But have some refreshments brought into the billiards room, if you would."

"They're already there, sir," Tomás said with a nod.

Salinas patted his manager on the back.

"Of course they are, Tomás. How could I have doubted it for a moment?"

Salinas sighed as he went into the air-conditioned house. Glancing to his right, he spotted the reason he had built the house, at an enormous expense, up here in the middle of nowhere.

The view of the Copper Canyon through his immense bay window had to be one of the most spectacular sights in all of Mexico, if not the world. His favorite aspect of the majestic vista was just a little bit off center, the thin, silver sliver of an eight-hundred-foot waterfall spilling down the face of one of the sheer canyon walls. He loved this house, this view. It was like living in an airplane.

He ducked into the hall bathroom outside the billiards room to relieve himself. He smiled and winked at his reflection in the bathroom mirror as he worked his zipper. What a day!

He was just about to urinate when he heard the distinct click of a billard ball. He zipped back up and went out and poked his head inside the billiards room. Unbelievable. A man in white linen, a staff member fucking off, no doubt, was bent at the table, about to take another shot. On the large-screen TV above the bar, a soccer match was playing with the sound off.

"Hey, you there! Asshole!" Salinas barked.

The man remained bent, surveying the lay of the balls before him. Was he deaf!?

"Are you having fun? Who the fuck do you think you are? Get your ass back to work before I break your legs with that cue."

Still, slowly and insolently, the man took his shot. The cue ball cracked into the eight, sinking it effortlessly. Then the man turned. Teodoro's eyes went wide. It took everything he had to keep his full bladder under control.

Because it wasn't a staff member.

It was Manuel Perrine.

"Oh, but, Teodoro. I am at work," Perrine said, chalking his cue. "Isn't that right, Tomás?"

Salinas felt something hard tap at the base of his head. It was the bore of a shotgun, pressed against his brain stem. Salinas suddenly felt like he was tumbling inside, a sudden free fall through the core of himself.

"Just as you say, sir," Tomás said, pushing Salinas into the room and locking the door.

Chapter 7

THE MARIACHI BANDS WERE resting and a DJ was playing some American dance music when the loud thump came from the stage. The music stopped immediately as a microphone squawk echoed throughout the tent.

As the crowd in attendance looked up from their plates, they could see that the entire staff of white-linen-clad Indians was now holding automatic rifles. The Tarahumaras went amid the crowd, knocking over tables, slapping people, sticking guns in faces.

The security men of the multiple drug dealers in attendance were quickly disarmed and handcuffed. Tables were moved aside, and all the chairs were lined up, like at an assembly. The gunmen sat the people back down roughly, threatening to kill on the spot anyone and everyone dumb enough to make the slightest move.

A moment later, Manuel Perrine walked out onto the stage, holding a microphone.

"Hello, friends," Perrine said in his most elegant Spanish, smiling hugely. "To those of you who know me, I can hardly articulate how pleasant it is to see you again. To those of you who are unfamiliar to me, let me say what a truly wonderful time this is for us to get acquainted."

He put his hand to his ear as he stared out at the pale, scared faces.

"What? No applause?" he said.

Some clapping started.

"Come, now. This is a party, is it not? You can do better than that."

The clapping increased.

"There you go. You did miss me. How touching. Now, at the risk of breaking protocol here at this beautiful *quinceañera* celebration, I would like to make a few announcements about another coming-of-age here today. The coming of the age of Manuel Perrine and Los Salvajes."

A terrified murmur passed through the crowd as Teodoro Salinas and the two other leaders of his cartel were brought into the tent from the house.

Salinas had a black eye. All three had their wrists bound behind them.

Three chairs were set at the edge of the stage, and the three men were seated with their backs to the crowd.

"Now, without further ado, the moment we've all been waiting for," Perrine said as one of the Tarahumaras handed him something long and thin.

The sickle-shaped, razor-sharp machete Perrine held up for the crowd to see had been his father's cane knife. The antique blade was beautifully weighted behind the cutting side, like a golf club, and had the manufacturer's stamp engraved in the blade, above the handle: COLLINS AXE COMPANY, CONNECTICUT, USA.

They just don't make 'em like this anymore, Perrine thought, hefting it lovingly.

The first man he stepped before was Salinas's second-in-command. The man had actually undone his binding, and he threw his hands up protectively as Perrine swung. No matter. The blade sliced the man's arm off neatly midway between his wrist and elbow and buried itself deep in the man's collarbone.

Several women in the crowd fainted as the man

screamed, blood spurting as he waved around his amputated stump. Perrine, after two tugs, finally worked the blade free. Then he stepped back and swung.

There. Much better, Perrine thought as the man's cleanly severed head rolled off his shoulders and off the stage.

That was when the second man kicked himself off the stage. It was the plaza boss, who actually thought he could take over Perrine's turf in Río Bravo. He managed to make it halfway across the dance floor before Perrine nodded to Tomás. Half a dozen automatic rifles cracked at once, cutting the man down. He slid across the dance floor in a thick trail of blood, followed by his Bally shoes.

Perrine had to tip his hat to Teodoro Salinas. The man didn't flinch in the slightest as both of his partners lost their lives. The big, handsome man looked like he might have been waiting for a bus as Perrine stepped forward. Perrine nodded respectfully, then swung and took the elegant host's head off with one swipe.

As his enemies bled out, Perrine turned toward the crowd. His face was covered in blood, his linen uniform, the blade of the cane knife. The women who were still conscious were completely hysterical, the sound of their babbling moans like that of people speaking in tongues.

Perrine lifted the fallen microphone.

"Please. I know all this is shocking, ladies and gentlemen, but facts must be faced," Perrine said, waving the dripping cane knife for emphasis. "These men thought I was defeated. They thought because I was in hiding that I was no longer valid. That they could take what was mine."

He turned and looked at the dead men behind him and smiled.

"Has anyone ever thought more wrongly? I cannot be defeated. I cannot even be diminished. The good news is, you are not as obstinate as these here, whom I have been forced to punish. The good news is that now, with the last of our detractors eliminated, we are one."

Perrine smiled.

"Don't you understand? We all work for Los Salvajes now. We have ambitions that transcend mere Mexico. In the next few weeks, you will see what I am talking about. I know this is a sad moment. You see this now as butchery, I can tell.

"But soon, you will change your mind. Soon, you will see the opportunity I have given you. You will come to realize this isn't the end but the beginning, and you lucky few are being let in on the ground floor."

Perrine checked his Rolex.

"Does anyone have any questions? Comments?"

He looked around. Not surprisingly, the only hand he saw was at the end of the disembodied arm lying at his feet.

"Excellent. All relevant parties will be contacted in the next few days with instructions," Perrine said. "You are all free to go now. Have a nice day."

Chapter 8

THE FOLLOWING MONDAY, WE'D just done the milking at Cody's and were getting out of the vehicles back at our place when we saw dust rising in the distance to the north. By the main road, a light-blue sedan I didn't recognize was approaching slowly.

Immediately, I could feel my heart start to pound. Despite our new, peaceful rural existence, I hadn't forgotten our situation for one second. Besides the mailman, we'd had exactly no visitors at all.

"Guys, inside, now. Seamus, Mary Catherine, go get them," I said immediately.

"Yeah?" Seamus said, looking at me.

"Yeah," I said. "I'm not kidding. Go help Mary Catherine now."

All the kids quickly went into the house. A moment later, Seamus and Mary Catherine came back out. Seamus was holding a shotgun, while Mary Catherine had two guns strapped over her shoulder. Then the door opened again, and Juliana and Brian came out, holding shotguns as well.

It didn't thrill me to see my young teenage kids standing there holding firearms, but it was what it was. Teaching the older kids how to use a gun was a thoroughly necessary evil. Because the thing was, Perrine really, really didn't like me. Not only had I broken his nose when I arrested him, but I'd actually killed his homicidal wife in a raid.

If the ruthless drug lord ever found out where we were, there was no way he would stop at killing just me. My children needed to be able to defend themselves.

Mary Catherine came down the porch steps and handed me the 30.06 deer rifle.

I quickly put it to my shoulder and peered through its telescopic sight at the car. It was a Ford Taurus. The driver seemed to be the only person in it. I couldn't be sure, but it looked like a woman.

The car disappeared briefly as it drove down alongside a small ridge below the house. When it reappeared, it was close enough for me to see the driver's face.

I squinted again through the rifle before I lowered it. I stood there, blinking, as I watched the car come. I actually knew who it was.

"What's up, Mike?" Seamus said.

"It's OK. Put the guns back into the cabinet. It's OK. We're safe."

"Who is it?" Mary Catherine said as the car pulled into the driveway. Before I could answer, the sedan stopped and its door opened, and a woman got out. My old pal and partner, Special Agent Emily Parker from the FBI, took off her sunglasses and smiled as she stared back at everyone glaring at her.

"Hi, Mike. Hi, Mary Catherine. Hi, Seamus," the FBI agent said. "Long time no see. So this is where you have been hiding yourselves."

Chapter 9

MARY CATHERINE PROMPTLY LEFT Mike and Special Agent Parker outside and went in to put on coffee.

After she locked up the shotguns in the front-hall gun cabinet, she went into the kitchen and washed out the coffee filter and threw in several scoops of Folgers. As she placed some scones in the oven to warm them, she heard a sudden commotion coming from the family room.

When she walked in, everyone was yelling and laughing as Ricky and Fiona flung each other around the room in an epic tug-of-war over the TV remote. The volume on an inanely cackling *SpongeBob SquarePants* episode rose and fell as they went sprawling onto the couch. Mary Catherine crossed the room and immediately turned off the blaring set.

"Out!" she said, snatching the remote and pointing it at the back door. "The lot of ya. No more TV. No more video games. I don't want to see hide nor hair of any of you in this house for the next hour, at least. I know your father ordered you inside, but this is ridiculous. The shame of it, to be in here like a tribe of screaming baboons, wrestling while your father is out there with a guest. Now get going out that back door!"

After they left, Mary Catherine tidied up the living room and went to the front door to see what was taking Mike so long. Mike and Agent Parker were still out by the car, talking. She folded her arms as she stood at the screen door, watching them.

Mary Catherine had met Emily Parker before, when Mike had worked with her on other cases, back in New York. She could see that the agent's coppery auburn hair was as thick and lustrous as ever as the wind tossed it around. Mary Catherine looked the agent over meticulously. She was so stylishly out of place in the farmhouse side yard, in her heels and nice office clothes. Then Mary Catherine looked down at herself, her hoodie, her old jeans.

"Coffee's ready," she finally called through the screen door.

Parker went into the powder room to freshen up as Mike came into the kitchen.

"Hey, something smells good," he said.

"Scones," Mary Catherine said as she split one with a butcher knife. "Fresh from the oven. So, what's the story with your FBI friend? Is something up?"

"I'm not sure yet. She said she needs to talk to me about a case," Mike said, taking a bite of a scone.

"Are the phones down or something?" Mary Catherine said.

Mike shrugged as he chewed, a puzzled look on his face like he actually wasn't sure what was going on. But Mary Catherine knew Mike. He was a bad liar. Playing dumb was definitely not his forte. Something was going on. Something bad. As if they needed that now. As if they needed more turmoil.

"Well, I've put on coffee for you two," Mary Catherine said, heading for the back door. "The kids are all outside, so you'll have the place to yourselves."

"Oh. Thanks for going to all the trouble, Mary Catherine," Mike said. "This looks great. I appreciate it."

Gone

"No trouble at all," Mary Catherine said quietly as she turned her back on him and went out through the shrieking back door.

Chapter 10

EMILY AND I BROUGHT the coffee and the scones into the dining room.

I stole a sidelong look at Parker as she reached into her bag. She was as attractive as I remembered. Besides being smart and quite pretty, even north of thirty-five, there was this delightful, hard-to-describe, brave, and bright-eyed girlish quality to her that made people—men especially—sit up quite straight when she entered a room.

Actually, she was more attractive than I remembered, I thought, as the light caught the copper in her hair. Had she lost weight? No, I realized. She had actually put on a little. Wow. It really suited her. I realized now that she had been too thin when we'd worked together, sort of bony. She was curvier now, more voluptuous.

She was also more chic than I recalled. Her looser, fuller hair was salon cut, her cream-colored blouse made of silk. My breath caught a little when I got a whiff of her perfume. Oranges? Flowers? It smelled expensive. Delightful indeed.

"This has to be about Perrine," I said quickly as she straightened up and placed a laptop on the table. "Something bad, or why would you come in person? Let me guess. He killed someone I know. One of my neighbors. The super of my building?"

She shook her head.

"No, Mike. It's almost worse than that," Parker said, slipping on a slim pair of red-rimmed reading glasses. "We're getting crushed. The massive federal and local task force put together to capture Perrine is in shambles after all these Mob murders. Each strike was carried out by highly trained professional mercenaries with an almost surgical precision. We have no forensics and absolutely no leads. That's why the assistant director himself sent me out here to talk to you. My mission is to, quote, 'pick your brain.'"

"Pick my brain?" I said. "At least this won't take too long. How long have you been on the task force?"

"Oh, about two days. There I was, happily

reading in my Behavioral Science cubicle at Quantico. Then somebody told the director that you and I had worked closely together on some other cases, and now here I am."

I stared at her.

"The FBI director told you to talk to me?"

"I guess they didn't know if you would want to cooperate. Apparently, you were dismissed pretty harshly by the bureau after Perrine broke out of the courthouse. I guess I'm what you would call an official Department of Justice I'm Sorry card."

"Well, I must say, the director has good taste in stationery, but 'pick my brain'? That's the new plan? That does sound pretty desperate."

Parker moved her glasses down to the end of her pert, upturned nose.

"Is it? You're the most tenacious investigator I've ever worked with, period. You're also the only one who's ever actually caught Perrine, Mike."

"Sure, I caught Perrine, but then I lost him," I said.

Something flashed in Parker's intelligent blue eyes.

"Bite your tongue. *You* did not lose him, Mike. He wasn't in your custody when he escaped. You and I both know that he bought off a whole bunch of people in order to get out of that courthouse. You weren't the one who was paid to drop the ball."

"If you say so."

"I say so," Emily said. "Anyway, since I'm here, do you think you could take a look at what we have?"

I squinted up at the ceiling, a fist under my chin.

"Sorry, can't do it. Impossible," I finally said, shaking my head vehemently.

I waited until her jaw finished dropping.

"Only kidding," I said. "Just a little tenacious-investigator humor. Let's see what you've got, Agent Parker."

Chapter 11

SHE HIT SOME BUTTONS that brought up a screen and then clicked on a video. It was black-and-white footage. Maybe military. It was an aerial shot of cars and trucks moving along an abandoned desert road.

"This footage is from exactly one week ago. It was taken from a high-altitude drone above Creel, Mexico, a tiny resort town near the Copper Canyon section of Chihuahua," she said.

"The FBI flies high-altitude drones now?" I said. "In foreign countries?"

"No, but the air force does," Emily said. "Is it that much of a shock that the military is involved in this, Mike? This is Homeland Security priority one. Just about everybody is involved."

I absorbed that with a nod.

"Who's in the cars?"

"We got intel that a high-level cartel meeting was taking place, so we had a plaza boss out of Río Bravo followed."

"A plaza boss?" I said.

"A plaza boss controls the centers of the border towns where the drugs and the drug mules congregate. After the drugs make it up from the south, they use these plazas as staging areas where they can organize, distribute, and prepare the product for smuggling across the US border."

The phalanx of cars pulled to a stop in front of a large, compoundlike building. What looked like tents were set up in the backyard. There were a large number of vehicles already there. There must have been fifty or sixty cars parked in a field beside the structure.

"It looks like a wedding," I said.

"Almost," Emily said. "It's the *quinceañera* of the daughter of cartel leader Teodoro Salinas."

I knew who Salinas was from the web news. He was the leader of the only cartel left that wasn't under Perrine's control.

Parker suddenly hit Fast-Forward on the video.

"Watch what happens."

She hit Play again, and suddenly people were

pouring out of the building, some of them running. There was a traffic jam in the parking lot as cars and trucks peeled out.

"A Mexican fire drill?" I said.

"It's something. We don't know exactly what. All we know is, our guy never came back for his car. Two of the other cars that were also left behind belonged to rivals of Perrine's Los Salvajes organization. And Teodoro Salinas is missing. There's been no word."

"That is a mystery. You think Perrine had something to do with it? You think he was there?" I said.

"We're not sure," Emily said.

I stared at the screen.

"Well, let's see. Three dirtbags enter, no dirtbags leave," I said. "Then a bunch of people suddenly flee in panic. Sounds a lot like the Manuel Perrine that I've come to know and love."

Chapter 12

"HOW LONG DO YOU think we have to stay out here?" Ricky said, watching as the beat-up Wilson football Brian tossed to him flew over his head.

"Agent Parker's car is still there, right? So at least until it leaves, dummy," Brian said, gesturing for the ball.

Ricky searched for the ball in the tall grass. It had been almost an hour, and here they still were, out in the back "yard." It was no yard. It was a field you couldn't see the end of. It was the size of Central Park—Manhattan, maybe. It had been cool at first, but now it was just like everything else out here in nowhere land. Extremely boring.

"What do you think they're talking about in there?" Ricky said.

"Probably how this place is too visible for us,

and they need to send us somewhere really remote," Brian said.

"This sucks," Ricky said as he finally found the ball. "Even with the delay, you know Mary Catherine is going to want us to do our schoolwork anyway. I wanted to catch *Matlock*. Now it'll be over by the time we're done."

"No," Brian said. "What really sucks is that you actually care if you miss a stupid, crappy eighties show about an old guy."

Jane, sitting with her back to the car shed, dropped her book and jumped up and intercepted Ricky's return pass right before Brian could catch it.

"It could be worse," she said.

"Give me the ball," Brian said.

"How the hell could it be worse, Jane?" Ricky continued. "New York had its downsides, but I had, like, friends, you know? Things I liked to do. Now I'm a hick. We don't even go to school! I mean, if we had a washboard and a jug to blow into, we could start a band."

"Give me the ball," Brian insisted again.

Jane finally flicked it to him.

"He's telling the truth, you know, Jane. Last week, I even busted Dad listening to country music. I'm starting to think there is no threat from that cartel guy. Maybe Dad's just gone crazy and turned the whole lot of us into a bunch of crazy backwoods hicks."

"But I thought you liked the animals, Ricky," Jane said, ignoring Brian.

"For about five minutes," Ricky said. "I'm going to be thirteen, Jane. Old MacDonald sitting on his stupid fence has lost his charm."

"Exactly," Brian said, overthrowing Ricky again by twenty yards. "It's bad enough we're living out here like doomsday preppers. Do we have to actually become farmers? In fact, I say we end this right now. If the peewees want to follow Mr. Cody around, more power to them. My days of waking at the crack of dawn and working for free are done."

"You said it," Ricky agreed, throwing the ball back to his brother. "Don't they have child-labor laws in this state? Only problem is, how are we going to get out of it?"

"He's right, Brian," Jane said, intercepting the ball again. "Mary Catherine won't sit still for that. You know how much she likes Mr. Cody."

All three of them turned as they heard the rental car start. Agent Parker waved to them before getting in and pulling out. They stood in the field, waving back until they couldn't see the car anymore.

"No! Come back! Take us with you!" Ricky said.

"Don't worry, little brother. I have a plan," Brian said, spinning the ball up in the air. "You just leave it to me."

Chapter 13

I WAITED ON THE porch until Emily Parker's sedan disappeared in the distance, and then I went back into the house and took the dishes into the kitchen.

In the corner, I saw that, despite her obvious annoyance at the federal intrusion, Mary Catherine had put on another pot of coffee. When I looked out the window, I could see her sitting on the fence behind the house, showing something green and fuzzy in her palm to Shawna and Fiona. Probably seamlessly weaving in some lesson about the life cycle while she was at it, I thought, teachable moments being yet another specialty of the ever-upbeat and unstoppable Bennett nanny.

Mary Catherine was handing the caterpillar off to Shawna when she looked up and saw me watching. She stuck her tongue out at me, but then she smiled and waved. I smiled myself as I waved back vigorously.

Friends again, I thought. Good. Lord knew I needed all the friends I could find.

I decided to pitch in and wash the dishes at the big porcelain sink. I'd washed a dish or two in my time working in restaurants when I was in college, but I couldn't remember the last time I'd actually washed any by hand. Then I did remember. It was when my mom went back to work when I was a kid.

She got a job cleaning offices downtown, and my dad and I had to fend for ourselves. My dad, no Bobby Flay, would char some pork chops in a big, black cast-iron pan and boil some potatoes, while I got cleanup detail. It was a grim time, to be sure, but I do remember how proud my mom was of my meticulous dish cleaning.

Remember, Michael Sean, she'd always say, *it's never the job you do but how hard you do it.*

I liked to think I'd taken her words to heart in the four-odd decades I'd lived on this planet. I had worked hard as a father, as a cop.

And now where am I? I thought, drying my hands. *Hiding out from a violent drug lord with my family in the wilds of Northern California.* I'd worked hard, all right. I'd damned near worked myself out of a job.

After I dried the plates and cups and put everything back in its proper place, I opened the tap and poured myself a glass of cold water. I took a long drink and then opened the tap again and cupped some water in my hands and splashed it over my face.

Only then did I go over the full significance of everything Emily Parker had told me.

I had hoped I was just being cynical about law enforcement's lack of information. I hadn't been. They really didn't know anything about the attacks on the Mafia. There were no witnesses, no DNA traces, and no leads.

That wasn't the only problem, unfortunately. Emily had told me some new, disturbing information that actually hadn't made the papers.

Throughout the Mexican border towns where the cartels were most active—Ciudad Juárez, Tijuana, Puerto Palomas, Reynosa, Nogales, and Nuevo Laredo—all the informants for both the DEA and Mexican *federales* were being systematically wiped out.

It was a veritable purge. In the middle of the

night, three or four pickup trucks would show up, and people would be dragged out of their houses by what seemed like army troops dressed in black. The informants' headless torsos would be found a few days later, dumped in front of police stations, the words *ESTO SUCEDE A RATAS* spray-painted across their chests.

This is what happens to rats.

It was unprecedented stuff. Some were saying that someone in US federal law enforcement had to be tipping off Perrine. It also had to be someone pretty high up in the FBI or the DEA, since the identities of the slain informants were top secret.

It was almost too incredible to believe that things were actually getting worse. Almost fifty thousand people had died in the last few years of the cartels' domination. Five thousand people were missing. Now, with the attacks on the Mob, our worst nightmare was coming true. Border be damned, the cartels were expanding into the Mob's territory. No different from terrorists or an invading army, they were here among us, killing Americans with impunity.

Emily had also explained the egregious political horseshit that was going on in our government. With the approach of an election year, the president, looking for the Hispanic vote, had backed off on strong border policies. In fact, the Justice Department had actually put some pressure on the state governments in Arizona and Texas to tone down their "aggressive border-related law enforcement."

No doubt about it. It was *Alice in Wonderland* crazy time. No wonder Perrine was on the rise.

And that wasn't even the only new terror-inducing bit of inside scoop Emily had given me. Apparently, an insanely toxic and strange white substance had been found at one of the Mob hits in Malibu.

Emily had actually shown me pictures of the Mob boss and his wife, who had been exposed to the substance, and it was something else. Their skin was a shade of purple I'd never seen before. It looked as if they had been turned inside out.

I was standing there, trying to get the frightening images out of my head, when one of the kids hit a Wiffle ball off the windowsill. I looked out the window at my kids, running around oblivious in the side yard.

Jane was in a lawn chair with her nose deep in a Pokémon encyclopedia, while Ricky and Eddie were shooting at each other with gun-shaped sticks. Brian had arranged a game of Wiffle ball for the younger kids, and as I watched, Chrissy hit the ball and began running toward third until Fiona grabbed her and turned her around.

After a second, I pulled open the back door and lifted a second foul ball before Shawna could pick it up. Shawna squealed happily as I actually picked her up as well.

"OK, butterfly girl," I said, forcing a smile onto my face. "Playtime's over. Who's going to be the first one to try to deal with Daddy's screwball?"

Chapter 14

MARY CATHERINE'S HAIR WAS still wet from her shower when she came down the stairs into the kitchen the next morning before dawn.

She smiled as she turned on the oven to warm yesterday's blueberry scones. The scones had been Juliana's idea: switch out the raisins in her Irish soda bread recipe with blueberries, and dust it with sugar. Could she be any prouder of Juliana? She was going on seventeen now, and instead of being a drama queen, the eldest Bennett just dug in every chance she got, with very little grumbling about it.

She'd be leaving them soon enough, Mary Catherine knew. Juliana had recently confided that she wanted to join the Coast Guard, of all things. She said she loved the ocean and thought it would be a great way to serve her country and learn something. She could also save money for college, knowing how difficult a challenge tuition would be for their huge family. *What planet do these kids come from again?* Mary Catherine thought.

She'd been worried about the transition for them, but they were adjusting. In the beginning, she'd had to peel them off the couch in front of the TV, but now they actually preferred being outside. They'd stay out there all day if she let them, running around in all that space or exploring the little stand of trees beyond the creek.

They really were a special bunch. They all had their quirks, of course, but overall, they were happy and obedient and well-mannered beyond their years. Sure, they liked to goof around, but the amount of general goodwill and fellowship they had for each other was quite remarkable.

Had Mike instilled that in them? Their deceased mom, Maeve? Whoever it was, they deserved a medal, because through thick and through thin, somehow these guys made it work. She'd never met a nicer, tighter, more down-to-earth group of caring kids.

She smiled as she looked around the room. She loved the old kitchen. The handmade cabinets, the huge pine table they used as an island, the pots and pans hanging on the rack above the new Kenmore stove.

There was even a real mudroom with a sink, where they stored the slickers and the wellies. The mudroom reminded her of the one on the farm where she'd grown up, in Ireland. So much so that on some dark mornings, coming down to get breakfast going, she would look through the mudroom doorway and could almost smell the acrid scent of turf smoke, almost hear the whistle of the kettle coming to a boil.

Even though we're in hiding, it actually is a good place here, Mary Catherine thought for the hundredth time. It felt warm, safe. It felt like home.

Chapter 15

FIVE MINUTES LATER, MARY Catherine had the big pine table covered with four different types of bread, spreading mayo here, peanut butter there, portioning out cold cuts.

She hadn't made the kids brown-bag lunches since New York and had almost forgotten what a Herculean feat it really was. It would have been fine if she could have made, say, just ten bologna sandwiches and been done with it, but of course they all had their idiosyncrasies. Shawna had to have a plain bologna sandwich, while Chrissy would tolerate only grape jelly with her peanut butter. Some would eat only turkey, others only ham. Ricky's order was the biggest pain: yellow American cheese (not white, heaven forbid) and mustard on wheat toast.

She'd already made potato salad and a couple of loaves of banana bread the evening before. It was all for the surprise picnic she had planned. After milking, Mr. Cody wanted to take everyone to a part of the ranch they'd never seen before, the rugged, hilly southeastern section. Cody had been out riding on his horse, Marlowe, the afternoon before and had spotted a huge, hundred-head herd of wild antelope that he wanted to show the kids.

Mary Catherine looked out at the sun, just cresting the top of the Sierras. She couldn't believe this place. Every day was like a new show on the Discovery Channel.

After she'd Sharpied each of the kids' names on their tinfoil-wrapped sandwiches, she went into Jane's room to wake her up. Jane was sleeping in the lower-left bunk of the girls' two sets of bunk beds. Mary Catherine smiled when she saw the latest Rick Riordan paperback on the floor over the flashlight Jane wasn't supposed to use to stay up late reading.

Mary Catherine gently shook her shoulder.

"Rise and shine, kiddo," she said.

Jane opened her eyes and stared up at her strangely. Then she let out a low groan.

"I'm not feeling well, Mary Catherine," she said.

"What is it? What's wrong? Do you feel hot?" Mary Catherine asked, putting a hand on her forehead.

"No, it's mostly my stomach," Jane said. "Maybe it's something I ate."

It's probably nothing, Mary Catherine thought, squinting at her. Too much popcorn from the *National Treasure* movie-a-thon the girls had watched the night before.

"I'll go and get you a ginger ale," Mary Catherine said.

Before she went downstairs, she went into the boys' room and shook the first foot she could find.

"Time to get up, Eddie," Mary Catherine said. "It's getting late. Could you wake the others for me?"

After a moment there came another low groan.

"Mary Catherine, my stomach's killing me," Eddie said. "I'm sick. I think I'm going to throw up."

"Me too," Brian said a moment later.

"Me three, MC. I really feel like I'm going to yack," called out Ricky.

What?! Mary Catherine thought, panicking. They'd had a turkey for dinner the night before. *Is it food poisoning?* she thought. *Salmonella?* That was all they needed. She hadn't even had a chance to find a pediatrician.

"Oh, no, guys. Jane's sick, too," Mary Catherine said. "Hang in there. You must have caught some sort of bug. I'll wake your father. We need to find you guys a doctor right away."

"Actually, you don't need to go to all that trouble, Mary Catherine," Brian said, sitting up across the room.

"What do you mean?" Mary Catherine said. "Of course I do."

"We're not that kind of sick," Brian told her.

Mary Catherine stared at him, confused.

"What kind of sick are you?" she asked.

Brian sat up against his headboard and folded his arms. "We're the sick-and-tired-of-doing-all-these-stupid-farm-chores kind of sick," he said. "Nobody asked us if we wanted to become agricultural slave labor, OK? We're hereby done with the milking. Hereby done with the whole cock-a-doodle-doo, crack-of-dawn hick routine. This is a strike."

Chapter 16

I WOKE UP TO a whole heap of commotion the next morning. It wasn't even the rooster this time. There was yelling at first. Then it stopped, and then came something that shot me out of bed like a skyrocket.

A loud, cacophonous clanging was coming from downstairs. It was amazingly loud, like an old school fire alarm or the hammering of a boxing bell after the last round.

I tripped out of bed and found my robe and headed down the stairs two by two. It was coming from the boys' room. What the hell now? I couldn't believe it. It was Mary Catherine. She was yelling like a drill sergeant as she banged two pots together.

"That's it! Out of your beds, you lazy so-and-sos! Everybody up now. I said up! And on your feet! You think you can sleep in, you're wrong! Every last one of you, rise and shine!"

Mary Catherine fired the pots into the corner and stood there sweating, her fists balled. I was about to say something, but when Mary Catherine glared at me, I immediately shut my trap.

"What the heck did you do?" I mouthed to Brian.

He just swallowed as he stood there, as wide-eyed as the rest of us. I'd never seen Mary Catherine so fired up.

"Trent!" Mary Catherine barked.

"Yes, Mary Catherine?" Trent said, like a nervous miniature recruit about to start marine boot camp.

"Get the girls in here, pronto! They're part of this. I know they are."

"Yes, Mary Catherine."

The girls came into the room sheepishly, followed by a groggy Seamus.

"Now, whose idea was this? Tell me now who organized this little work stoppage."

Everybody glanced at each other.

"We all did," Brian said after a moment.

"Oh, you all did? How creative of you. That's

just great. After all I do for the lot of you, you plot behind my back? That's just a real fine how-do-you-do after the nice meal I cooked for everyone last night. Speaking of which, I have a question for you. Where did that food come from?"

"Mr. Cody," Eddie said, raising his hand.

"Wrong," Mary Catherine snapped at him. "Also, you all slept warm in your beds last night under this roof. Where did this house come from?"

"Um, Mr. Cody?" Eddie tried again.

"Wrong again, wise guy," Mary Catherine said. "Food, houses, everything good that you use in this world, comes from one place: work. Men and women worked to put food on your plate. Men and women worked to put this house together. Now, let me ask you another question. Where would the lot of you be if all those men and women decided to claim that they were sick and sleep in?"

"Up a creek?" Eddie said with a shrug.

"Finally, Eddie, you got one exactly right. Without people working, we'd all be up a certain type of creek without a paddle."

Mary Catherine circled the room, staring into each of the kids' faces one by one.

"I think you guys know me pretty well by now.

I try to help everyone. Sometimes I even let things slide."

She stopped in the center of the room.

"But what I will not do, by God, is sit idly by and watch all of you become a lot of lazy, useless ragamuffins. While I live and breathe, you will do three things. You will work. You will help. And you will pitch in. Or I'm out of here. You'll never see me again. Understand? No work, no food, no house, no nanny. Is that perfectly clear?"

"Yes, Mary Catherine," a few of them said.

"What? I can't hear you!" Mary Catherine yelled.

"Yes, Mary Catherine," everyone said loudly, including me and Seamus.

I stepped back as my young, blond nanny hurried out of the room, her blue eyes sparking. I actually had goose bumps on my arms.

Whoa, Nelly. Talk about a wake-up call!

"Exactly," I said to the kids after Mary Catherine left. "Exactly what she said, and don't you ever forget it!"

Chapter 17

THE NEXT MORNING, I awoke with a start as my bedroom door creaked open. It was early, I saw, as I glanced with one eye at the still dark-gray window, and someone was out in the hallway.

Something was up. Of course it was. Something was always up.

"Hark! Who goes there?" I said into my pillow. "If it's you, Mary Catherine, please, no pots and pans this morning. I'll be up in a second, I swear."

"Good morning, Michael. Are ye awake?" Seamus whispered.

"I am now," I said, sitting up in bed. "What is it? Let me guess. The kids are occupying the barn."

"No, it's not that," Seamus said, stepping in and closing the door behind him.

"How are you this morning?" he said sheepishly. "Sleep well?"

I noticed that he was showered and wide awake and wearing his formal black priest suit with his Roman collar.

"I was, Father. I was sleeping as well as you please. I remember it quite fondly. What is it? Are you here to give me last rites? What in the Wild Wild West is going on?"

"Well, I—" he started. "What I mean to say is that . . . I guess you could say I have a confession to make."

"A confession?" I said, sitting up. "That's a switch. Wow, this almost sounds good enough for you to wake me in the middle of the night. Please, my son, confess away. Unload thy soul."

"Well, you know how you told us all repeatedly to keep a low profile?" Seamus said, wincing.

I stared my grandfather solidly in his not-so-innocent blue eyes.

"Yes. I believe we were all there for the conversation with the witness protection folks."

"Well, I haven't been exactly following the rules. I was talking to Rosa, and she was telling me about the local priest in town. She kept telling me what a nice man he was, and I gave him a call. She was right. Father Walter is a very nice man. Actually, we've been talking back and forth for a couple of weeks now."

What a thoroughly nutty situation this all is, I thought. Seamus felt guilty about talking to another priest?

"OK," I said. "You and the local guy are talking shop. Did you tell him who we were?"

"No, of course not," Seamus said.

"Why do I have the feeling that there's another shoe about to drop?" I said.

"Well, being the only priest in the parish, he's swamped. I guess I let it be known that I might be available under extreme circumstances to help out. One of those situations just came up. His father had a heart attack, and he asked if I could fill in today for early-morning Mass."

"Holy cannoli, Father," I said. "Why would you say that?"

"Fine. I'll admit it. I want to say Mass. Is that a sin? I haven't said Mass in a while, and I want to."

"But you say Mass for us here at the house every Sunday morning."

"That's not the same thing as saying Mass in a church, at an altar, Detective Bennett. I really miss it, Michael. I feel utterly, completely useless out here in the middle of nowhere."

I looked at him. I knew how that felt.

"Listen, Father. I feel useless, too, but this guy who's after us is not messing around. He's spending a lot of money to find us. We can't risk it."

"I know. You're right," Seamus said. "I'll tell him I can't do it. What do people's souls really matter anyway, right?"

I sighed.

"Where's the church?"

"It's Our Lady of Sorrows, in Westwood."

"When is Mass?"

Seamus looked at his watch.

"Starts in an hour."

"OK, Father Pain-in-My-Ankle," I said as I finally stood. "Put on some coffee and let me hop in the shower. I wouldn't want to be late for Mass."

Chapter 18

ABOUT TEN MILES TO the northwest, Westwood was a quiet, tiny mountain town that didn't stand on too much ceremony. There was a farmer's market, a post office, a couple of streets of small, neat houses with pickups in the driveways and grills on the front porches.

"Hey, look, Dad," my eldest daughter, Juliana, said from the backseat. "That's a pizza place coming up."

Juliana had overheard Seamus and me in the kitchen and insisted on coming along to be Seamus's altar server. She claimed that she wasn't just trying to get out of her homeschool classes, but I had my doubts.

"And oh, darn, there the pizza place goes," I said, driving past it. "We're in hiding, Juliana.

No town pizza. If this weren't a four-alarm Catholic emergency, we wouldn't even be here."

There were more pickups in the parking lot of Our Lady of Sorrows, beat-up work vans with ladders on top. Seamus had explained that the congregation included a lot of farmworkers, many of them unemployed after environmentalists in the state legislature had head-scratchingly cut down the rural area's water allowance for the year. Without the water, farmers had been forced to let fields lie fallow, and now there were a lot of unemployed people hurting.

Thanks, government, I thought, parking Aaron Cody's seventies muscle wagon in the corner of the lot. *Take a bow. Another job well done.*

"Our Lady of Sorrows, indeed," I mumbled when I saw the food-bank notice on the bulletin board beside the door of the tiny white church.

The inside of the church was very plain. Definitely not St. Patrick's Cathedral, but there was something nice about it, something serene. Instead of an organ, there was an old piano beside the altar, currently being played beautifully by a thin, red-haired middle-aged woman.

"That's Abigail, the parish secretary," Seamus

said. "Juliana and I better get going. She's supposed to show us where everything is."

"I guess it's OK," I grumbled as I looked around at the blue-haired congregation. "Not too many gangbangers around."

"Exactly, Dad," Juliana said, rolling her eyes. "Everyone knows the gangbangers just go to Sunday Mass."

I knelt at a pew at the back of the church after they left. I hadn't been to early-morning Mass during the week in ages.

I used to go all the time in the months after my wife, Maeve, was diagnosed with ovarian cancer. Before or after my shift at work, every chance I got, I would head to Holy Name Church, a couple of blocks from our building. The youngest person there by decades, I would sit in the front and pray with everything in me for my wife to somehow be OK, for God to grant me a miracle.

Because, while people talk about their wife being their better half, Maeve was more like my better three-quarters, my better seven-eighths. She was the saint who'd put our crazy, wonderful family together. *Mike, we need to adopt another one*, she'd say. And I'd look over at her, at the holy look in her eyes, and I was suddenly the farm boy from

The Princess Bride, and it was "As you wish" time.

But, prayers or no prayers, God wasn't having any of it. Maeve died almost six months to the day of her cancer diagnosis. It had been years now since she'd passed away, but her spirit was very much alive, and she was still such a source of strength for me.

"Hey, babe," I whispered up at the rafters. "What do I do now?"

The church filled up more than I'd thought it would. In addition to the requisite white-haired old-timers, there were quite a few able-bodied young white and Hispanic men who looked like they worked outside. Praying for work, no doubt. For some hope, I thought, feeling bad for them. I checked my wallet and fished out a twenty to slip into the poor box on the way out.

It was just before the gospel when a strange guy with a gray ponytail and a scraggly white beard came into the church behind me.

"Well, what do you know? It's actually true," the guy whispered as he climbed into the pew beside me. "Open the door, and here's the people."

I looked him over. With his camouflage hunting anorak over his greasy jeans, and with suspiciously glassy eyes, the old hippie had a very strong resemblance to a homeless person. Or maybe to Nick Nolte about to get a mug shot taken.

"*Welcome to the Hotel California,*" I thought, rolling my eyes.

My cop radar thought Nick Gra-Nolte might pass out or cause some trouble, but as the Mass went on, he knelt when he was supposed to and knew all the prayers. He even knew all the annoying changes in the prayers that the church had just dropped on everyone out of the blue.

But as I stood to line up for Communion, I couldn't help noticing what he was carrying at the back of his worn jeans.

It was a pistol, a Smith & Wesson semiauto, not in a holster, just tucked there, happy as you please.

Peace, love, and a nine millimeter? I thought, my cop radar clicking up to DEFCON 3.

Chapter 19

I WAS READY TO tackle the guy the whole way up the aisle. As it turned out, nothing happened. I breathed a sigh of relief as the old hippie left right after Communion.

But, of course, it wasn't over. Nick Nolte was pretending to read the bulletin board when I went out with Seamus and Juliana ten minutes after the end of Mass.

What will happen now? I thought, my hand tracing the line of my back where my gun was located. A postservice Wild West gunfight? I mean, give me a break. My blood pressure really didn't need this.

"Hi, strangers," the hippie said, smiling.

I noticed for the first time that the guy was in pretty good shape—broad shouldered, with big hands. I instinctively put myself between him and Juliana.

"Nice service," the guy said. "Are you guys new to the parish?"

"No," I answered for Seamus. "We're just passing through."

"Passing through?" the hippie said. "In Aaron Cody's station wagon?"

"You ask a lot of questions," I said. "I got one for you. You always carry in church?"

"Carry?" the hippie said, his bleary eyes squinting. "Oh, you mean the ol' *pistola* here," he said, giggling as he patted the small of his back after a beat. "Oh, sure. All us rootin' tootin' cowboys up here like our Second Amendment rights. That goes without saying. How about you? You always carry in church?"

"Get in the car, guys," I said to Juliana and Seamus as I walked over to the still-giggling weirdo. Despite my initial paranoia and the guy's roscoe, I could tell he was just a high California goofball.

"It's been really fun talking to you, bro," I said, smiling as I stared into his red eyes, "but don't you think it's time for you to grab a bag of Doritos and go watch *Jerry Springer*?"

He burst out laughing at that.

"I like you. You're funny," he said, going into his anorak pocket.

"Tight-lipped, too," he said, removing a fat joint and lighting it with a Zippo as if it were the most natural thing in the world. He blew some rancid smoke in my direction.

"Around here, tight-lipped works just fine," he said. "Actually, I was just trying to be neighborly. The priest's accent reminds me of my grand-pap. I'm Irish, too. They call me McMurphy. There's a little bar down the road a bit called Buffalo Gil's. Why don't we meet up? I'll buy you a Guinness."

I stared at the lit weirdo, wondering why this kind of crap always happened to me. I mean, talking to drugged crazy people was fun, but I had cows to milk.

"Sounds like a plan, McMurphy, but I actually have a better idea," I said as I turned to walk toward the car.

"Yeah, what's that?" my new dope-smoking hippie friend wanted to know.

"How about we don't meet up, but we just tell everyone we did?" I said as I climbed into the station wagon.

He stared at me blankly as I started the engine,

but just as I pulled past him, he suddenly got it.

In my rearview mirror, I watched as the nut broke up, laughing in the empty parking lot, the joint in his hand falling to the gravel as he slapped at his greasy thigh.

Chapter 20

VIDA GOMEZ KEPT THE stolen Cadillac Escalade at a steady sixty as they rolled east on the San Bernardino Expressway in El Monte, east of downtown LA.

They were nearing their exit when a motorcycle gang roared past out of nowhere. Completely startled, she cursed violently as a dozen black-leather-clad motorcyclists on big Jap bikes screamed around both sides of her SUV like a fusillade of just-missing guided missiles.

Assholes, she thought, seething, as one of the devil-may-care speeding bikers popped a wheelie. She could have shot one of them. All of them, in fact. The thing she hated most on this earth was to be snuck up on.

Trying to roll the tension out of her neck, she

glanced back at the six buzz-cut men seated behind her to see if any of them had witnessed her blow her cool. But they were calm, oblivious, half of them dozing as usual.

Though all of Perrine's handpicked cartel soldiers had obeyed her so far, she never once forgot that they were killers of distinction from a place where killers were a dime a dozen. Any sign of weakness, even the slightest hint of fear, could be fatal in her line of work.

What was up with her today? she wondered. It definitely wasn't like her to be so jumpy. This morning she'd woken up with a bad feeling. It was something in the air that wouldn't quit, a brooding sensation that something unpleasant was about to occur.

Or was she just being paranoid? Having a bout of stage fright? She didn't know. The only thing she knew was, this was definitely the part she hated the most, the space between the plan and the execution.

The latest task given to her elite squad was to deal with an Asian gang out of El Monte called the Triumph Dragons. The Vietnamese gang, though quite small, ran one of the busiest docks out at the Port of Los Angeles, down in Long Beach. Perrine had made a deal with them to let a large shipment through, but at the last second, the Dragons had reneged, causing the seizure by the US Coast Guard of an entire shipping container filled to the brim with premium Colombian heroin.

Manuel had not been pleased. Yesterday afternoon, the cartel boss had forwarded to Vida a very simple instruction by encrypted text message.

Slay the dragons, his text had said. Each and every one.

She weaved through the dense El Monte neighborhood until she found the location she was looking for, a deserted parking lot behind a shuttered supermarket on Cogswell Road.

The young man slouching in the passenger seat beside her loudly slurped at the last of his McDonald's chocolate shake as they came to a stop.

"You're going to do this now, right, Jorge? Not having any second thoughts on me, right?" she said in Spanish.

"Please," Jorge said, looking at her, his brown eyes soft in his even softer face.

Youthful appearance aside, Jorge was an up-and-comer in the cartel's newest ally, Mara Salvatrucha, the brutal Hispanic gang otherwise known as MS-13.

Jorge had dealt to the Dragons before, so his job had been to set up a dope deal. Five kilos of coke at the cut-rate price of $12K per. There weren't any drugs, of course, and the only thing cut-rate was going to be the lives of the Vietnamese gangbangers, as soon as they showed up.

Vida looked out on the El Monte neighborhood as they waited. Low stucco houses, palm trees, chain-link fences. California shabby, minus the chic. Above it all, dark clouds rolled against the fast-fading gold of the sky.

More waiting, she thought, feeling like a bubble about to pop. It was driving her mad.

Vida sat bolt upright as Jorge's phone finally rattled in the silence.

"Is it them?" she said hopefully.

"It's them," Jorge said with a nod. "They just got off the expressway."

Chapter 21

AT JORGE'S CONFIRMATION, THE inside of the truck was immediately filled with the meticulous, oiled click and snap of guns being loaded and readied.

Music to my ears, Vida thought.

Vida put a hand to her brow. Even with the AC jacked, she was sweating, amped up beyond belief. She had to slow things down and concentrate. She counted backward from ten as she carefully dried her hands and face with a McDonald's napkin.

Then she reached back and accepted her trusty MGP-84, which the cartel soldier behind her handed up.

"Let's go over it one more time," Vida said to Jorge, who was nervously playing with the door latch.

The young man sighed.

"I roll up, make nice, make sure the gang's all there," he said quickly. "Then I whistle over to you like I want you to bring the stuff, right?"

"Then duck, Jorge," Vida said, showing him her Peruvian machine pistol as she draped a motherly arm over his shoulder.

The rough men behind them in the SUV chuckled as they polished gun sights and tightened weapon straps over their burly forearms.

"You don't want to forget that last part, homey," one of them said in a low voice as Jorge finally swung open the door.

Jorge was sitting up on the abandoned supermarket's concrete loading dock as a car pulled into the lot. The new black Audi A4 with tinted everything pulled up directly in front of Jorge, and three Asians immediately got out, leaving the driver behind the wheel.

Vida scanned the men quickly with a pair of binoculars. The young, heavily tattooed Vietnamese thugs might have hidden handguns, she thought, but that was it. So far, so bad. For them, at least.

Vida peered closer at the tallest of them. She quickly looked at some pictures on her phone, comparing. *Well, what do you know?* A stroke of good luck. The tall forty-something Asian with the handsome, angular face looked an awful lot like Giang Truong, the head Triumph Dragon honcho who, after the port fiasco, had personally told Manuel to go fuck himself. Manuel said if they took out Truong, their crew would split a bonus of $50K!

All of her anxiety had been for nothing. Her and her superstitions. Everything was coming together just fine.

Jorge wasn't through with the hand slapping when it started. From one of the cruddy houses across the street came a loud bang. Then, all of a sudden, out of nowhere, there was a group of large men wearing blue Windbreakers, running across the street toward them. At the same time, two marked and two unmarked cop cars rolled out from behind the supermarket like they were some kind of circus trick.

"Everyone on the ground!" a bullhorn cried as the first cop car raced toward them. "This is the Los Angeles Police Department! Turn off your engines and exit your vehicles! We have you completely surrounded!"

Chapter 22

"SHIT! SHIT! SHIT!" VIDA cried as she watched the cops advance and the world end.

When she turned back toward the loading dock, she watched as the Triumph Dragons piled into the already-moving Audi. The sports car squealed past the SUV, almost hitting it as it headed east.

They were running. *Good idea,* Vida thought. Jorge wasn't completely in the car when she slammed the SUV into drive and the accelerator into the floor.

She almost collided head-on with the first cop car as she roared out of the lot, heading west. In her rearview, she could see one of the unmarked cars fishtail and hammer after her, its blue light bubbling. It must have been some kind of souped-up copmobile, she thought, because after a minute, it really started gaining on them.

I can't have that, Vida thought, instantly taking a left in the middle of the house-lined block.

The SUV lurched and almost tipped as it skidded sideways over a grassless lawn. Its big, screeching wheels caught a driveway, and then the front air bags went off in two loud, white puffs as the grille smashed through a chain-link fence into a backyard.

Wood crunched as they blurred through a play set and another wooden fence. Then they swerved alongside another stucco shitbox, veered onto another driveway, and were bouncing over the curb onto the street opposite the first.

Vida checked her mirrors. The following cop car was nowhere, at least for the moment. Wheels smoking, the big-block, four-hundred-horsepower engine howling, she hooked a right at the next corner, back toward the expressway.

Less than half a minute later, they'd made it. They turned another corner, and the on-ramp to the westbound San Bernardino was right there. In a minute, they would be on it and gone.

Instead of gunning it, though, Vida, biting her lip in concentration, pulled over on the shoulder under the expressway overpass beside the on-ramp and put the SUV into park.

"What are you waiting for?" Jorge said, banging on the dashboard. "Are you out of your mind? The cops are coming! I don't want to go to jail. We need to get the hell out of here. Let's go!"

Vida shook her head as she lifted her phone.

"Calm down. I won't tell you twice," she said. "You let me handle the cops. We can still get this done."

Chapter 23

EVERYONE IN THE SUV except Vida turned and looked back as the cop car that was following them screamed past on the perpendicular street behind them. Then they watched as it hit its brakes and swung around.

"They saw us! How about now? Can we go now?" Jorge wanted to know.

Vida shook her head.

"Out, men," she said calmly. "Lay down suppressing fire."

"Suppressing fire?!" Jorge yelled.

Vida placed her machine pistol to the young man's temple.

"That means you, too, Jorge. Time to grow some hair on that chest. Get the fuck out of this truck!"

In the falling dusk, in the middle of the busy

city street, the cartel hit team poured out of the vehicle and immediately opened fire on the approaching Crown Victoria. Against the iron-and-concrete tunnel of the overpass, the sudden rattling blast of the half-dozen fully automatic AR-15s and AK-47s going off at once was pants wetting. The oncoming cop car swung sideways and halted in the middle of the street, its perforated hood smoking, its windshield torn to shreds.

Still the cartel soldiers fired, without letup. Their shooting stance was textbook, rifle stocks tucked high in the shoulder as they smoothly squeezed off round after round after round.

Despite the war thundering around her, Vida's eyes were wide open as she put the SUV into drive.

Seconds later, the Triumph Dragons' Audi A4 appeared in the cross street in front of her, from the east. It was headed directly toward the on-ramp on her left, like she'd predicted. She stomped the accelerator into the floor.

She timed it perfectly. The Cadillac Escalade plowed directly into the side of the small, speeding Audi in a horrible crunch of metal. The Audi, spinning in a dog squeal of rubber, hit two other cars waiting at the light before it came to a stop.

Amid the automatic gunfire and screaming

citizens, Vida exited from the now-smoking Escalade with the machine pistol. The Triumph Dragons in the crumpled Audi were moaning as she walked over the broken glass. She emptied a clip into the wreckage, then reloaded and gave each man another short burst in the head just to be sure.

She dropped the machine pistol and took out her phone. People who had been waiting at the light abandoned their vehicles. Between the pauses in the gunfire behind her, she could hear sirens approaching in the distance. Then the phone was finally answered.

"Where are you?" Vida said. "We are in El Monte, just before the Peck Road on-ramp. We need you here now."

"Thirty seconds," a voice told her.

Moments later, she could hear them coming. The dozen-strong motorcycle pack that had passed her earlier suddenly poured off the expressway, their big Ninja and Hayabusa bikes raging and growling like starving grizzlies.

They were the insurance plan, Jorge's buddies, MS-13 members, their backup in case things went to shit. And, boy, had things gone to shit.

Her soldiers, still under the overpass, dropped

their guns and rushed forward and hopped onto the backs of the now-halted bikes. Vida counted heads and waited until Jorge and everyone else was accounted for before she hopped onto the back of one of the Jap bikes herself.

Then they all were accelerating, leaving the wreckage and dead Triumph Dragons and sirens behind as they roared out onto the expressway.

That's the way it's done, Vida thought as they zipped down the shoulder, the hundred-mile-an-hour wind ripping at her short hair. *Stick and move. Get in, do damage, get out.* Manuel wouldn't have done it any other way.

Vida allowed herself a tiny smile as she snuggled tighter into the driver. He opened it up, and LA warped into long streaks of white lines and yellow light.

Chapter 24

SIX HOURS LATER, COMING on two a.m., Vida Gomez was behind the front wheel of a new stolen SUV, a Toyota Land Cruiser that was parked in West Hollywood about three blocks south of the iconic HOLLYWOOD sign.

No rest for the weary, she thought, listening to music thump from a brightly lit glass house up the scrubby hill from where they were parked.

Keeping her eyes glued on the raucous Hollywood party, Vida took a sip from the stainless steel travel cup at her elbow. Instead of coffee, the cup contained *tejate*, a traditional energy drink from her native Oaxaca. Made from corn, cacao beans, mamey seeds, and *rosita* flowers, it was far more potent than anything from Starbucks.

With the unflagging pace she was clocking, she

needed the energy. There'd been barely enough time for a shower and a hastily eaten dinner at the safe house in La Brea. Now they were back at it, back out again on the street.

They had one more job tonight, one more hit, which was even more audacious than the last one, if that was possible. The house just up the winding road belonged to none other than celebrity rap music performer and producer Alan "King Killa" Leonard.

Some rap music record producers only fronted like they were gangbangers, but King Killa was actually the real deal. In addition to being a celebrity, he was the leader of a Bloods contingent that ran most of the cocaine trade in the Greater Los Angeles area. It was said that his influence even ran into the LAPD's infamous CRASH gang unit, where he had several officers on the payroll.

Like most of the gang leaders in the city, King Killa had recently been approached by Manuel's cartel to become his gang's new drug supplier. The gang leader had immediately and vehemently refused. Killa had even roughed up Manuel's representative and had gone so far as to put a gun in his mouth.

Bad move. That was why they were there.

Decisions had consequences. Manuel's order was explicit. Grammy awards or no Grammy awards, tonight, King Killa was to be executed.

At the safe house, Vida had reached out to Manuel via encrypted cell phone to make sure that he felt this second scheduled hit was prudent, after the unscheduled firefight with law enforcement in El Monte that was all over the news.

Manuel had texted back immediately.

Prudent? It is now more necessary than ever!!!! You are in Hollywood, Vida, are you not? The bigger the splash, the better!!! The biggest mistake when you are winning is to stop! Forward, my beautiful Vida. Forever forward.

Vida brought up the message on her phone again and frowned. She'd been afraid he would say something like that. They had gotten lucky once tonight. In her opinion, they were pushing it.

But what did her opinion matter? Nothing. She was smart enough to know not to question or even to comment on an order, however odious, if it came from Manuel himself.

Chapter 25

THE MUSIC SUDDENLY SUBSIDED ten minutes later, and the first of the cars triple-parked in front of the ostentatious glass house started down the hill.

They waited another half hour, until the traffic jam of limos and Jags and Mercs and vintage Porsches and other obnoxious automobiles rolled down, away from the house, before they stepped out of the Cruiser and into the darkness.

It was only a four-person job this time. The driver, Vida, her most trusted soldier, Estefan, and a pudgy soldier named Eduardo, who was an expert with the materials.

It took about half an hour to infiltrate. They would have done it much more quickly, but they encountered a thick chain-link fence at the rear of the property's perimeter that they had to bolt-cut through as slowly and quietly as they could. Past the hole in the fence was the basement door, which Vida scrub-picked herself in less than a minute.

Then they were actually inside King Killa's famous Hollywood house, which had been featured on MTV's *Cribs*. Vida had watched the episode several times in order to memorize the interior layout.

They found the utility room next to the one for the swimming pool pump. The HVAC unit was forced air, its blower humming busily as it circulated cool air throughout the house.

Eduardo knelt beside it and then gave an A-OK sign.

At the signal, Vida and her men quickly put on the Airhawk breathing suits they'd brought. Then Eduardo shut off the HVAC unit and unclasped the silver hardpack case containing the material.

They had used canisters at the mobster's house in Malibu, but they now used the deadly material in a very fine powder form. Eduardo removed the air filter from the unit and then dusted the filter liberally with the poison. Then he carefully slid the filter back into the unit and turned the blower on high.

Vida checked her watch as the fan hummed. They sat in the dark, waiting. After ten minutes, Eduardo repeated the process, powdering the filter a second time. Exactly twenty minutes after that, Vida nodded, and they headed up the basement stairs.

Inside the first bedroom they entered on the top floor was quite a surprise.

The surprise wasn't that the room's occupant was dead. They'd used enough poison to easily kill a hundred people, so of course she was dead. The surprise was that the woman lying in her own blood and snot in a fetal position on the carpet was Alexa Gia, the famous singer.

Was she seeing King Killa? Vida wondered. She didn't know. She only knew that the beautiful woman known as the Latina Madonna had recorded eleven number-one dance music hits in the eighties and nineties. Vida had actually danced to one of the singer's pop hits at her own *quinceañera.* Go figure.

Manuel wanted a big splash? Vida thought. He was about to get one. The death of the singer would be huge. About as high profile as it got.

Vida made sure to get a close-up of the singer's face with the video camera before they left. Of course, she was filming everything, as per the plan. Why Manuel wanted the grisly footage, she was unsure. She knew better than to inquire.

Well, if anything, the substance had worked even more potently than it had the last time, Vida thought as she toed King Killa's cheek, resting on the floor of his bathroom down the hall. The six-foot-six, three-hundred-thirty-pound man had made it only halfway to the toilet before he'd bled out of all his orifices like a butchered hog.

"OK, that's it. All the other rooms are empty," Eduardo said, tapping her on the shoulder. "Time to go."

"Wait, one thing. Just a moment," Vida said, spying something.

She carefully stepped around the blood pooled around the fallen rap impresario and knelt and removed his sparkling signature twenty-one-carat diamond earring.

Though it wasn't part of the plan, she would make sure to ship it out to Manuel first thing tomorrow morning via FedEx.

Manuel will like that, she thought with a small smile. The only thing he appreciated more than subtle gestures was unexpected gifts.

Chapter 26

THE NEXT MORNING—EARLY, of course—we were at Aaron Cody's farm, getting the milking going, when the old farmer pulled me and the rest of the Bennett boys aside.

"Gentlemen," Cody said, looking us over, "I got a call early this morning, and I was wondering if you all might be able to help me with a special assignment."

A special cattle-farm assignment? I thought. What could that mean? Sounded organic, and not exactly in the Whole Foods kind of way. Where was that guy from *Dirty Jobs* when you needed him?

"Involving?" my skeptical son, Brian, asked.

"Touchdown," Cody said solemnly.

"Touchdown?" Trent said, suddenly wide-eyed. "Oh, no. That's bad."

"Bad? What do you mean? What's *touchdown?*" I said.

"He's the bull, Dad," Trent said. "That big boy I showed you the other day. You know, the orn-ry big boy."

"That's right," Cody said. "Like it or not, Touchdown needs to go on a road trip today, and I was hoping you could help me get him out of the bull pen and into his trailer."

After we helped Cody hitch a trailer to his pickup, the boys piled into the truck bed, and we drove over to the bull pen.

Cody backed the trailer opposite the gate of the bull pen and got out and dropped the trailer's ramp.

"Trent?" the farmer said to my son as he removed a stafflike metal pole from the truck bed.

"Yes, Mr. Cody?" Trent said.

"I see that Touchdown is way over there on the other side of the field, grazing. Why don't you hop on over that fence and see if you can't get his attention."

"Really? Oh, wow!" Trent said. "Can I really? Dad, is that OK?"

"I guess," I said. "But you better be ready to do some quick climbing back when he sees you."

"This is going to be good," Eddie said, hopping up onto the fence as Trent lowered himself into the pen.

"Hey, Touchdown!" Trent called as he did some jumping jacks.

The truly massive black Angus bull kept on grazing until Cody made a yodeling call. At the sound, Touchdown suddenly stopped chewing and popped his head up and over in our direction like a dog being called by its master.

It was obvious Cody hadn't needed Trent's help but just wanted to get my seven-year-old involved. I smiled. The more time I spent with Cody, the more I liked the old farmer.

"Ah, you don't scare me," Trent said, waving at the bull some more. "I'm over here, dummy! Nanny, nanny!"

Trent hadn't gotten the third *nanny* out when Cody yodeled again, and the bull turned and started to approach. We laughed as Trent shot up the fence. A squirrel couldn't have done it quicker.

As Touchdown drew up, I suddenly understood why spectators screamed so loudly at bullfights. They were terrified. It was truly monstrous, a ton or more of pure muscle snorting viciously as it trotted toward us.

I instinctively stepped back from the fence while Cody stepped forward. He shot a hand out over the railing and grabbed the huge, door-knocker-sized ring drooping from the beast's nose. Then he attached the ring to a clip on the end of the metal pole he was holding.

I thought the thing would go nuts and rip Cody's arm off, but instead it just grunted a few times and placidly looked at the farmer.

"Good morning, sunshine," Cody said calmly to the bull as we all stood there in shock. "Mike, could you get the pen gate open so I can lead Mr. Touchdown into his trailer?"

I ran over and followed instructions. Pulling on the pole like it was a leash, Cody walked the bull along the fence and out the gate. The bull paused for a moment on the trailer's ramp, but then Cody let out with a cowboy "Yeehaw!" and the bull moved his massive bulk the last few feet into the creaking metal trailer like he'd been booted. The septuagenarian slammed the trailer gate closed and ran the bolt. Only then did he unclip the pole and pull it out through the slats in the trailer.

"OK, everybody," he said. "Count all your fingers and toes. All there?"

We nodded.

"Excellent job, then. Well done, boys. Trailering a dairy breeding bull is about the most dangerous thing done on a cattle farm. Thanks for the backup."

"How'd I do, Mr. Cody?" Trent asked.

A wide smile creased Cody's weather-beaten face as he put his big hand on Trent's head.

"You did fine, son," he said. "Just fine. We just might make some good country stock out of you city boys yet."

"Mr. Cody, where is Touchdown headed, anyway?" Trent wanted to know.

Cody looked at me. After a second, he took off his hat and scratched at his bald head.

"Well, he's got a . . . well, a date, I guess you'd call it."

"A date?" Eddie said, giggling. "Touchdown has a girlfriend?"

"He sure does," Cody said, nodding. "Why, just two farms over, the prettiest little cow you ever saw is right now waiting for him to get over there."

"What are they going to do when he gets there? Hold hooves and go bowling or something?" Trent asked, beginning to really crack up.

Great. Here we go, I thought. It was too early in the morning for cows and bulls, let alone the birds and the bees.

"Something like that, Trent," I chimed in before Cody could explain things in more minute detail. "Look at the time. Last one back in the truck is a rotten Homer!"

Chapter 27

AS WE WERE BUMPING our way back to Aaron Cody's farmhouse, towing the four-footed, twenty-five-hundred-pound bachelor of the month behind us, I noticed on my phone that I'd missed a couple of calls.

I blinked at the screen, not knowing what to think. I didn't get many calls these days. Actually, I guess I had a bit of an idea. Both of the calls were from the same person, Emily Parker of the FBI.

I wanted to call her back right there and then, but I knew I needed some privacy. My little, and not-so-little, Bennett pitchers had big ears, and if it was something important, I didn't want to get everyone riled up. Or more riled up than usual.

When we met back up with Seamus and the girls, who were done with the milking, I told Mary

Catherine that I was going to walk the mile and a half of country road back to our house.

"Any particular reason for the sudden return to nature?" my sharp-as-a-tack nanny wanted to know.

"Just need a little exercise," I said.

"Is that right?" Mary Catherine said, her blarney detector obviously going off like gangbusters. "Whatever you say, Mike."

Gravel sprayed as she drove away with my brood. I slipped my phone out of my pocket as the car crested the hill.

"Mike," Emily answered on the second ring. "I assume you've heard what happened."

"Assume I live with cows, Parker," I said. "I couldn't be more out of the loop if I tried. What's up?"

She proceeded to tell me about the previous night's amazing events in Los Angeles. A half-dozen men with automatic rifles had opened fire in a suburb east of the city. Two LA County narcotics detectives, along with four members of a notorious Vietnamese gang, had been murdered in the middle of a busy street.

I hadn't even begun to digest that when she told me about the even bigger news, the home invasion and murder of the celebrity rapper King Killa and singer Alexa Gia.

"I'm at the home invasion right now, Mike. It's the same exact M.O. as with the mobster in Malibu. The victims were poisoned with the same still-unknown substance, through the ventilation system. I've been to crime scenes, but never in an astronaut suit borrowed from the Centers for Disease Control."

"So it's Perrine," I said.

"No question. The Vietnamese and the rapper both had strong ties to the drug trade. Perrine has some kind of elite paramilitary hit team treating LA County like it's a war zone."

"It sure seems like it," I said. "So how do I fit in?"

"Don't be obtuse, Mike. My phone's been ringing off the hook. The director himself wants you put on this now, more than ever. We need you to come back. Perrine needs to be stopped. He needs to be found—not tomorrow, but now."

I let out a breath as I kept walking. I looked out at the miles and miles of Cody's completely empty, tan-colored land. The reddish mountains in the distance beyond. For all my griping, we were safe here. Being in the middle of nowhere had its benefits.

"Mike? Hello? Are you still with me?"

"What about my family, Emily?" I said. "You know the price Perrine has put on my guys. I go traipsing out hither and yon, looking for this bastard, who's going to watch my family? I can't risk something happening to them if I'm not here. I won't do it."

"Please, Mike. Perrine is outgunning us, out-thinking us. Screw the bureau. I need your help. Can't you come down and just talk with our people, at least for the sake of morale? I'll get them to fly you down, you give a pep talk, and I'll have them fly you back. You'll be gone two days. I promise."

I let her hang for a few seconds.

"I'll call you back," I said, and hung up.

Chapter 28

"OK, FAMILY MEETING!" I yelled when I finally made the last country mile back to the farmhouse. "Listen up, people. I need to talk to you."

I poked my head into the kitchen and saw all my guys already arrayed around the kitchen table. They were all staring at me, too. I was waiting for them to yell *Surprise!* or something, except it wasn't my birthday. What was this?

"Oh, there you are. What's this? A second breakfast?"

"No," Seamus said. "We're sitting here waiting for you to tell us what's about to happen next, Detective. You don't think we can tell when something's up? Find out anything on your little nature walk that you want to share?"

"Yeah, where to now, Dad?" Juliana asked. "Alaska?"

"Kazakhstan, probably," Jane said.

"Yeah, Dad," Eddie said. "Do we need to brush up on our Mongolian now?"

"Hold up, wise guys, would you please?" I said. "Where's Mary Catherine?"

"Here I am," she said, coming into the kitchen. "What is it? Come on. What's the news on the Batphone? Lay it on us. We can take it."

"Exactly," Ricky said. "We've been out here in Nowhereland for eight months, Dad. We can take anything."

I let out a breath. My, my, was everybody pissed at me all of a sudden. Getting kicked by Touchdown would have been less of an assault.

"It's nothing, OK?" I said. "Some people wanted my advice on a case. That's it. That's the big mystery. So don't worry about it. Situation normal. How are the chickens doing, Chrissy? How's Homer? Any eggs today?"

"'Advice on a case,' my posterior," Seamus said. "Spill it."

"The FBI wants me. They want me back on the Perrine case. There been a number of new incidents throughout the country, and for some reason, they think I need to be on the case. But I told them that my job is to be here with you guys. I'm not going anywhere."

"Wait a second, Dad," my eldest girl, Juliana, said. "What are you talking about? Perrine is the guy who forced us all to come out here, isn't he? You get him, we go home?"

"She's right, Dad," Brian said. "Perrine wants to hurt us. He's the one making us hide. If they can't find him, then you're going to have to be the one to do it. It's actually a good idea. Once you get him, we all get our lives back."

"And this will all have been a strange dream," Eddie said.

"It's not as simple as that," I said.

"It's not?" Seamus said. "Listen, I don't mean to hurt your feelings, Michael, but you've been about as useful as a . . . a . . ."

"NYPD detective on a cattle farm?" Ricky suggested.

"Exactly. Or that rusting hay rake on the porch," Seamus said. "Ever since we got here, you've been walking around, mumbling to yourself. And, frankly, your moping around is flat-out depressing for everyone involved. We love you,

Mike, but get the heck out of here, would you?"

I had to admit, they had a point. Emily herself had told me that the investigation had stalled. Maybe I really could get it going in the right direction. The fact that Perrine was trying to kill me and my family was certainly strong motivation. As was the fact that once he was taken care of, we really could get our lives back.

"Wow," I said, staring at them all. "I didn't know how, uh, supportive everyone would be about my leaving. Thanks. I think."

"Seriously, Mike," Mary Catherine said. "Of course we don't want you to go, but we know that you need to do this. You really need to bag this creep. It's time."

I stared at my crazy family, shaking my head. It was like I was the subject of an intervention or something. But what was I addicted to? Being a cop? I thought about that. Maybe they weren't so crazy after all.

"Well, if that's how you feel, I guess I could be reluctantly persuaded to go back to work. If that's what you guys want, of course. Because I'm perfectly fine out here, farming and living off the fat of the land."

That got them going. I smiled at the barrage of

eye-rolling *boo*s and Bronx cheers. I guess they knew me pretty well.

Better than I knew myself, that was for sure.

Chapter 29

MARY CATHERINE CAME INTO my room with a stack of laundry as I was packing.

"Don't tell me. The kids called me a cab," I said as she laid my underwear down on the bed, next to my carry-on.

"Please, Mike. Those kids love you more than life. You know that," Mary Catherine said. "They're just frazzled. The one thing in life kids crave is stability, and it's been about as stable as a house of cards in a wind tunnel lately. Plus, they know how good you are at what you do. They don't have a single doubt that you'll be able to find Perrine."

"Oh, sure," I said, tucking my shaving kit into a zippered compartment. "I'll be back by dinner. Don't forget to leave the porch light on."

"Well, before you go, I have something to show

you," Mary Catherine said, reaching into the back pocket of her jeans.

When she opened her fist, I saw what looked like a tiny white pebble in the palm of her hand. I grinned. It was a baby tooth.

"Shawna's eyetooth!" I said, smiling as I held it to the light like a jeweler with a gem. "It finally wiggled free, huh?"

"With a lot of wiggle help from Shawna," Mary Catherine said, smiling back at me.

"Quick," I said, opening the closet door. "To the fairy box."

From the top shelf, I took down a small box. It was an old, plastic Macy's jewelry box that my wife, Maeve, had painted over with white and gold, with generous amounts of glitter. On its lid was a dainty, smiling fairy with elaborately swirling butterfly wings. I smiled at it. It was just a few strokes, but Maeve had been an artist, in addition to so many other things.

I handed it to Mary Catherine, who held it open as I placed the tiny tooth on the little white silk pillow inside it.

"Make sure she sees it before she puts it under her pillow," I said. "And don't try to do the switcheroo until after midnight. You know what an unbelievable skeptic that kid is!"

"Aye, aye, Detective Tooth Fairy," Mary Catherine said, laughing as she looked at me.

Our eyes met. Mary Catherine and I had gotten closer and closer after she'd become part of our family. But right before we went into hiding, we'd gotten into a huge fight, and that had made things pretty tense. In fact, ever since we'd landed in California, she'd been all business, had kept things strictly professional.

But for a second, as we stood there, looking at each other over the jewelry box, we were suddenly back the way we used to be. It felt good. Better than good. Like suddenly finding something you'd thought you'd lost forever. "You know," I said, staring at her, "I don't have to go, Mary Catherine. I really don't."

"Oh, yes, you do, Michael Bennett," Mary Catherine said, closing the jewelry box shut with a loud snap before leaving the room.

Part Two

BACK IN THE SADDLE

Chapter 30

TWO US MARSHALS SHOWED up at the farm-house less than two hours after I called Emily back with my agreement to join the hunt for Perrine.

I'd met some marshals, since the US Marshals Service was the branch of the Justice Department that ran the witness protection program, but this young team, Agents Leo Piccini and Martha McCarthy, was new to me. They must have had orders to step on it, because after Martha dropped my overnight and duffel into the trunk of the Crown Vic, Leo dropped the hammer.

The best news of all was that after I caught my flight, the marshals would be heading back to the ranch to guard my family. My kids would be getting extra-special, round-the-clock protection while I was gone. Their safety was paramount, the priority for me. I wanted Perrine bad, but my guys came first. If anything ever happened to them while I was away, I didn't know what I would do.

Leo told me we were headed to a place an hour southeast of Cody's ranch, along the California-Nevada border, called the Amedee Army Airfield. As we drove, I wondered if *Amedee* was Indian for *end of the world,* because the area was hands down the most desolate place I had ever seen in my life. On both sides of the faded two-lane blacktop was nothing but mountain-rimmed scrub desert beneath a sky so huge and bright and blue, it hurt my head.

"Is this where they tested the atom bomb?" I asked as we slowed and turned onto a dirt road.

"No, sir. I believe that was down in New Mexico," Leo said from behind his aviator shades.

"I knew I should have made a left in Albuquerque," I mumbled as we bumped along.

We slowed and stopped about five minutes later. I looked to the left and right for the military airport that was our destination, but there was nothing. No planes, no control tower, no buildings. There was nothing but more desert.

"Um, I thought I was supposed to catch a plane," I said, scanning the bleak landscape.

The young agents looked at each other, smiling.

"You're about to," Agent McCarthy said, opening the door.

"But where's the . . . you know, buildings and TSA gropers and everything?" I asked, stepping out and spotting for the first time the macadam runway in front of us.

"That's at an airport," the female fed explained as she checked her watch. "This is an airfield."

"Aha," I said, pretending like that explained something.

When I turned to her partner for clarification, he was pointing up at the sky.

"Here comes your ride now," Leo said.

Far in the distance to the east, a plane began to make a whistling descent out of the wild blue yonder. Though unmarked and military charcoal gray, it looked sort of like a corporate jet.

The plane made a wide turn to land from the west. I was almost surprised that the plane didn't start buzzing me like the crop duster that goes after Cary Grant in *North by Northwest*.

The sleek, rumbling jet aircraft landed and taxied up, close enough for me to reach out and touch the razorlike edge of its wing. Its jets were rumbling so loud that I couldn't even hear myself when I thanked the agents who handed me my bags.

Instead of a stewardess, a green-fatigues-clad soldier wearing a beret dropped the door and helped me aboard. As the soldier resealed the door, I could see that the plane's resemblance to a G6 ended at the steps. Inside, it looked like a cargo plane, with netting and jump seats, and smelled frighteningly like spilled gasoline. A female pilot gave me a wide smile and a thumbs-up from the forward cockpit.

"Can I get you anything, sir?" the soldier asked after he expertly strapped me and my bags to the wall.

Still in a state of shock and awe, I just shook my head as the jets fired and the desert outside the window started to roll.

The soldier didn't offer me any peanuts or headphones, but he did snap out a large brown paper bag and handed it to me as we left the ground.

"Just in case," he said.

Chapter 31

AS WE HEADED SOUTH, the friendly soldier-steward told me his name was Larry and that the plane was called a C-26 Metroliner.

What he failed to mention was why I was on a military aircraft, but I had a feeling I was about to find out.

It had been just under an hour when we touched back down to earth. Not bad, considering that Cody's ranch was almost six hundred miles from LA. Even in a military cargo plane, I decided flying private was the way to go. No one had even once made the suggestion that they wanted to touch my junk.

When I looked out the porthole of a window, not too far off I spotted a couple of parked Chinook cargo helicopters. *Where are the Delta and Southwest planes?* I wondered. *Where are the guys driving the luggage carts?* Instead of these usual airport sights, beyond the runway fence were rows of two-story dormitory-style buildings. It looked like we were on some sort of military base.

"I take it this isn't LAX," I said to Larry.

"No, sir. We're at SCLA, Southern Cal Logistics Airport," he said.

Emily Parker was sitting waiting for me in a Gator XUV, a golf cart on steroids, as Larry dropped the door. She was checking her phone and trying to look all nonchalant, like private jets were the most ho-hum thing in the world to her.

But after I thanked Larry and the pilot and started to walk over, she cracked a smile and started giggling. When she wanted to, Agent Parker could look as steely as the snub-nosed Colt .45 automatic she packed, but when she smiled like that, she looked like the girl you were too afraid to ask to your high school prom. I'd forgotten what a great smile it was. Almost.

"Hey, what do you think? Pretty cool, huh?" she said, elbowing me as I sat. "I told you they wanted you. How does it feel to get the Nancy Pelosi treatment? You're a real government VIP now."

"I didn't fill the barf sack on the ride here, so I guess that's a start," I said, dropping my bags in the back of the Gator.

We started to drive. The army MP on duty nodded at us as we came through the airfield gate. Which wasn't easy, since the young man was trying to look down Emily's shirt at the same time. On the other side of the fence was a road with the dormlike buildings I'd seen from the plane.

"OK, Parker. Give it up," I said as we hummed along. "What is all this? I didn't know I was joining the army. Are we going to the hangar where they have the aliens now? I mean, what's up with the Area Fifty-One routine? What the heck is going on? What is this place? An air force base?"

"Kind of. It used to be George Air Force Base, but it was mothballed in 'ninety-two. They turned half of it into Southern Cal Logistics, a municipal airport, and kept the other half of it—the dormitories and surrounding area—for multiple military use, mostly training."

"OK, but why are we here?"

"Let's get you settled first," Emily said, swinging into a parking lot.

She took me through a door and up a flight of stairs, and dropped my overnight on a cot in a little room halfway down the hall. She locked the door and handed me a key.

"Are you the RA?" I said, taking it. "Where do I get my meal card? Or do I have to report for boot camp? Help me out."

"Head's a couple of doors down, on your left," she said, all business now. "There's a general meeting in about an hour. Why don't we get a bite to eat, and I'll bring you up to speed."

Chapter 32

BACK DOWNSTAIRS, WE GRABBED a couple of Cokes and plastic-wrapped turkey clubs off a tray in the dormitory's kitchen. We were taking them outside to a picnic table beside the parking lot when a short, wiry, black-haired man dressed in camo came through the front doors. Though short in stature, he carried himself with a physical grace, like an old-time baseball shortstop.

"Emily," the soldier said, smiling as he stopped in front of us. "I thought I heard you come in. And you must be Michael Bennett."

"This is Colonel D'Ambrose, Mike," Emily said. "He's in charge of this . . ."

"Shindig? Fiasco? I haven't quite figured out what it is myself yet," D'Ambrose said, shaking my hand. "Have you brought Mike up to speed?"

"Just about to, over lunch." She smiled.

"Excellent," D'Ambrose said. "Let me grab some grub and join you."

"I probably shouldn't be telling you this until you sign the paperwork," D'Ambrose said at the picnic table a few minutes later, as he speared some potato salad onto a plastic fork, "but large things are afoot, Mike. Forty-eight hours ago, the president signed a national security directive targeting Perrine as a clear and present danger to the security of the United States. Now, instead of just local and federal law enforcement, my military boys are on board.

"As of seven this morning, the Department of Justice is now working hand in hand with my covert-ops guys, the Navy SEALs and Delta Force, and the airborne-signal intelligence-gathering unit known as Gray Fox, as well as the CIA and NSA."

I stared at him, taken aback. I'd seen investigations ramped up before, but I'd never worked with the actual military.

"Did this little order suspend *posse comitatus?*" I asked, squinting at him. "You know, the federal statute that says the military can't operate within the continental US?"

"They finally eject California from the Union?"

the feisty colonel said, smiling.

"The colonel and his men aren't actually operating on US soil," Emily said, turning to me. "See, we believe Perrine is hiding somewhere in Mexico. Because of the rampant amount of bribery and corruption in the law enforcement agencies and even the military of our sister republic, the Mexican president has reluctantly agreed to let us into Mexico to act as special advisers in the hunt for Perrine."

"Which is not something the Mexican president is ready to crow about, since it's an election year," the colonel added. "Because discretion is mandatory, this base is the military's rallying point for airborne sorties over the border."

"OK, I think I'm getting the picture," I said. "Go on."

"That's just one side of the blade," D'Ambrose said. "Perrine's people are now operating in LA, so we're going to be working with the LA FBI and DEA, and the LAPD as well."

"Don't forget the Mexican authorities," Emily said. "The *federales,* and even CISEN."

"CISEN?" I asked.

"The Mexican intelligence agency, equivalent to our CIA," D'Ambrose said.

"Exactly," said Emily. "We're going soup to nuts, from street cops to the feds to the intelligence community and the army."

"In two different countries?" I said, and shook my head.

"Yep," D'Ambrose said. "Starting to feel my pain now? You don't speak Spanish, by any chance, do you?"

I nodded and looked up as one of the Chinook helicopters went by close enough to land on the roof of the barracks. Half the napkins we had brought went flying as well.

"This thing is a real mess," I said.

"What are you talking about?" Emily asked. "I thought you'd be pleased. Action is finally being taken. Perrine is being looked at like the international terrorist that he is. You're not happy that they're finally going after Perrine in a serious way?"

"It didn't have to come to all this, Emily. How many years was nothing done about the border? About the cartels? We let this fester. Now things are so bad, we have to bring in the military? It's a disgrace. Everybody is goddamn asleep at the switch these days."

"Not everybody, Mike," Emily said. "Colonel D'Ambrose has been working tirelessly on this for the last three months. Before that, he and his men at the Joint Special Operations Command helped redefine counterinsurgency tactics in Iraq, bringing in the CIA and NSA to sort through the electronic pocket litter that the Special Forces teams found on the battlefield. There's no one better on the planet to head up this kind of international manhunt."

The colonel smiled as he wiped his mouth.

"Thanks for the defense, Emily, but Detective Bennett here is more correct than he knows. I'm disgusted, too, Detective. We needed to keep our house clean, but we didn't. Letting things go to the point where the exterminator has to come to your house is pretty damn embarrassing."

Chapter 33

AFTER WE FINISHED EATING, D'Ambrose left for a meeting, and Parker took me over to Building 14. The huge open room on the ground floor was being used by D'Ambrose's JSOC guys as the multiple-agency task force command center.

There were desks everywhere, several large PowerPoint boards and flat screens, a podium. Everyone on the task force must have been taking a break to eat, because except for a couple of soldiers running some wires through the drop ceiling, we were alone.

We grabbed a couple of coffees from a well-stocked table, and I followed Emily over to a desk.

"We found this footage two days ago at a safe house we raided with the *federales* in Durango," Emily said, tapping at a laptop as we sat. "It's of a dinner Perrine held for his top cartel people. We had it closed captioned. You have to take a look at this."

I let out a breath as Perrine appeared on the screen. He was wearing an impeccably tailored tuxedo, standing at a podium in what looked to be some kind of ballroom.

The last time I had laid eyes on him, he was in a prison jumpsuit, escaping from a Lower Manhattan courthouse in a construction-crane basket. It made my blood boil to see him back in his stylish finery, dressed to the nines again.

I also noticed that he had gotten his nose fixed. Which sucked. I was the one who had broken it for him in a scuffle we'd had before I placed him under arrest. I had the funny feeling we would have another scuffle before this thing was done. *But is that a good thing?* I wondered.

I watched as the psychopathic murderer smiled pleasantly, adjusted the mike, and cleared his throat.

"I see myself as a historical figure," Perrine said from the dais without the slightest hint of irony. "Like Pancho Villa or Che Guevara or the great Simón Bolívar, I am here to continue the Southern Hemisphere's great tradition of rebellion. Only, I am more honest, more defiant, because I refuse to hide my ambitions behind the bullshit con game that is socialism.

"I do not need to justify my actions. Especially to the Americans. *Borders and laws,* they cry. *Supply and demand* is my reply. They disrupt my business while it is their decadent sons and daughters who are my very best customers.

"It is time," Perrine said. "Time to stop fucking around. That is what I learned during my stay in the great United States. My brief stay."

The audience broke into applause and uproarious laughter at that one.

I wanted to put my fist through the screen.

"I see the US finally for what it is," Perrine continued. "Just another rival, just another meddlesome obstacle to our ambitions. Where the Americans are weak, we will show our strength. We will not stop until the border itself is meaningless. We will spur on chaos until it is manifest everywhere, until even the American authorities are as cowed as the Mexican ones. Then and only then will we have free rein.

"And by *we,* be sure that I do not mean old Mexico. I do not mean the sorry downtrodden, the blessed poor. Fuck the forever-useless, sniveling, ever-present poor once and for all, I say.

"By *we*, I mean you and me—all the people ruthless and lucky enough to be in this room at this present moment. *Tout le monde* is ours for the taking, my friends! The world is turning, readying itself for new borders, new laws. I say we write them with the blood of our American enemies. What do you say? Who is with me? Who wants to be a billionaire?"

Chapter 34

THE SCREEN FADED TO black, and Parker closed the laptop, cutting off the sound of more applause.

"Wow, I'm impressed," I said. "That has to be the Gettysburg Address of maniacal narco-terrorists."

Emily nodded. "One of our informants who was at the dinner said that after his speech, Perrine expertly directed a PowerPoint presentation in which a precise military-insurgency plan of attack on the southwest US was laid out," she said.

"What?" I said, laughing.

Parker nodded somberly.

"I'm not kidding. Like a general, he referred to the cartel's current troop strengths and provisions, its recruiting efforts. Ho Chi Minh was mentioned often and fondly."

"Ho Chi Minh? Now, please. I know he's a

threat, Emily, but Perrine's out of his cocaine-smuggling mind. Or he's just trying to get his guys going. There's no way he can operate in the US the way he's been doing it in Mexico. He knows that would be suicide.

"Believe me, Emily. This guy is smart. You saw him there with his manicure and his silk bespoke attire. His tastes are pure French. He's a gourmet, a real bon vivant with joie de vivre. He likes being alive."

"What you say is true, Mike, but he's making some pretty audacious moves nonetheless," Emily said. "Those two cops in El Monte were blown to pieces by highly trained paramilitaries— mercenaries, probably. Which is troublesome when you consider that some of our analysts are saying the cartels employ upward of fifty or sixty thousand people.

"Plus, you heard the speech. Drugs seem to be almost beside the point. He's high on his own power. He seems like he's drifted from egotistical drug smuggler into megalomaniac world conqueror. He's French, all right. It seems he thinks he's Napoleon."

"You have a point there," I said.

"Well, the good news is, this really isn't the first

rodeo for the US military against these narco nuts," Emily said, twirling a pen in her fingers. "In Colombia in the eighties, Pablo Escobar actually went to full-blown war with the Colombian government. He blew up government buildings and an airliner before the Colombians asked for our help. The first George Bush sent in Delta Force, which tracked down the maniac for the Colombian army, who ultimately took him out."

"You're right. That's true," I said, brightening. "I forgot all about that. You've been around awhile, Parker. Were you involved in the Pablo Escobar takedown?"

She turned and stabbed me in the arm with the pen.

"Ow!"

"Screw you, Bennett," she said, affronted. "I'm younger than you are. In the nineties, I was in high school, dancing to Depeche Mode."

"It was a joke, Parker," I said, rubbing my arm.

"About my age," she said.

"My bad," I said. "How about a toast?" I said, raising my coffee cup. "To history repeating itself."

"Hear, hear," Parker said, tapping Styrofoam. "To Perrine in a body bag."

Chapter 35

THE MORNING AFTER HIS dad left, Brian Bennett opened his eyes as he heard soft footsteps in the hallway. After a moment, the bedroom door slowly opened and Grandpa Seamus poked his head in.

Uh-oh. *Chore time. Has to be*, Brian thought, immediately shutting his eyes and making what he hoped was a natural-sounding snore.

"You're up, Brian. Excellent," Seamus whispered as he tugged hard on Brian's earlobe. "Get dressed and grab Eddie and Jane, would you? I need to talk to you goslings in the kitchen about something."

"Are we in trouble?" Brian whispered back. "I already told Mary Catherine I was sorry about the strike, about a thousand times."

"No, no. It's nothing like that," Seamus said. "I

just need to talk to you. You have five minutes. Move your butt."

Seamus had an apron on over his priest suit and had some scrambled-egg tortillas waiting for them when they entered the kitchen. Brian hesitated at the door when he smelled the bacon. Bacon was trouble. The bribe of bacon meant they were about to be made to do something even more heinous than he had imagined.

"There you are! Carpe diem! Come in now, Brian. Be not afraid," Seamus said.

"What's up, Gramps?" Brian said, finally taking a seat.

"Funny you ask that question, Brian," Seamus said, raising his bacon fork. "I just got a call from my priest friend in town. Father Walter needs help in accomplishing a corporal work of mercy this morning, and I think I've found just the people for the job."

I knew it, Brian thought, rubbing his tired eyes. *All aboard. Next stop, Chore City.* He wasn't sure what the word *corporal* meant, but work was something he had become infinitely familiar with in the family's rural exile.

"Now," Seamus said jovially, "who can tell me what the corporal works of mercy are?"

"Visit imprisoned people like us," Brian mumbled.

"Very good, Brian. Visit the imprisoned. Anyone else?"

"Um, clothe the naked?" Eddie said, trying to keep a straight, pious face, and failing.

"Yes, Eddie. Clothe the naked. Why did I think you of all people would remember that one? Anyone else?"

"Feed the hungry," Jane said, eyeing the bacon.

"Bingo, Jane. Feed the hungry. That's the one Father Walter needs our help with. Father just received a large shipment of donated canned goods and needs help with distribution. We have to go to the rectory and run the supplies over to a remote food bank in a tiny, poor part of the county and dole them out. I thought it would be a nice opportunity for the three of you. I know you've been complaining about not getting out."

"But what about Dad?" Eddie said. "Didn't he say we have to stay on the farm? No exceptions?"

"I'm in charge, Eddie," Seamus said, pouring himself a cup of coffee. "People need our help, and we're going to help them. Evil wins when good men do nothing."

"We're not men, though, Gramps. We're kids,"

Brian complained. "And I thought you said we weren't in trouble."

Seamus smiled as he lifted a pan off the stove and brought it over.

"Thanks for volunteering to help, Brian," he said as he piled some bacon onto Brian's plate.

"There's a special place in heaven for young saints like yourself."

Chapter 36

THE FOOD BANK WAS in a little town called Sunnyville, a few miles south of Susanville.

Getting out of the van with Seamus, Jane wondered if the town's name was supposed to be ironic. Because there wasn't anything sunny about it. It wasn't even a town, really. Just a collection of ramshackle houses, a barnlike building that looked like a bar of some kind, and a place that sold snowmobiles and dirt bikes.

What it looked like was something from a serial killer movie, she thought. Right down to the creepy, weird sound of an unseen wind chime tinkling as they got out of the station wagon. Even the shedlike building they used for the food bank looked weird, she thought as she grabbed a case of Chef Boyardee. It looked like a caboose.

The caboose of a train that was smart enough to cut out of this godforsaken place a long, long time ago, Jane thought.

They were going up the stairs with the heavy boxes when she saw that there was another collection of buildings, to the rear of the food bank. It was a trailer park. A huge, excessively run-down one. As she watched, there was a sudden roar, and a heavy woman riding a motorcycle shot out from between two of the decrepit structures.

If they got out of this alive, she'd never complain about the farm again, she decided as she dropped off the cans and went back for more.

It took them about half an hour just to get the boxes inside the food bank caboose and unpacked. The food was mostly divided between canned stuff—Campbell's soups, SpaghettiOs, Del Monte fruit—and dry goods: macaroni and cheese, ramen noodles, hot cocoa. When they were done arranging the shelves, it looked like a grocery store.

A line of people from the trailer park formed quickly. It was obvious they were in bad straits. Whites, blacks, Hispanics. All of them poor. All of them about as desperate as migrant workers out of work got.

Jane and Eddie ran around behind the counter, putting together the orders, while Seamus and Brian worked clipboards, checking IDs of people who were on the church's food bank giving list.

They were just about all out of food when the gang of trailer-park kids came around. There were about seven of them, ranging in age from eight to thirteen, as desperate looking as their parents. They wore filthy T-shirts and jeans, filthy sneakers. One of them, a dopey-looking white kid with an Afro puff of curly brown hair, didn't even have shoes, Jane noticed in horror from behind the counter.

"Hey, you guys like baseball?" the oldest of them, a short Hispanic kid, said with a nice-enough smile. "I'm Guillermo. We got a little field back here, and we were wondering if you guys wanted to play."

Before they could answer, Guillermo turned to Seamus, showing him the dinged-up aluminum bat he was holding.

"Would that be OK, Father? Could they play some baseball with us?"

"That would be fine, kids. Just don't go too far. We'll be leaving soon enough."

Jane stood behind the counter, frozen. She

stared at her grandfather like he was crazy. She didn't want to play baseball with California's version of *Children of the Corn*. She was twelve! *And a girl!*

"C'mon, now. Jane, Eddie, c'mon out from behind there," Seamus said. "You've been a big help today. You can play for a little while with them while Brian stays here with me to clean up."

Jane and Eddie looked at each other.

"Yeah, c'mon," Guillermo said, patting Eddie on the shoulder as they left the food bank. "It's this way."

They went behind the food bank caboose, toward a stand of pines and oaks. Behind about twenty yards of trees was their field. It looked comically bad. There was a flat plain of red dirt with a tree for first, a large, dangerous-looking rock for second, and a rusted hunk of metal that might have once been a motor for a refrigerator for third base. The newest-looking object in sight was a tall fence that bordered the outfield, with barbed wire running along the top.

Eddie looked at the fence and then at the circle of poor kids standing around them, staring silently. For the first time, he noticed that none of the kids had a ball. Did they use rocks or something?

"Um, you want to choose sides or what?" Eddie said to Guillermo.

Guillermo laughed.

"No," he said, shoving Eddie hard in the chest. "I want your money. Cough it up, you little bitch."

Chapter 37

"WHAT?" EDDIE SAID IN amazement. "Wait, you're joking, right? C'mon, are we going to play, or what?"

Guillermo shoved him again, harder.

"I'm not kidding. Give me your money."

"Don't forget his iPhone, G," said the kid with no shoes. "You know some do-gooder city kid got an iPhone, dawg."

Guillermo grabbed Eddie roughly by his shirt and poked him hard in the chin with the tip of the grungy metal bat.

Jane started crying then. This wasn't happening. How could this be happening?

"Give me everything you have, or I'm going to knock the shit out of you," Guillermo said.

"I knew it!" Brian yelled as he came running

from behind the trees off to the right.

Guillermo froze in place as the six-foot-one former Fordham Prep nose tackle grabbed him by his shirt and shoved him, sprawling, onto the ground.

The trailer-park kids scattered immediately into the woods as the kid and his bat went flying. Jane stood there, wide-eyed. She didn't know what she wanted to do more: wrap her arms around her big brother's neck or do a cartwheel.

Brian picked up the bat.

"Hey, it's OK, man. I was just playing around," Guillermo said, dusting himself off as he finally stood. "Now give me the bat back, OK? I was only kidding."

Brian hefted the bat.

"This bat?" Brian said. "You want this bat back?"

Brian turned and hurled it as hard as he could. It made a whistling sound as it spun through the air like a thrown airplane propeller. After a while, it landed out of sight, in the vegetation on the other side of the barbed-wire fence.

"There's your bat back, punk," Brian said. "Go fetch."

"Hey, why'd you do that?" Guillermo said in honest shock.

"I wonder," Brian said, squinting at him. "You think you can mess with my little brother and sister? You're lucky I didn't return the bat upside your head."

The kid looked at Brian, then at the fence, and suddenly started crying.

"I need the bat back. It belongs to my brother, man. Now he's going to kill me."

Brian eyed the kid.

"Then go get it, you little baby."

"I can't. Look where you threw it, man. Right into the middle of Cristiano's patch."

"So what? It's a fence and some bushes. Start climbing."

"Just some bushes? You crazy? Open your eyes. That's weed, yo! That whole thing is a cash crop of premium weed. Cristiano don't play. He's got dogs, man. Rotties in there. Booby traps, too, people say. What goes in there, stays in there."

"Did you say *weed?*" Jane asked. "As in *marijuana?* You can't grow weed. That's illegal."

"Hello? Where the hell are you from? That's all they grow around here," Guillermo insisted, wiping tears from his eyes.

"And that makes you what? Cool or something?" Brian said, shaking with anger. *This place is*

America? he thought. He really felt like punching the kid right in his face.

"Eddie, Jane, come on. We're getting the hell out of here now," Brian said.

"But what about my bat?" the kid screeched. "My brother, man. He's going to go crazy!"

Brian turned to the kid and pointed a finger in his face.

"To hell with your bat, and to hell with you, too, you evil little runt. I hope your brother does kill you. He'll be doing the world a favor."

As they ran back to the food bank, Brian knew what he'd said wasn't very Christian, but he was sick of this. These weird hippie families and messed-up poor people. All the drugs everywhere. I mean, they'd come here to help this morning, and Eddie had almost gotten beaten by some juvenile delinquent? How'd that make sense?

Seamus was closing the back door of the station wagon when they got back to the food bank.

"Did you win?" he asked as the kids quickly piled into the car.

"Oh, we won, Gramps," Eddie said with an innocent smile. "Could we go now?"

"Is everything OK?" Seamus asked, staring at them.

"Fine," Brian said, nervously looking over his shoulder, back at the trailer park. "Could we get going, though, Gramps? I, uh, really need to use the bathroom."

"So do I," said Eddie.

"And me too," Jane said. "Really bad."

"OK, then," Seamus said, trying to turn the old car's engine over. It wouldn't catch.

No, Brian thought. *Please, God. Please help us.*

"Hold your horses, and, um, everything else," Seamus said as he tried again.

The engine churned and chugged, but again there was nothing.

We're going to be stranded, Brian thought. Stranded, and then the *Lord of the Flies* kids would come.

Then it caught. The big old muscle-car engine finally fired up, rumbling happily.

In the backseat, Brian crossed himself as Seamus got their rear in gear, and they finally pulled out.

Chapter 38

IT WAS FIVE-THIRTY A.M. when Mary Catherine led the horse out of the barn behind Aaron Cody's house. It was still dark, and cold enough to see the plumes of the horse's breath. She turned as a cow mooed forlornly somewhere off in the darkness to her left.

"And a fine good morning to you, too, madam," she said over her shoulder. "Wonderful weather we're having, don'tcha think?"

She smiled. When she could squeeze it in, her early-morning ride was by far the best part of her day. It was a moment to be still, a moment to be sane and serene before the kids got up and the chaos began.

"OK, now, Spike. Here we go," she whispered soothingly as she gently mounted the gray quarter horse. As usual, the four-year-old gelding had been a little skittish about getting saddled, but once they got on the trail, she knew they'd get along fine.

It took the better part of half an hour to get up the range to her favorite spot. Spike knew it by heart by now, slowing by the high ridge's edge even before she pulled the reins.

"You get me, Spike, don't you?" she said, patting his scruffy head. "Now if only you were a man, all my dreams would come true."

She watched in silence as the sun came up over the distant Sierra Nevada. As it did every morning, it literally put a chill down her spine. All that land. All that sky. The holy whistling of the cold wind as light split shadow and spilled down the rutted slopes.

It was the America right out of a children's book, she thought. Any moment now, down from the mountain, she'd see some cowboys chasing Indians alongside a steam locomotive with a little red caboose.

As she took out the thermos she'd brought, she wondered what the daft, ever-wisecracking boyos in her hometown back in Ireland would say if they could see their skinny Mary Catherine all grown up and drinking her tea high in the saddle out here in the Wild West.

Nothing was the answer to that one, she thought, taking a sip, since every one of those ragamuffins would be struck speechless for once in their miserable lives.

Who was she kidding? She could hardly believe it herself, the way her life was turning out.

When she'd heard about the nanny job in New York City, she'd originally envisioned taking care of some megawealthy power couple's two children, wheeling them in an expensive stroller through Central Park when she wasn't taking them to art museums or helping them with their French. The gig she got instead, of course, couldn't have been further from her expectations. Instead of the power couple, her boss was the NYPD's busiest detective, and he didn't have two kids but two kids multiplied by five.

But she'd done it. That was the funny part. By hook or by crook, over the last several years, she'd learned to effectively manage the rambunctious Bennett clan. Not only had she kept them mostly fed (those teens were bottomless pits), cleanly clothed, and educated, but what filled her with the most pride was that she was actually making strides in teaching them to take care of each other and themselves.

Though her work was at times quite painful and sometimes seemed hopeless, she was managing to accomplish the hardest, most important, and most unsung job on the face of the earth—raising a large crop of good human beings.

And just when she was cruising, just when she had achieved the mammoth task of getting down everyone's schedules and tics in New York City, what happens? A criminal from one of Mike's cases targets them all for assassination, and they're ripped from their lives and deposited three thousand miles away, on a California cattle farm.

It was the most recent events that seemed the most impossible. That someone was actually out to kill her and the kids, someone she had never met, had never done anything to—she just couldn't understand how any human being could actually be that inhuman.

But she knew it was true, of course. It certainly terrified her. Her dreams these days were mostly nightmares where she woke up expecting figures to be standing in the dark beside her bed. It had gotten so bad that she'd taken to loading one of the shotguns and laying it on the floor next to the bed, under a blanket. That helped, at least a little.

She flung the dregs of her tea on the ground

and tightened the cap on the thermos. She let out a sigh as she tucked the thermos back into the saddlebag. *Sleeping with one eye open, with a shotgun under the bed,* she thought, shaking her head. She was out in the Wild West, all right.

As if reading her thoughts, Spike suddenly snorted out a kind of sigh himself.

Mary Catherine laughed as she scratched Spike between his ears.

"C'mon, old friend," she said. "It's getting late. I guess it's time for us poor workhorses to get going. Time to head them off at the pass."

Chapter 39

MARY CATHERINE GOT LOST on her way back to Cody's farm.

It was her own dumb fault. As she led Spike through a stand of cypress and black oak, she'd spotted a smaller trail off the main one that she thought looked like a shortcut. But it wasn't. After a while, the path started going up instead of down and turning in the wrong direction, north instead of south.

She was just about to give up on it, about half a mile in, when there was a rustle on her right and a man stepped out onto the trail behind her. Spike, startled, wheeled around, rearing back on his hind legs, almost throwing her.

Mary Catherine managed to calm the horse and get him completely turned around. She sat there, blinking at the figure. He was a scraggly, thin, young white guy in jeans and a plaid shirt with the sleeves cut off. Beneath his khaki bush hat, long brown hair fell to his shoulders.

There was also an olive-colored strap over his arm, and then she saw the black barrel of the rifle sticking up over his back.

Gun! she thought, freaking out. *The cartel! They were here! We've been found out!*

"Can I help you?" the young man said, something sharp in his voice.

Not the cartel? Some maniac, then? Mary Catherine thought, still round eyed and frozen in the saddle. *An off-the-reservation militia person?*

Then she realized it. Why he seemed angry. She actually clapped a hand to her forehead.

"Oh, no. I rode onto your property, didn't I?" Mary Catherine said. "I'm so sorry. I'm staying at Aaron Cody's place, and I went out for a morning ride. I thought this was a shortcut back. I'm such an idiot. I didn't mean to trespass."

"Oh, Mr. Cody's. I see," the guy said, the tension in his voice immediately gone.

He tipped back his hat and smiled, and Mary Catherine suddenly noticed how young he was. He was just a cute sixteen- or seventeen-year-old kid.

"I didn't mean to startle you," he said. "I'm Kevin. Kevin Norberg, Mr. Cody's neighbor. You did wander onto our property, but don't worry about it. The property lines are tricky. There actually is a shortcut back to Mr. Cody's ranch, through our farm. I'll show it to you if you want."

Mary Catherine paused for a beat, then took a breath.

"OK," she said. "Thanks."

She followed the kid off the path. She stared at the gun. It looked like a deer rifle. Was he out hunting? Spike hesitated once as the dirt trail descended through a gap in an outcropping of rocks, but she finally encouraged him to go through.

When they came out on the other side, Mary Catherine saw what at first she thought was a grove of tightly grown baby evergreen trees. But as she got closer, she could see that the long, neat rows of green weren't trees at all but plants. Plants about nine feet high, with leaves that had long, thin light-green fingers and purplish buds with a strong, sweet smell, almost fruity.

It was marijuana, Mary Catherine realized when she took a breath. Acres upon acres of pungent marijuana.

She remembered then what Brian had told her about the encounter at the food bank. The kids there claiming that marijuana was the area's largest crop. She looked out at the green sea of pot they were skirting. She knew that California's Central Valley grew a huge amount of the country's food, but that wasn't the only thing the valley was supplying to the nation, apparently.

Is it actually legal? she wondered. *A medical-marijuana farm?*

Kevin, leading the way ahead of her, certainly didn't act like his family farm had anything to hide. He couldn't have been calmer if they had been strolling through Central Park. Or was that because of the rifle on his back?

Mary Catherine decided to keep her questions to herself.

"You sit that horse well, ma'am," Kevin said as they walked through the forest of cannabis. "Are you working for Mr. Cody?"

"No, just, um, visiting," Mary Catherine said as calmly as she could.

"From where? Scotland?"

"Ireland, actually."

"Oh," Kevin said with a nod, blushing a little. "I love the accent."

"Thanks," Mary Catherine said brightly.

"How you liking your stay so far?"

"It's a beautiful country," Mary Catherine said.

"You like country," the kid said, "you've hit the jackpot."

They came upon a greenhouse. It was swathed in white plastic and had a table inside, covered with Styrofoam cups. Each cup had a little pot plant in it, like it was part of show-and-tell at a hippie kindergarten.

On the other side of the building, in the distance, there was a white-haired woman in a gardener's smock, squatting in a ditch. She was attaching some PVC pipes together in the middle of an elaborate irrigation system. She waved, and Kevin waved back.

"That's my mom," Kevin said.

Mom was also armed, Mary Catherine couldn't help but note. In a holster on her hip was one humongous, long-barreled silver revolver. It was a .44 Magnum, Mary Catherine realized. She'd never actually seen one outside of a Clint Eastwood movie.

This really was the Wild West, she thought, feeling a little dizzy.

After another hundred yards, Kevin let her out

through a cattle gate and pointed down the red dirt road.

"You follow this till you get to the creek, and then you'll see Mr. Cody's silo down the hill."

"Thanks, Kevin," Mary Catherine said, riding Spike through the gate. "It was nice meeting you."

"You, too, ma'am," the polite young dope farmer said, with a tip of his hat, as Mary Catherine rode away.

Chapter 40

WHITE LIGHT FLASHED IN the pitch black and began fluttering. After a moment, a low and insistent electronic buzzing began sounding off, the measured pulses synched with the flutter of the light.

Vida Gomez woke in the back upstairs bedroom of the safe house on South Alta Vista Boulevard in La Brea. She sat up and unplugged the charger from the encrypted cartel cell phone as she lifted it from the nightstand.

For a fraction of a second, she stared at the green Accept and red Reject buttons on the smartphone's screen. *The more accurate choice would be Live or Die,* she thought, finally accepting the call with a callused thumb.

She didn't say hello. In fact, she didn't speak

once. She just sat in the dark, automatically listening and memorizing the new orders she was being given.

A half hour later, they were rolling backward down the suburban safe house's cobblestone drive-way in the team's only legitimate vehicle, a black Honda Odyssey, Touring edition. Like Vida, the men were wearing shorts and T-shirts and sneakers. Instead of sporting their usual Kevlar vests and long guns, they were armed with small conceal-carry pistols, Glock 26 and Taurus PT 24/7 subcompacts in 9 mm. The orders were explicit that they keep a low profile.

Avoiding the freeways, they headed south and then west along side streets, Venice Boulevard to Lincoln to Washington Boulevard. Vida, behind the wheel, had to consult the onboard GPS only minimally in order to find the way. She'd been utterly lost in the confusing city the first week she had been here, but now she was getting the hang of it.

With the lack of traffic, they arrived at Marina del Rey in under thirty minutes. Vida had never been to the upscale seaside area before. The pastel-colored high-rises and palm trees reminded her of a trip to Miami she had taken as a child.

They left the van in a parking lot and went out along one of the docks. It was an enormous marina, the berths containing at least a thousand vessels. The forty-two-foot sportfishing boat they were looking for was the third one down on the left of Dock 29. In the predawn murk, Vida could just make out its name on the stern, *Aces and Eights*.

The middle-aged American loading the bait bins on the deck was scruffy and blond and had a beer belly and enormous, scarred hands.

"Help you?" he said, dropping his bucket to the deck with a hollow bong.

"Are you Captain Scanlon? Thomas Scanlon?"

"I am," the big blond man said.

"We're the Raphael party," Vida said.

Captain Scanlon looked at Vida, then at the six hardfaced killers behind her.

"Permission to board granted," he said, waving them on.

Everything was all set up, the rods and reels, the charts. Even fishing licenses for all of them had been provided in case there was some kind of problem.

Vida stayed with Scanlon up in the flying bridge as they cast off. The American completely ignored her as he piloted the boat, humming to himself as he checked his charts and the compass on the computer in front of him. She wondered how many runs like this he had done for the cartel. This wasn't his first. She was sure of that.

They met other sportfishers as they headed for the mouth of the marina. One of them, carrying a party of what looked like female college-volleyball players, hailed Scanlon with a horn blast. Scanlon honked back twice, laughing merrily.

"Enjoying yourself?" Vida said coldly.

"Siempre," Scanlon told her with a wink. "Always."

That makes one of us, Vida thought, grasping the cool railing of the bobbing ship and trying to keep down the churning contents of her stomach.

Chapter 41

SCANLON CUT THE ENGINES when they were eleven miles out. He went down and started setting the baits on the sea rods and parceling them out to the men.

"That won't be necessary," Vida told him, still up on the flying bridge.

"No?" Scanlon said skeptically, looking up at her. "Coast Guard has drones now, sweetie. Attached to them are cameras that can see through your pants and count the dimples on your ass from five miles up. What do you imagine the Coasties are going to think if they see your buddies here, out on this fishing boat, standing around?"

"Fine," Vida said, checking her watch. She went back to scanning the horizon with her binoculars.

"You're sure we're in the right place?" she said.

"As if my life depended on it," the captain said as he showed Eduardo how to cast.

The ship came into view from the south a little over an hour later. It was huge, a Handymax-class oil tanker, its rust-streaked black hull two football fields long from stem to stern. There wasn't anyone visible on its deck. It was flying a Guatemalan flag.

This is it, Vida thought. *It has to be.*

She thought the ship would stop, but it didn't even slow as it passed, about a hundred yards from the starboard side of the fishing boat. She craned her neck up at the deck.

Shouldn't there be someone up there? Or is this the right ship?

The ship passed on. As the fishing boat bobbed in the tanker's swell, Vida scanned the choppy surface to see if something had been tossed from the opposite side. But there was nothing.

Scanlon was opening the cooler on the deck below when she placed the barrel of the Walther to the leathery back of his red, sun-beaten neck.

"What is this?" she said. "Where is it? You brought us to the wrong place."

Scanlon, unfazed by the gun, cracked his can of Bud as he slowly turned around. "Why would I bring you to the wrong place?"

"To double-cross us," Vida said. "We weren't given the coordinates. Only you were. You bring us here, to some bullshit point, then send another boat to the correct spot to grab the shipment for yourself."

Scanlon laughed and swigged his beer.

"Lady, you have absolutely no idea what you're talking about," he said. "Listen, Perrine and I go way, way back. We got drunk together in Paris at a NATO thing back when I was a SEAL. Ask around. Your buddies on the ship got spooked or tipped off or something, OK? I've been doing this shit for twenty years. It happens all the time. We go back to shore. You call your people. You'll be—"

"Ahhh!" someone yelled behind him.

The men were crowded at the back of the boat, yelling at one another.

"What happened?" Vida asked, rushing up.

"Eduardo!" one of them said. "He was sitting there a second ago, and then I don't know what happened. It seemed like something pulled him into the water!"

A moment later, Eduardo broke the surface, ten feet off the stern.

"¡Ayúdame! ¡Tiburón!" he yelled. "¡Algo está agarrando el pie!"

Help me! Shark! Something's grabbing my foot!

"You gotta be shitting me," Scanlon said as Eduardo went under again.

The water broke again a moment later. It wasn't just Eduardo this time. Vida jumped back, elbowing Scanlon in his beer belly. Beside Eduardo was a man in a full black scuba-diving suit!

"Surprise!" Manuel Perrine said as he peeled off the face mask and chucked it onto the deck. "How is everyone? Vida, you're a sight for sore eyes."

Everyone stood there, blinking, trying to catch up. Vida was completely flummoxed. The call had said they were there to receive a shipment. She hadn't thought it would be the boss himself.

"I got you, didn't I? I can tell," Perrine said, swimming toward the rear of the boat.

"You actually jumped off the deck of that rust bucket, didn't you, you crazy son of a bitch," Scanlon said as he hauled Perrine up onto the deck.

"What can I say, Scanlon?" Perrine had a twinkle in his light-blue eyes. "I still got it."

Vida kept on staring as the rest of the men fished Eduardo out of the drink. Perrine was back in the US! What did that mean? Nothing good. How could it?

Eduardo was right, she thought.

There actually was a *tiburón*. A two-legged one, now on board.

Chapter 42

EVEN WITHOUT THE AID of a rooster, I woke up on the air base bright and early the next morning.

The afternoon before had been hectic. Parker had me fill out some paperwork that officially made me a government contractor with top secret intelligence clearance. I was given temporary FBI credentials and, even better, a Glock 17. After dinner, she'd also handed me a pile of files to take back to my room. I'd pored over them until almost one in the morning.

I'd never seen a CIA report before, and I was surprised to see how similar they were to the NYPD ones I was used to. The gist of what I'd read was that, though there were a lot of leads and tips as to Perrine's whereabouts, so far they hadn't amounted to much.

Usually paperwork in cases drove me nuts, but I was actually pretty jazzed about the whole thing. I wasn't exactly back at my Major Case Squad desk at One Police Plaza in Manhattan, but at least I was doing something positive, for once in the past eight months. Something constructive.

I was even psyched about giving my talk. Public speaking is usually on par with a root canal on my list of favorite things, but that morning, I was actually raring to go to give my speech about Perrine to the US troops who were after him.

But, as it turned out, my enthusiasm was short-lived. After my shower, I was in a towel, shaving in the dormitory head, when my phone rang.

"Hey, Parker," I said, holding my phone away from my mouth to avoid covering it in Barbasol. "I'm almost done with the first draft of my speech. Think one part Gettysburg Address, one part St. Crispin's Day speech from Shakespeare's *Henry the Fifth*."

"Sounds . . . ambitious," Parker said. "But you'll actually have to put it on the back burner, Mike. Tip came in last night, late. Apparently, someone spotted Perrine over the border in Tijuana. The army scrambled Gray Fox to check it out. The rest of the gang is on standby."

Gray Fox, as Parker had explained to me the day before, was the code name of a division of the army's Special Ops. They were an airborne unit that worked with the CIA on covert operations. Using small, single-engine aircraft or drones, they scanned search areas with sophisticated listening equipment. They could tap as well as pinpoint the location of any and all cell-phone transmissions in a given area on the ground.

The rest of the gang she was referring to included the Delta Force and SEAL Team Six members who had been assigned to the task force to do the actual boots-on-the-ground arrest once Perrine was found.

"Well, I hope it's credible. Where does that leave us?"

"I just got off the phone with the LAPD federal task force working the cartel murders in LA. They need bodies. I know I said it would just be a couple of days down here, Mike, but if you want, we can get on board there."

"But what about my military speaking engagement?" I said. "I've been working on my Patton impression all night."

"The troops can wait for now, General Bennett," Parker said. "How about pretending to be a cop again for a couple more days? Last time I checked, you were pretty good at it."

"I was, wasn't I?" I said, finally putting the phone back down on the shelf. "When can you get here?"

"I already am," Parker said from the open doorway of the bathroom behind me.

I spun around, blushing, as I gripped my towel, but she was already turned, laughing as she hurried away.

"Not funny, Parker!" I yelled. "No girls allowed in the boys' room!"

Chapter 43

A FEW HOURS LATER, after I was allowed to put on some pants and we'd grabbed some breakfast, we were on Interstate 10, speeding west toward LA.

It was a long, strange sort of trip from the air base to the city. First, we went through the edge of the Mojave Desert, then up and down through the San Gabriel Mountains. I didn't spot one yellow cab or dirty-water-dog/tube-steak cart on any of the blocks. Actually, there weren't even any blocks.

As we neared the LA city limits, Parker pointed out the spot in El Monte where the two LA County detectives had been gunned down with automatic fire.

I couldn't believe it. There was a Burger King on the corner, beside a furniture store, and a car dealership across the street. It looked like your typical suburban strip. It definitely didn't look like a war zone.

As we drove closer to downtown LA, I sat looking out at the blue sky and palm trees, the San Gabriel mountain range now in the hazy distance off to my right. I had actually been to LA once, the summer before college. After watching a bunch of Stanley Kubrick films, me and a buddy of mine had gotten it into our heads that we would come out here, find work, and become either screenwriters or directors.

What happened instead was that we got depressingly drunk for three days in a row in a crummy, run-down motel near Hollywood Boulevard, found no work, and eventually had to have our parents wire us money for a ticket home. Aren't eighteen-year-olds brilliant?

Watching the glittering downtown LA skyline come into view in the forward distance, I just hoped my second visit to La-La Land would prove more successful.

The task force HQ was set up at the LAPD's Olympic Station, a new glass, metal, and brick building located on South Vermont Avenue, in the Wilshire neighborhood business district. The multi-agency squad had originally been housed at the LAPD's Hollywood Station, but the paparazzi and media, who had camped out after the deaths of the rap mogul King Killa Leonard and pop singer Alexa Gia, had been such a nuisance, they had decided to move.

Upstairs, in a conference room, Parker introduced me to FBI agents Bob Milton and Joe Rothkopf. The veteran agents couldn't have been more welcoming or accommodating in setting us up. They'd already dragged in some desks from somewhere and placed them in the corner, with a couple of computer monitors.

Agent Rothkopf was placing a file about the Mob-boss killing in Malibu on my desk when a group of burly LAPD detectives swaggered in. *Coming in from a late lunch*, I thought, checking my watch. A semiliquid one from the looks on their red faces.

Parker had already given me the rundown on the task force. There was a large federal presence. DEA, ICE, and even the ATF, but senior detectives from LAPD's Major Crimes and Robbery-Homicide divisions were running the show. And didn't let anyone forget it, apparently.

The tallest of the detectives eyed me coldly,

then suddenly smiled as he broke off from his buddies and walked over.

"Here we go," Agent Rothkopf said to me, under his breath. "Hope you're wearing a cup."

"I'm Terry. Terry Bassman," the large thirty-something detective said, shaking my hand too hard. "You're Bennett, right? Your federal friends here were telling me all about you. They said they were bringing in some more help, and what do you know? Here you are. The guy who lost Perrine in the flesh."

The cop grinned back like a fool at his giggling buddies as I broke his grip. He was six foot four, about two-fifty, broad shouldered, in good shape. He popped a piece of gum into his mouth, the expression on his lean face that of a man who didn't take too much shit from anyone. Which was pretty convenient, since he was so big that he probably rarely had to.

But what the hell? I decided to give him some shit anyway.

"It's true, Terry," I said, loud enough for everyone in the crowded room to hear. "I lost Perrine. But you know what? I figure it's better to have caught him and lost him than to never have caught him at all. You know, like you crackerjack LAPD guys so far."

That stopped the giggling pretty quick. In fact, it got so quiet, you could have heard a firing pin drop. I glanced at Rothkopf, who was biting the inside of his cheek to keep from cracking up.

I stared back at Bassman innocently. I don't like to bang heads, but, like any cop worth his salt, I can when I have to. With the best of them, actually.

Bassman stared levelly at me, his square jaw working as he chewed his gum. Then he clapped a hand painfully on my shoulder as he smiled again.

"Well, if you need anything, Mr. Bennett—directions to Disneyland, star maps, anything at all—remember, the LAPD is here to protect and serve," he said.

Chapter 44

AFTER THAT ROUSING ENCOUNTER with the welcome wagon, I pored over the case files on all the murders.

The most disturbing photos by far were of the crime scenes at the Licata home and at rap mogul Alan Leonard's house. The pale and naked bled-out bodies were so chilling, like something out of a documentary about Nazi human experimentation. And we had no idea what had killed them. The FBI lab was still working on the toxicology of the lethal substance.

Parker stared at the horror-movie stills with me.

"I wonder if shock value is the point," she said, letting out a frustrated breath.

"Probably," I said. "Things have gotten so

bizarre of late that Perrine has to get creative in order to grab people's attention."

"He certainly has mine," Emily said. "I mean, this is simply incredible. I've read reports that indicate the cartels turned to all these horrors, like beheadings and body mutilations, after seeing them performed by Islamic terrorists on the Internet."

"Bull," I said, turning over a photograph. "Narco traffickers south of the border have always been famous for incredibly brutal killings. Where does the Colombian necktie come from? My pet theory is that this recent, really sick garbage has more than a little to do with Santa Muerte, the spooky quasi-religious death cult that many of the cartel soldiers adhere to."

"So you're saying it's like a cycle," she said. "The more the cartels rise in power, the more and more its members want to satisfy Santa Muerte's thirst for blood?"

I nodded.

"That's a little out there, Mike. Isn't this about money and drug trafficking, not Perrine's evil cult?"

"If it's about just money and drug trafficking, what's up with all the bodies, Parker?" I said.

"Twenty-nine dumped in Nuevo Laredo. Forty-nine in Juarez. They're hung from bridges. Bags of heads are found along highways. The victims aren't even cartel members. They're innocent migrant workers or people trying to cross the border into the US. To kill a mule for stealing a load is one thing, or to go after a witness. I'm telling you, this is new. Or, more accurately, old."

"Old?" Emily asked.

"Have you ever heard of the Thuggee cult?"

Parker rolled her eyes. "Had a lot of reading time on our hands up there on the prairie, Detective?"

"A little, Parker. Anyway, in India there used to be this criminal cult called the Thuggees. They were a secretive organization of robber-murderers. They'd strangle their victims and then bleed them, offering their blood to Kali, the goddess of death. Some say Santa Muerte is a modern incarnation of Mictecacihuatl, the Aztec goddess of death."

"So what are you saying? It's us versus the goddess of death?"

"Kind of," I said.

"You've been watching too much History Channel," she said.

"Have I?" I said. "These cartel people are

engaging in the kind of unhinged, deranged behavior usually reserved for serial killers. Is it that crazy to believe that there's some sort of ideology behind it? I think we have to at least consider it. We have to stop thinking that this is just about a bunch of greedy dope dealers."

Chapter 45

ABOUT AN HOUR LATER, on our way to get a bite to eat, I knocked on the dash of Parker's metallic-brown Crown Victoria as we pulled out of the Olympic Station lot.

"What's up with this ride, Parker?" I complained. "As my preteen daughters would say, this car is 'so not cool.' You'd think, this being LA, that they'd assign you some kind of convertible, at least."

Parker smirked at me from behind her Ray-Bans.

"Tell you what, Mike," she said. "You bag Perrine, I'll see to it you get first bid on his Bentley at the government auction."

"Bentley, huh?" I said, scratching my chin. "How many passengers can a Bentley fit? I need

Gone

seating for a dozen, two of them car seats."

Parker laughed.

"Just a dozen? Aren't you leaving someone out? What about Seamus?"

"We usually put him in the trunk, or on the roof with the cat."

Parker shook her head, sighing.

My chop busting was, of course, just show. I actually loved the Crown Vic, the FBI radio crackling beneath its dash, even the bad gas-station coffee in the holder beside me. In fact, it felt fantastic to be back at work.

I was even more excited about our dinner plans. Parker had spoken to Agent Rothkopf, who, with the help of a cousin or something, got us reservations at some hip restaurant called Cut, in the Beverly Wilshire Hotel. It was a Wolfgang Puck steak house where Tom Cruise supposedly ate from time to time. I couldn't wait.

It was our LAPD hosts who had been less than accommodating. As I'd watched them read reports and brood about them, it'd become painfully obvious to me that the cops in this clique of LAPD heavy hitters were doing their own thing, working their own leads, their own contacts, while completely leaving the feds in the dark.

219

Though I'd been pretty tribal myself about my home turf back in NYC, the fact that I was now among the feds being boxed out kind of pissed me off. I didn't come in off the farm to be a benchwarmer.

Parker's phone rang.

"One second," she said. "I'm driving. Let me hand you to Detective Bennett."

"Who is it?" I asked, holding her BlackBerry against my thigh.

"Bassman."

"Gee, thanks," I said, lifting the phone. "Bennett here. What's up, Detective?"

"Hey, where'd you guys go?" Bassman asked. "I've been looking all around for you."

Yeah, right, I thought. We'd been sitting there for hours, twiddling our thumbs. My guess was that he'd somehow heard about our reservation and had finally come up with a way to ruin it. A goose chase, no doubt. The cartels were blowing people away, and the only thing Bassman was interested in was more chop busting. This guy was the full package, a complete ass.

"I don't know how they do things in New York, Bennett, but this task force is a team. Anyway, I have a lead for you and Parker. A guy arrested for

DUI involving a fatality swears he saw Perrine this morning. How about you guys run down to the hospital and talk to him."

"Hospital?"

"Yeah, he's in the psycho wing at the Metro State Hospital in Norwalk. Apparently, this guy is on speed or ecstasy or something."

I knew it. The task force was getting thousands of useless calls a day about Perrine's locale, and here Bassman was sending us to talk to some guy who was drugged out of his mind. *Sure, he saw Perrine. Riding a giant green velvet bumblebee over a rainbow, no doubt.*

Whatever, I thought. Tom Cruise would have to eat his Kobe fillet without us. We had to start somewhere.

"No problem. Hit me with the address."

Bassman harrumphed. He seemed upset that I wasn't complaining. As if I'd actually give him the satisfaction of squirming.

"Here you go, Bennett. Ready? I'll make sure and go real slow so you can type it clearly into the GPS."

Chapter 46

THE METROPOLITAN STATE HOSPITAL in Norwalk was due southeast from our location, a full forty-minute ride down Interstate 5.

As we rolled along haltingly on the traffic-filled six-lane superhighway, it wasn't really the traffic but the immense sprawl of the city that made me stare in astonishment. Back east, as an NYPD cop, I only had to worry about five measly, cramped boroughs. Here in LA, they had to cover five *counties*.

The state mental hospital was housed on a large, leafy, wooded piece of land that might have resembled a college campus if college campuses had ten-foot chain-link, barbed-wire-topped fences running their perimeter.

"Didn't they film *The Silence of the Lambs* here?"

I asked as we pulled into the driveway. "Or *Terminator Two*? No, wait. It was *One Flew Over the Cuckoo's Nest*."

"I'd advise you at this point in to keep a lid on it, Bennett, or they might not let you back out when we're done," my trusty partner said.

After calling ahead, we badged our way through the gate and met California Highway Patrol Sergeant Joe Rodbourne in the front vestibule of the new administration building. The burly, bald sergeant got right to it. He slipped on a pair of granny reading glasses as he freed his notepad from the bulging breast pocket of his khaki uniform shirt.

"OK, here's what we got. At four twenty-five or thereabouts this afternoon, a BMW tried to make an illegal U-turn at a highway patrol turnaround on the Seven Ten near the Santa Ana Freeway in East LA. As the car made the turn, a southbound Peterbilt hauling a trailer ran right over the top of the Beemer, killing the female passenger instantly. Witnesses say the truck and the tanker rode the median for a quarter mile, throwing sparks, but luckily came back down without going over and killing God knows how many other people driving home from work in the middle of rush hour."

Rodbourne licked a callused thumb and turned the page.

"The driver of the BMW, named Scricca, Mathew J., was miraculously unscathed. He's a deep-sea fishing-boat captain down at Marina del Rey. He gets around some, apparently, by his priors. His last one was attempted assault with a deadly weapon outside a Sunset Boulevard strip club on New Year's Eve last."

"Scricca is on something, they said?" I said.

The weather-beaten cop studied me over his bifocals.

"The attendant at the ER swore it's GHB. You know, that nifty new date-rape drug all the lovely young clubgoers are experimenting with these days? Makes sense. Scricca reportedly had some, eh, visual disturbances at the scene. Kept going on about flowers. 'Keep the flowers off me. Get the flowers out of my stomach.' Interesting stuff like that. That's why they sent him here.

"We called you guys in when he came down, a little over an hour ago. Make that came down a lot, after he was informed of the fatality he was responsible for. He immediately asked to deal. He said he had something big. Something about Manuel Perrine."

Parker and I looked at the veteran cop, then each other. We could practically read each other's minds. Boats. Smuggling. Perrine. So far, so interesting.

"Take us to him, if you would, Sergeant," Parker said with a smile.

Chapter 47

SERGEANT RODBOURNE FOUND AN orderly, and we went in through the administration building and then out through a covered passageway to an older, one-story brick dorm.

We were buzzed through a gate and went down a long, worn, once-white corridor. The hospital's emergency lockup was lined with the kind of heavy doors usually seen on walk-in freezers. The blast doors had peekaboo windows in them, with thick crisscrosses of chicken wire beneath the smudged, shatterproof glass.

"Are you still dreaming of the lambs, Clarice?" I whispered to Parker, who immediately elbowed me in the solar plexus.

As we stopped at a door near the end of the hallway, I looked through the screened window to see Scricca, shirtless and on his back, handcuffed to a hospital bed.

I was surprised to see that he was good-looking. He was deeply tanned, with long, shiny black hair and pale-gray-green eyes, and was muscular in a wiry, rock-climber kind of way.

Even the creeps have to keep up appearances out here in the land of make-believe, I thought.

I saw ubiquitous tattoos, inked only on his torso in a vestlike pattern. It looked like he was wearing a paisley blackjack-dealer vest of snakes and soaring eagles and eight balls and evil clowns.

"Style. I like that in a man," Parker mumbled as the orderly cracked the clasps on the door.

What Sergeant Rodbourne said was true, I thought, quickly scanning Scricca's face as we went into the room. Though his eyes were bloodshot, he didn't look deranged. If anything, his tired, forlorn expression was quite sober, that of a man who had just awakened to find himself as far up shit's creek as one could go, and without a paddle in sight.

"Hi, Mr. Scricca. I'm Agent Parker," Emily said with the slow, deliberate speech one would use with a toddler or a stoned-out junkie. "I work for the FBI."

"Yeah, well, I'm sorry that girl is dead," Scricca

said, nervously chewing on the thumbnail of his free hand. "I got two girls of my own. One of them near her age, but, like I told them, she was the one with that mind-bending shit. She told me it was coke. It was bath salts or something, right? To tell you the truth, she was the one who suggested I make the U-turn. She dared me, in fact. Said I didn't have the balls."

"You're a piece of work, Scricca," Sergeant Rodbourne said, stepping toward him. "First you throw your date under a truck, now you throw her under the bus."

Sensing trouble, I took a quick step sideways, into the brawny and angry cop's path.

"Thanks, Sarge," I said, steering him toward the rubber-room door. "We'll take it from here."

"We're not here about the accident," Parker said after I pulled the door shut. "You made a claim that you saw the wanted cartel leader Manuel Perrine here in LA. Where did you see him?"

"It's not a claim," Scricca said, folding his arms as he slowly looked back and forth at us. "I saw him this morning, before all this happened. He was with someone I know."

"Let me get this straight," I said, peering at him. "This morning, Manuel Perrine, the world's most wanted and most ruthless killer, just strolled past you with a buddy of yours? That's what you're trying to tell us? Because when I meet people who have crossed Perrine's path, it's usually in a funeral home, not a loony bin."

"He didn't *see* me. I was a couple hundred yards away," Scricca said, knocking hard on the bed railing with a knuckle. "I saw him with binoculars. I even looked at my cell phone at the FBI website to double-check the face. I'm not shitting you. It was him. Mr. Public Enemy Number One himself."

"This was on the water?" Parker tried. "You saw Perrine when you were out on your boat?"

Scricca took a deep breath, his handcuff scraping on the bed rail as he squirmed back against the wall.

"I can't tell you that until I get a deal. I'll tell you everything I know when you write up some immunity and my lawyer OKs it. Being a rat makes me sick, but I can't go back inside. My old lady tried to kill herself last time. I can't do her like that. Not again."

"OK, Mr. Scricca. I see. We'll be back," Parker said, ushering me out.

"What a noble guy, to consider his wife like that, don't you think?" I said as we hit the hallway.

"After he kills the girlfriend he's been out drugging with and gets busted, his old lady is the very first person he thinks about."

"The question is, what do you think of his story, Mike?" Parker said. "You think this waste of life might actually know something?"

"Yes," I said, after a few seconds of looking back in at him. "Other than his taste in three-piece-suit body art and his obvious self-destructive tendencies, oddly enough, he actually seems like a pretty sharp cookie."

"That's what I was thinking," she said. "Screw it. Let's bite. Offer him a deal based on Perrine's arrest and capture. If it doesn't pan out, then what do we have to lose? It's not like we have any other promising leads."

"I'm down," I said. "As long as there's no cow milking involved, I'm pretty much down for anything."

Parker took out her phone. She smiled mischievously as she waited for the line to get picked up.

"What's so funny, Agent P.?" I asked.

"This goose chase that jackass Bassman sent us on," she said. "How hilarious would it be if we just found the one that lays the golden egg?"

Chapter 48

AS IT TURNED OUT, we did strike gold out here in California.

After Emily called back to the task force with our hunch, Bill Kaukonen, the LA County assistant district attorney on call, came to the hospital, and a deal was quickly struck.

Captain Scricca made out like a pirate. He would get a suspended sentence and a six-month stint in rehab for his role in the vehicular homicide if his information led to the capture of Perrine.

It was a sickening arrangement, I thought as I watched Kaukonen leave. The young woman who had been killed was only twenty-eight. But with Perrine out there trying to turn Southern California into the Vietnam War Part Two, it was easy to see that these were desperate times that called for some pretty desperate measures.

After the ADA left, we went back into Scricca's cell and got his statement. The gist of it was that a little after noon, he had spotted Perrine in Marina del Rey, on a deep-sea fishing boat called *Aces and Eights* owned by a man named Thomas Scanlon. Scanlon was a sketchy character, he said, and it was an almost open joke among the fishermen down at the marina that he was involved with drug running.

Scricca's story seemed to pan out further when we went back up to our HQ at Olympic Station and Emily put Scanlon into some of the Big Brother federal databases she was privy to.

Scanlon was, in fact, a sketchy character. In 1995, he had gotten booted from the Navy SEALs for a hot drug test. Soon after, Mr. Scanlon's passport started appearing in some pretty strange places: South America, the Netherlands, Central Africa, the Middle East. It was a lot of world travel for a man who didn't seem to have any visible means of support.

"This guy was in Qatar for a year and a half," Parker said over the diner takeout piled on our desks. "When was the last time you went to Qatar, Bennett?"

"Went to Qatar?" I said, cracking the lid of my coffee. "I can't even play one."

"Then Scanlon just disappears off the grid for five years, and pow! Out of the blue suddenly pops up in SoCal as a deep-sea fisherman?" Parker said. "How's that work?"

"You're right. Overall, this guy seems pretty fishy," I said.

Agent Parker tossed a sweet potato fry at me, which I deftly caught without spilling my joe. I took a bite and then, remembering it was a vegetable, promptly chucked it into the wastepaper basket.

"So what now?" I said.

"Now we call the bosses in to see how quickly they can spin our gold into straw," Emily said.

"Ouch," I said with a smile as Emily started texting people. "That sounds like something a burnt-out, jaded NYPD detective would say after a bottle of twelve-year-old Irish wine."

"You're a bad influence on people, Bennett," Emily said, smiling broadly without looking up. "You should seriously think about talking to somebody about it."

All the bells and whistles started going off after Emily and I sent the info up both the civilian and military chains of command. Wiretap subpoenas for all Scanlon's phones were immediately put into motion, as well as round-the-clock surveillance for Scanlon's boat and his house in Brentwood. The head FBI honcho working with the CIA and military folks up at the air base seemed especially excited, as the Tijuana tip they'd been following had dug a hole as dry as the Mexican desert.

A massive task force meeting was called for eight the next morning. It would be teleconferenced with the military folks at the air base. In the meantime, Emily's immediate boss, the assistant special agent in charge of the FBI's LA office, Evaline Echevarria, ordered us to Scanlon's house for the first shift of surveillance.

Though we'd been running pretty hard since the a.m., we both leaped at the assignment. I know I was pretty jazzed. After being out of commission, out in the sticks, I had a deep store of untapped adrenaline to run on.

As we drove over to the FBI HQ to get a better surveillance vehicle, it was my turn to start laughing.

"That's a real personal gigglefest you're having over there, Mike," Emily said. "You losing it on me already? If you want, I could swing you back to

Metro State Hospital for an eval. I noticed the rubber room next to Scricca was free."

"Not yet," I said, finally getting myself under control. "It's just that I pictured Bassman's face when he heard the news about our little gold strike. That obnoxious bozo is going to be so freaking pissed."

Chapter 49

SCANLON'S HOUSE WAS IN Brentwood, on Chaparal Street, a quiet, high-hedged lane behind an all-girls private school. It was an old, tasteful brick Tudor house hidden behind a lot of shrubbery, with a wrought iron gate across its driveway.

There weren't too many parked cars on the secluded street, and, even with the silver Mercedes crossover we were using for an unmarked, it definitely wasn't the best setup for surveillance.

"Nice crib for a chum chopper," I said from where we parked, a couple of houses down.

Parker nodded. "That house easily goes for a million, maybe a million and a half."

There was a security light on above the garage when we got there. We scanned the windows with binoculars, but there was nothing. No movement anywhere, even after another half an hour. There was no way to tell if Scanlon was home.

Parker fixed that, and quick. She made a phone call, and about twenty minutes later, a plain, white panel van pulled onto Chaparal. It passed us without acknowledgment and then slowed to a brief stop in front of Scanlon's house before pulling away.

Parker's phone dinged a couple of minutes later.

"It's clean," came a voice from the speaker, "but there's a dog, Parker. A big son of a bitch. Good luck."

"Gee, thanks," Parker said, hanging up.

"Infrared?" I said.

"Close," Parker said. "That was the LA office's portable X-ray van. We use it at the ports sometimes, and on presidential visits. Two techs in the back of it work equipment that can see right through just about anything."

"Like a TSA team on wheels? I take it that's a pretty much all-male detail. Tell me, Parker. Can federal contractors apply for the job, and what's the waiting list like?"

Parker raised one of her auburn eyebrows.

"You'd be surprised how many female agents are in the unit, Bennett."

I blinked at her.

"Well, in that case, remind me to head to the supermarket before we go back to the hotel. I need to make a supply of tinfoil boxers for my stay here in LA."

Though Parker tried to hide it, I noticed she actually laughed a little at that one. My war of attrition was taking its toll. As usual, I was wearing her down with my charm.

"Now, if Scanlon isn't home trying not to let the bedbugs bite at this time of night, where do you think he is, Mike?"

"That's the sixty-four-million-dollar question, isn't it?" I said. "If I were an international fugitive sneaking into an unfriendly country, I'd probably want to keep everyone who knew about it on a tight leash. At least until I left. If I were a betting man, I'd put my money on it that Scanlon is chilling with the big boss for the duration of his trip."

"Which means, if we find Scanlon, we find Perrine," she said.

"We can only hope and pray," I said.

Chapter 50

AFTER IT WAS DETERMINED that Scanlon wasn't home, phase two of the operation was put into play.

Parker got on the horn again, and then, twenty minutes later, a beat-up Dodge Ram pickup with a camper bed pulled up behind us.

"More friends of yours, Parker?" I said. "What does this truck do? Test your cholesterol?"

As she shushed me, I noticed that the two men who got out of it were dressed head to toe in black. I also noticed that the cabin light in the pickup failed to go on when the men opened the doors.

Parker zipped down her window as they approached. One of the agents was stocky and older, with a dark mustache. The other one was blond and looked like he'd just started shaving.

I thought they looked like a father-and-son team of American ninjas.

"Which is it?" Junior wanted to know.

"The one with the gate," Parker told him. "There's a dog, apparently."

"No problem," said Senior, patting the bag he was holding with an evil grin. "We love puppies."

Junior kept his eyes on the house as he put a chaw of chewing tobacco between his cheek and gum. There was a light jingle of metal on metal when he tightened the knapsack on his back. He checked his watch.

"We'll call you in . . . seven minutes?" he said, cocking his head at his partner.

"Six," the older partner said with a nod before they walked off.

"The wheels of justice are moving so much faster than I remember. This must be some sort of land-speed record for a search warrant," I said, watching the FBI agents scale the driveway gate like squirrels.

Parker ignored me. I'd only said it to tease her. This was an illegal, unauthorized black-bag job if there ever was one.

One I thoroughly approved of, actually. Following the letter of the law when Perrine was out there wiping out families and cops would be like obeying the traffic laws while driving a dying relative to the emergency room. In a word, stupid.

We needed information, the faster the better. We needed to be on Scanlon, on his phone, neck deep in his life, before he had the slightest inkling of what was what. My eyes were locked firmly on the prize, namely, a world without Manuel Perrine. I'd cut more corners than a miter saw to take out the son of a bitch who was still out there on the loose, trying to kill my family.

It was actually only five minutes from when the FBI Watergate plumber guys hopped the fence until it slowly started opening. The older agent opened the door formally, like a butler, as we came up the drive.

"Where's Fido?" Parker asked.

"Out like a light. After we picked the lock and tossed him a treat, he got real sleepy all of a sudden. Funny, huh?"

Chapter 51

PARKER HANDED ME SOME gloves and night-vision goggles from a bag of goodies she had brought with her, and we proceeded to toss the house. We were careful not to disturb anything. Not just because we didn't want Scanlon to know, but because there were guns everywhere. A Taurus .380 in the bathroom cabinet, a .45 M1911 under the sink in the kitchen. A locked-and-loaded, fully automatic MAC-10 was taped to the underside of the night table in the master bedroom.

"Mr. Scanlon seems like a fairly cautious individual," I whispered as I showed it to Agent Parker.

The treasure trove we found was in the closet of a bedroom that Scanlon used for an office.

On top of a case of printer paper, we found a dozen boxes of portable disposable cell phones. Half of them were empty.

The phones were the unregistered kind that narcotics dealers liked to use and throw away. What got our blood pumping was that the boxes with the missing phones still had the serial numbers on them. Our techs could contact the company, and we could put a trace out on every single one of them. If Scanlon had one in his pocket, we could find him, even if it was off.

"Please let this work," Parker said as she snapped picture after picture of the boxes.

We spotted some guy crossing the street toward the house just as we were about to go out.

"Is it Scanlon?" Parker asked.

I quickly checked the passport photograph we had. The guy coming toward the gate looked young and was too dark and thin to resemble the blond, bearlike Scanlon.

We fished out our Glocks as the guy punched a code into the keypad beside the gate. It was evident that the guy was in his early twenties as he came through the buzzing gate and up the driveway. He was wearing white iPod earbuds.

"Whoever this guy is, he doesn't seem to have a care in the world," I whispered.

We stepped back as the guy keyed open the door.

As he closed the door behind him, I put my Glock to his brain stem. He bolted forward like he'd been Tasered and head-butted the door. A hiss of N-word-laced rap drivel cut the silence as I pulled out his earbuds for him.

"Don't move," I said.

"What is this? Who the hell are you?" the young man said.

"Who the hell are we?" I shot back, full of attitude. "Who the hell are you?"

"I'm Donny Pearson, from up the street. Tommy just called and said he'd be out of town for a few days and asked if I'd feed Christobel, man."

Parker took out his wallet and nodded. I showed the guy my badge and holstered the gun.

"I got nothing to do with anything illegal. I swear to God!" Pearson said.

"Just listen to me, Mr. Pearson," I said. "Did he call you on your cell or your house phone?"

"My cell," he said, taking out his iPhone.

Parker took it and quickly compared the phone number Scanlon had phoned in on with the ones we'd found in the closet. Then she gave me a palm-stinging high five.

"Bingo was his name-o," she said.

Chapter 52

WE WERE HOMING IN on Perrine now. We could feel it.

On the way back to the hotel, I drove while Emily disseminated the intel to just about every card in the multi-jurisdictional Rolodex. The LAPD phone people got a call, as did the FBI, CIA, NSA, and even Gray Fox, the army Special Ops communication specialists.

Back in my hotel room, I stripped, sleepwalked through a hot shower, and proceeded to crash like the Hindenburg. I was facedown, still stone-dead asleep in the hotel bathrobe, when my phone rang ten hours later.

As it trilled, I blinked out the window at the bright sky behind a palm tree. Was it morning? Afternoon? I couldn't figure it out. *No wonder they call this place La-La Land,* I thought, finally answering my phone.

"The goose just laid a four-hundred-troy-ounce gold bar," Parker said excitedly. "They just got the signal on Scanlon's phone. He's in Orange County."

Parker clued me in as we raced south down the Pacific Coast Highway.

The signal on Scanlon's phone was coming from Newport Coast, a ridiculously affluent town an hour south of LA. The Gray Fox army com unit had done a flyby, and the house where they had triangulated Scanlon's phone was in a development of ten-thousand-square-foot-plus houses off Newport Coast Drive, not too far from the world-renowned Pelican Hill Golf Club.

As Parker drove, I flipped through an old Realtor.com file the FBI had dug up on the massive mission-style mansion. I read in the report how the premier property had been owned by an energy-company billionaire but had recently been put up for rent due to ongoing divorce proceedings.

"Huge pool," I said, nodding. "Ocean view, check and double check. It also says the interior decor was imported from an eighteenth-century château in Monpazier, in the south of France. This is feeling righter and righter, Ms. Parker.

This seems to fit Perrine's billionaire boulevardier tastes to a capital tee."

Our rallying point was behind a Trader Joe's off the Pacific Coast Highway, three miles south of the target. The assemblage of law enforcement officials that came together over the next hour was nothing short of dumbfounding. There was a command bus on site when we got there, and for the next hour, a nonstop wagon train of unmarked cop and federal-agent cars pulled into the lot. And this was just the civilian staging area.

A series of white vans brought in the FBI's hostage rescue team. Watching them disembark, I noticed that there were two men with them who weren't wearing FBI fatigues. They stood together, apart and aloof, big, fit-looking men with shaved heads and beards, dark sunglasses on under their drab olive ball caps.

I didn't need Parker's help to figure out that they were military, probably Delta Force. They were likely coordinating radio signals and whatnot between the civilian and military forces. Parker had already told me that the military was gathering somewhere else to coordinate an air assault.

As the invasion force mounted, Emily and I touched base with the other task force members.

At a card table stacked with ammo, LA-office FBI agents Bob Milton and Joe Rothkopf were busy handing out vests and requisitioning M4 automatic rifles. Despite the obvious building pressure, the young agents were fairly unflappable. Serene, laid-back, California cool. They were acting as if they were waiting for a surfing competition to start down on the beach, on the other side of the PCH, instead of World War III.

I spotted Detective Bassman, on the other hand, pacing around the parking lot like an expectant first-time father. He was completely keyed up. He wouldn't even make eye contact with Emily and me, let alone talk to us. I could just about read the big man's mind as he bounced around in a state of semi-shock. He'd had his hands on perhaps the greatest rocket boost his career would ever know, and he'd gone and handed it away to a Feeb and a bum from the NYPD.

If I had any last qualms about how serious the authorities were in dealing with the Perrine problem, they were fully put to rest when I saw what swung into the parking lot just after dark.

On the back of a flatbed truck came none other than a twenty-ton-plus Bradley Fighting Vehicle. I stood there, gaping at the caterpillar-treaded troop-carrying tank, at the 25 mm gun mounted to the front of it.

"Well, well," said Agent Rothkopf as he polished the lens of a nightscope beside me. "I don't believe we'll be getting outgunned on this one."

"This is impressive," I said, getting a little nervous at all the commotion. "I mean, we don't even know if Perrine's here."

"Better to have some backup if he is," Rothkopf said.

"Perrine wanted a war," Emily said. "Time to see how much he can handle."

Chapter 53

PLANS WERE MADE AS the clock ticked and it got darker.

The armed-to-the-gills LA-office SWAT teams, along with Hostage Rescue, were geared for a full frontal assault, while we task force members were assigned slightly safer, perimeter positions in case Perrine tried to mosey out the back door.

At a little after eleven, Parks Department personnel were inserted into Crystal Cove State Park, a little south of the development. We had to hike a mile down a dark horse trail, alongside scrub willow and oak, using night vision. Though it was pretty temperate, with all the gear on and my rifle, I was sweating like a pig in about a minute and a half. Parker looked as fresh as a daisy.

When I turned, far away over the trees, I could

see the shiny surface of the Pacific. *Wow, do I have a weird job*, I thought.

We were under strict radio silence. Too bad there wasn't voice silence. Up ahead in the dark, Emily and I could overhear Bassman complaining about what a bullshit detail this was and how, since it was LA cops who'd been murdered, it should be the LAPD kicking in the front door.

Emily and I shook our heads at each other. I'd heard blowhards before, but this guy was something else.

It took us almost twenty minutes to get into position along the horse trail at the bottom of the shrub-and-loose-dirt-covered slope behind the rented mansion. We spread ourselves out in two-person teams along the bottom of the slope, one team every ten or twenty yards. If Perrine came down the hill, he'd be nailed. I prayed that he would.

When I checked my watch, it was a quarter to twelve. The breach team was due to go in at 12:20 on the nose. It was exactly 12:15 when the bullshit started. We turned as Bassman, who was stationed on the trail to the right of Parker and me, started climbing up the hill with his partner. "Bassman," I hissed, rushing down the trail toward him. "What the hell are you doing?"

"Getting into a better position," he hissed back.

"That's not the plan, Bassman. You're gonna get your ass shot."

"What are you? My mother?" he said, dismissing me with a wave as he continued up the slope.

After another minute, he disappeared over the crest of the hill with his partner.

The moment he disappeared, I looked up to see the huge form of an MH-60 Black Hawk helicopter appear out of the night. It passed extremely low, directly over my head, making no more noise than a Cuisinart mixer. I knew that the military teams were being inserted into the compound by air, in conjunction with the SWAT teams. What I didn't know was how discreet their entrance would be.

Less than a minute later, up over the ridge in the distance, there came several sharp, loud bangs that must have been the SWAT teams breaching the house's wrought iron gate. There was a roar of engines that had to be the SWAT vans. Over the tactical mike, I could hear cops—or maybe they were soldiers—calling out a jumble of shouted directions amid more bangs.

That was when the firing started. From everywhere at once, it seemed the silence burst with the unmistakable metal-hammering-on-metal sound of automatic gunfire. The dark sky above us lit up, suddenly glowing with muzzle flashes as the jumble over the radio became confused screams.

The firing was becoming heavier when I heard an unmistakable voice over the cacophony.

"I'm pinned down!" Bassman was yelling. "By the pool house! Cop pinned down! Somebody help!"

"Of course he is," I said to Parker as I started up the loose-dirt hill.

When I peeked over the ridge, I didn't see any sign of Bassman, but I did see a figure on the deck. He was a short Hispanic guy in tighty whities, with a tribal tattoo on his shirtless chest, and he was staring straight at me as he raised a pump-action shotgun.

Before I could duck, get my hand onto the pistol grip of the rifle strapped to my back, or say my act of contrition, a half-dozen FBI SWAT guys appeared in the backyard from the side of the house, firing. The glass doors on the deck blew in, along with most of the gunman, as a fusillade of MP5 fire ripped open the entire front of him, from his crotch to his throat.

I stood there, frozen, watching helplessly as

the SWAT team rushed in through the back doors.

If they hadn't come, I would have been dead, I thought. *A second later, I would have been gone.* I knew it in my bones.

I shook all over.

I'd never been to war.

Until now.

Chapter 54

I PULLED MYSELF TOGETHER by the time Parker arrived behind me. I raced with her around the pool and around the dead guy on the deck, into the house.

"Down! Freeze!" cops were yelling. From somewhere a woman was crying.

As we passed a bathroom, Parker tapped me on the back.

"Mike! Oh, shit, Mike! It's him!"

"Who? Perrine? Where?"

I turned. It wasn't Perrine. It was Scanlon. I recognized him from his passport photo. Barely. He was on his back in the tub, on top of the torn shower curtain. His hands were handcuffed behind him, and his throat was cut to the bone.

We scoured the house for another twenty

minutes before one of the ATF SWAT guys found the trick door in the wine cellar. Beyond it was a steep set of circular stairs, with faux castle walls and candelabra, leading toward a Gothic, dungeon-like door on the bottom.

"What the hell is this?" Emily said as one of the hostage rescue guys in front of us pushed it open.

"They left this out on Realtor dot com," I said.

The door led to a large octagonal room with benches along the crimson walls and a huge platform bed in the middle of it. Strapped on the bloodred silk moiré walls were lots of very interesting objects. Whips, handcuffs, leather hoods, and other assorted adult devices that, when bought off the Internet, probably arrived in plain brown packages. There was a sophisticated sound system and even a mounted camera in the ceiling.

"Now I think I know why the previous owner got a divorce," I said.

One of the commandos pushed open yet another door, on the other side of the room. There was another long corridor behind it. It dead-ended at a brick wall with a little ladder bolted into it. At the top of the ladder was a hatch. An open hatch.

I poked my head out. The escape hatch opened up onto the trail, not twenty feet from where we'd been stationed behind the house. I shook my head. Then pounded my thigh with my fist.

No! If we'd still been in position, we would have heard Perrine escaping. Now Perrine could be anywhere.

"He's in the woods behind the house," one of the commandos called into his radio. "Get the chopper! Light the park south and east of the target house, and, dammit, get K-nine into the park!"

When I went back into the underground sex chamber, Bassman was standing there, examining one of the curios on the wall. I just stared at the jackass, about as pissed off at anyone as I'd ever been in my life.

He finally noticed me staring. *No wonder he made detective,* I thought.

"Can the eyeballing, Bennett," he said, puffing up his already pretty puffed-up self. "You need to get something off your chest, open your trap."

Actually, I did need to get something off my chest. But I forgot to use my words. I took two steps forward and punched him as hard as I could in the mouth.

He grunted as his head snapped to the side. Then he screamed as he rushed forward and rammed his shoulder into my chest, knocking out my breath as he bulled me backward. He was about to get me down when I wrapped a leg around the back of his ankle and spun us both sideways. Bassman landed hard on his back, beside the bed, with me on top of him. I punched him three times quick again in his face before two of the SWAT guys could peel me off him.

"What are you, crazy?" Bassman yelled, thumbing blood on his lip.

"We could have had him!" I screamed back, going berserk. "He was here! We had him! But you had to charge the hill, didn't you? Had to screw things up like the two-bit flake that you are!"

"Screw you, Bennett!" he screamed. "You're full of shit! Screw you!"

"You already did it for me," I told the dumbass. "Don't worry, Bassman. You already royally did."

Part Three

TROUBLE ON THE HOME FRONT

Chapter 55

IN THE MORNING, MARY Catherine left Trent in charge of pouring the pancakes and went down into the cellar to find another apron. Rummaging through a packing box, she glanced up as she heard soft footsteps coming down from one of the upstairs bedrooms.

"Hey, Chrissy," she heard Trent say.

Oh, boy, let the games begin, Mary Catherine thought, moving some Christmas ornaments over to get at another U-Haul box. Trent was at the age when his goal in life, the very purpose of his existence, in fact, seemed to be teasing the girls as much as he possibly could. And Chrissy, being the youngest, was his favorite target.

"Good morning, little sister," Trent continued

sweetly. "So nice to see you this happy day. Sleep well?"

"What are you doing?" Chrissy said skeptically. "You're not supposed to have the oven on. Where's Mary Catherine?"

"Who knows?" Trent lied. "I'm doing an experiment, Chrissy. See how this batter is running off the spatula and splattering onto the pan? This is exactly like when somebody gets shot and all the blood goes flying all over the place. Imagine I was just shot, OK, and I'm bleeding to death, and this pan here is covered in my blood. Isn't it awesome?"

Mary Catherine shook her head, smiling. *What is it with boys?* she thought. *How do they even come up with this stuff?*

"Stop it, Trent!" Chrissy said. "Blood doesn't even do that. You're lying."

"No, it's true," Trent said sagely. "Blood splatters like crazy. Way worse than this, especially if a bullet nicks an artery. I saw it on TV."

Note to self, Mary Catherine thought. *Change the TV's parental channel locks as soon as possible.*

"You know what else?" Trent continued. "I bet Dad is right now looking at blood splatter on a wall next to a dead body. I mean, that's what Dad does, right? He's a cop. So whenever they find a dead guy with bullet holes in him or a knife sticking out of his neck, they call Dad in to the scene. Isn't he lucky? Isn't that so cool?"

Mary Catherine winced, waiting for Chrissy to start screaming or crying, but was surprised when nothing came out.

"Actually," Chrissy said calmly, "it's not cool. It's just really gross, like you."

Yes! Mary Catherine thought. Chrissy was learning to defend herself. One good thing about being a member of a family this big was developing the ability to use the occasional sharp elbow. *Excellent job, young lass,* Mary Catherine thought. Offense was always the best defense.

"Mary Catherine!" Trent yelled down the cellar stairs a second later. "Chrissy called me stupid!"

"Stupid?" Mary Catherine said, winking at Chrissy as she made it back into the kitchen. "I believe the term I heard your sister use, young man, was *gross.*"

Chapter 56

THE COFFEE MACHINE'S BEEPER went off as half the sleepy Bennett clan fed on flapjacks. Mary Catherine took a porcelain cup out of the cabinet over the sink and filled it, carefully pouring in some half-and-half before she took it out the front door, onto the porch.

She always loved going out in the morning, right before sunrise. The creak of the old screen door. The cold of the wind coming down from the mountains, the feel of old porch floorboards under her bare feet.

The deputy US marshal on watch, Leo Piccini, stood abruptly from the camp chair he was sitting in and placed a copy of James Dickey's *To the White Sea* on the railing of the porch, beside a Toughbook field laptop.

The other men brought smartphones to while away the hours on watch, but Leo always had a book with him. Mary Catherine wondered how he read in the dark until one time she peeked out the window and saw him wearing night-vision goggles.

After Mike had left, the marshals had come and beefed up security even more than usual. In addition to the now round-the-clock watch, yesterday they had come and put in high-tech motion detectors along the property's perimeter, as well as night-vision video cameras. She didn't know what would be next. Trip wires, maybe, and mines.

She glanced at his weapon, an M4 automatic rifle, lying on the floor of the porch in its open case, with a towel covering it. It was scary to have to receive military-grade protection now. But Mike had called the day before and told her about the raid. About how they thought Perrine was in the US now. There really was no choice but to put up with it.

"Oh, you didn't have to do that," Leo said as Mary Catherine handed him the coffee.

Oh, yes, I did, Mary Catherine thought.

In addition to being polite to a fault and seemingly intelligent, Leo was six one, lean, and really quite cute. From their brief conversations, she'd learned he was from Baltimore and about her age. She had already noticed that he didn't wear a wedding ring.

And why shouldn't I notice such things? she thought. Ever since she and Mike had taken a sabbatical on their on-again, off-again relationship, she'd been pretty darn lonely up here on the prairie with the kids. She could bring Mr. Strong, Sensitive, and Silent his coffee, couldn't she? She thought so. All day long, in fact.

They stood, staring at each other.

"So, how goes it? All quiet out here on the western front?" Mary Catherine said.

"So far, so good," Leo said, showing deep dimples as he smiled. "Though on one of the cameras, around three a.m., I did see a couple of owls duke it out with one another. I'm surprised it didn't wake you up. It sounded like people screaming."

"Two males fighting. Over a lady owl, too, no doubt," Mary Catherine said, shaking her head. "Isn't that the way? Just like men. Maybe owls aren't as wise as they say."

"Oh, I don't know about that," Leo said thoughtfully after a sip of the coffee. He smiled again, his twinkly eyes twinkling.

"Sometimes the lady in question is worth a fight," he said.

Mary Catherine felt heat rise in her neck as the young marshal looked at her again for an extended beat with his light-brown eyes. Then he turned away, blowing on the coffee as he scanned the crooked line of the distant mountains.

"If you say so, Marshal," Mary Catherine managed to sputter as she turned back toward the porch door, hiding the blush rising into her face.

"Carry on," she said.

Chapter 57

THERE WERE A BUNCH of lessons to go over in pretty much each of the children's curricula, but Mary Catherine, after hearing the warm-weather forecast, decided to make a command decision. As principal of the Exiled Bennett Western Academy, she was officially calling a day off.

After breakfast, she left the older guys with Seamus and packed lunches, along with most of the younger kids, into the station wagon and headed to Cody's farm. Everyone cheered as they pulled up in front of the horse barn.

Though the kids complained about so many things, every last one of them loved riding Cody's three horses, Spike, Marlowe, and Double Down. Not as much as she did, maybe. But almost.

As Mr. Cody came out of the barn with Double

Down already saddled, he put a startled look on his wrinkled face.

"Why, what is this?" he said in mock surprise. "Where'd all you kids come from? Aren't you supposed to be doing your lessons? Let me guess. The gang's had it with everything, is that it? Y'all picking up stakes and hightailing it out of here for greener pastures?"

The kids stared at the old farmer silently, their wide eyes on the saddled black horse. They wanted to ask if they could ride, of course, but Mary Catherine had forbidden them ever to ask for anything from their long-suffering host. If he offered, they could accept, but they could never do something so rude as to ask. In the silence, Chrissy and Shawna stared up at Double Down like they were going to explode.

"Cat's got all you guys' tongues this morning, I see," Cody said, peering at them. "Well, before you leave, could you do an old man one last favor? These horses of mine need to be rode, and I can't find a cowboy or even an Indian anywhere to give them some exercise. I know it's last-minute and all, and I do hate to impose, but do you think you crew could ride 'em for me?"

"Oh, I don't know, Mr. Cody," Mary Catherine

said as the kids bounced up and down by the horse-yard gate. "These kids do love the horses, but there is their schoolwork to consider. Maybe we should just head back to the house and get our lessons out of the way."

"No!!!" they all squealed, unable to contain themselves another moment.

"Horse. Need to ride horse," Trent chanted like the goofball he was as he pretended to pass out.

"OK, OK," Mary Catherine said, finally relenting. "Form a line, children. Excellent. There you go."

She turned as a car came into Mr. Cody's side yard. It was Leo, in his government-issued Crown Vic. *What now?* Mary Catherine thought as she rushed over.

"What is it, Leo? Is something wrong?" she said as she got to the passenger window.

"No, no. Everything is fine, Mary Catherine. Sorry, I didn't mean to scare you. I just thought I'd see if you guys were OK one more time and say good-bye."

Mary Catherine blinked at him rapidly.

"What do you mean? You're leaving? You're not going to be working here anymore?"

"Oh, no, of course not," Leo said, smiling. "I just meant that my shift is over."

"Oh, oh, of course, Leo," she said, fingering a strand of blond hair behind her ear. "You didn't have to go to all the trouble of coming out here."

"No trouble. I wanted to," Leo said softly, smiling as he stared into her eyes. "By the way, Juliana and Jane were saying that you guys haven't had pizza in about a month, and I was wondering if it would be OK to pick up some for you guys for lunch today and bring it back."

"Oh, sure. That would be nice, Leo. Really nice. The kids would love you."

Maybe not just the kids, thought Mary Catherine.

"I'll see you later, then, Mary Catherine," Leo finally said.

"Later, then," Mary Catherine whispered to herself as she watched him drive away.

Chapter 58

TWO DAYS OF SIFTING through the disaster in Newport Coast had yet to uncover hide or hair of Manuel Perrine. Even after we went back to Brentwood and tossed the rest of the dead smuggler Scanlon's house and went through his phone records, we didn't come up with one lead.

The only high point, if you could call it that, was a fresh palm print in one of the upstairs bathrooms that matched the one we had in Perrine's file. That proved, at least, that he had been in the house and was probably still in the country.

There was some grumbling in both the bureau and the LAPD that someone in our task force might have tipped off Perrine, but I wasn't buying it. It wasn't so much that there couldn't be a mouse in the house as it was that I knew Perrine was an extremely paranoid individual. There were a hundred different ways he could have learned about our siege on the house in enough time to sneak out via what Parker had come to refer to as the mansion's "crazy man cave." I preferred to call it the California billionaire sex chamber escape hatch myself, but I guess that was like the man we were searching for: neither here nor there.

For all my griping about the LAPD, the entire task force had come together after the botched raid and redoubled its efforts. They were all, even Bassman, extremely dedicated, extremely professional cops. It wasn't their fault that Perrine was such a slippery fish.

On the third day after the fiasco, Parker was called off the hunt to do her FBI mandatory pistol qualification. With my partner out of commission for the day, I decided to take a much-needed break. I woke around seven and took a shower and got dressed and headed out on a self-guided day tour of LA.

Our Santa Monica hotel was on Ocean Boulevard, right across the street from a park that had enormous palm trees. As I was standing there, staring out at the Pacific glistening between the palms, a Harley chopper pulled up at the light beside me. Riding it was a white-bearded, tuxedo-clad guy with a little white Benji-like dog panting happily in his lap. A moment later, a neon-teal lowrider with an elaborate Virgin Mary painted on the hood arrived behind it.

How do you like that? I thought, watching the vehicles rumble off. One foot out the door, and I'd already spotted a random act of randomness under the sunny Cali sky.

Following the recommendation of the guy at the hotel desk, I walked over a few blocks to the Third Street Promenade. It was a really neat pedestrian-only outdoor mall lined with shops and restaurants. After a block or two of window shopping, I stopped in this place called Barney's Beanery.

At first, I thought it was a coffee shop, until I spotted the large screens blaring a soccer game, license plates on the walls, and the line of car seats that were used as bar stools. It turned out the zany sports bar actually did have breakfast, though, so I sat and tore into a massive delicious Mexican breakfast of shredded beef and eggs and chili on flour tortillas.

After breakfast, I walked back toward a Hertz I

had spotted near the hotel and rented a car. Staying off the highways, I drove around aimlessly at first, then headed inland, east up Santa Monica Boulevard. When I got to Beverly Hills, I hooked a left and somehow found myself on a twisty road called Coldwater Canyon Drive. I took it north, marveling at all the cutting-edge architectural-glass houses up and down the slopes of the Hollywood Hills.

I made a right after a while onto iconic Mulholland Drive, then another onto Laurel Canyon Boulevard. When I came to the intersection with Hollywood Boulevard, I found a garage and parked and walked around.

I did the full tourist tour. I stopped at the TCL Chinese Theatre first and looked around, smiling down at Old Hollywood's hand- and footprints. I found the Walk of Fame, and when I came to Elvis's star, embedded in the cement, I laughed as I snapped a pic of it for Mary Catherine, who couldn't get enough of the King. Then I bought some postcards for the kids and, for ten bucks, had my picture taken with a Jack Sparrow pirate look-alike who was walking around.

I texted the pictures to Mary Catherine:

Just me and Johnny on the set. We're heading over
to Tom's later to do lunch and play some hoops.
How's your day going?

She texted back:

Not as good as yours, apparently, Mr. Movie Star.
Don't let all that fame go to your head. ☺

I texted back, for some unknown reason,

But you'll always be my number-one fan, won't you?

Actually, I did know. I was missing home, as
well as the great relationship Mary Catherine and I
had had up until pretty recently.

I knew I'd probably pushed it when she didn't
text back. Then my phone beeped as I was starting
the car.

?

was Mary Catherine's reply.

Chapter 59

I DECIDED TO HEAD back to Santa Monica and Barney's Beanery for lunch. In the midst of washing down a slice of white pizza with a pint of Guinness, I received an e-mail from Emily. It was some good news, for a change. Sort of.

The FBI lab had finally isolated and identified the poisonous white substance found at the two Los Angeles crime scenes. Apparently, it was some kind of weaponized fentanyl, an incredibly powerful narcotic over a hundred times more potent than morphine. The Russian special forces had used a similar offshoot of the extremely toxic drug to gas some Chechen terrorists in a Moscow theater takeover in 2002, and the fentanyl ended up killing 117 people.

It was chilling to think Perrine had access to

such an incredibly sick and deadly weapon, but at least now we had another lead to follow.

After that not-so-cheery note, I ordered another Guinness and found a booth in the back and decided to call home to see how everyone was doing.

"*Hola,*" I heard Seamus say in a bad Spanish accent after the second ring.

"*Hola?* You didn't just say *hola?*" I said.

"Oh, it's you," Seamus said. "Of course I said *hola,* Michael. It's called tradecraft, ya know. The art of deception. Even an infirm old man like your grandfather needs to develop some when he's running for his life. *Hola* is what you've reduced me to. Now, please tell me you've finally bagged the devil himself."

"Not yet," I said. "How are you holding up? How are the kids?"

"Oh, keeping me on my toes, as usual. They're out there now, playing Wiffle ball with the new fella. What's his name? Leo."

"Leo?" I said, baffled.

"He's the tall, nice-looking young fella. The marshal who works the night watch. He just showed up here about an hour ago with a Wiffle ball and a bat and some pizzas. Turns out he pitched in the Astros' farm system, he did, until he tore something in his shoulder. He's teaching the boys how to throw sliders. He's a real wizard, like. I can see Mary Catherine laughing out there right now from the window. She's having more fun than the kids, looks like."

I nodded. *Aha.* So that was what the question mark was all about.

"That's just grand," I said.

"'Tis," Seamus agreed.

"'Tisn't, old man. I know your game," I said. "You want me jealous so I hurry up and catch this guy already so we can all go home."

"Now that sounds like a plan, young Michael. Stick with that one," Seamus said. "Gotta go now. They're waving to me. It's my turn to bat."

Chapter 60

DODGER STADIUM, DOWNTOWN LA

RAYMOND BOWIE, ARMS FILLED with beers, had to open the glass door of the luxury suite with his butt in order to get out onto the patio.

"That's OK, guys. Really. I got it," he said sarcastically to the three folks completely ignoring him as they leaned and cheered along the field-side railing.

"Here, let me help you lighten the load, bro," his best friend, Kenny Cargill, said, winking as he grabbed a brew for himself and his wife, Annie.

"Hey, you're welcome, jackass. Really, anytime," Ray said, laughing.

It had been a whopping twelve grand for Ray to rent out the Dodger Stadium luxury suite for

opening day, but Kenny was leaving at the end of
the month for a finance job on the East Coast.
Kenny, Ray's oldest and best friend, had introduced
him to Denise, had helped him to turn his life
around. It was the very least he could do.

Ray's wife, Denise, was sipping her Coke when
they heard the crack. Down on the field. Dodger
second baseman Mark Ellis took off as the frozen
rope of a line drive he'd just hit skidded off the
grass in right and headed for the corner. Ellis made
the turn at first, then laid on the speed as the
Giants' right fielder scooped it.

Oh, no! Ray thought. The right fielder couldn't
hit for shit, but he had a gun for an arm. It was as if
the entire stadium, the entire City of Angels, was
holding its breath as the ball lasered toward
second.

Ellis's headfirst sprawl and the ball arrived
simultaneously. Ray groaned as the second baseman's tag swept toward Ellis's outstretched left
hand. But no! At the last instant, Ellis pulled his
hand in. He sailed past the bag and, at the final
moment, hooked it with the toe of his spike. The
umpire spread his arms wide. Safe! No outs, game
tied, 3–3 in the seventh, and now they had a runner
in scoring position!

The whooshing freight-train roar of the crowd rose and then rose again as the Giants manager walked out of the dugout, toward the mound. Lincecum, the Giants' freak of an ace pitcher, was being taken out!

Ray's breath caught as the air crackled with the hair-raising energy of fifty thousand people going nuts all at once. Annie pulled the Dodger-blue bandanna she was wearing off her head and started whipping it around as the stadium DJ busted out the *"Ya'll ready for this?"* anthem.

"Yeah! Wooohahoooo!" Kenny screamed as he pounded Ray on the back.

Ray, smiling and getting beer spilled on him, soaked it all in. The churning sea of Dodger blue and white, the checkerboard pattern in the outfield grass, his best friend on one side, his wife on the other.

As the crowd continued to roar, Ray dried a palm on the leg of his shorts and reached under Denise's vintage Piazza jersey and cupped her belly, where their child was growing inside her.

At eight weeks, their son or daughter had fingers now. Wrists and ankles, facial features, tiny eyelids squeezed shut. Its brain and lungs and liver were starting to form. He'd read all about it in the stack of baby books they had bought after Denise had shown him the two blue lines.

Dodgers versus Giants. *Doesn't get any better than this*, Ray thought, feeling the warmth under his hand. Hell, life didn't get better. Especially when you considered other alternatives.

Up until a year ago, Ray had been heavily involved in the LA nightclub drug scene. He'd bounced at first, then started dealing. Then he'd made enough to buy a club. Then two more.

High on ecstasy and coke, paranoid and soul broken, he had awakened one afternoon after five years of the fast lane and put a gun in his mouth. As he was sitting there, searching desperately for a reason to keep on going and coming up empty, he had glanced at his phone and seen that he had gotten a text the night before from his old buddy Kenny.

Once extremely tight, they had lost touch in the decade since high school. Kenny's father had died, the text explained, and Kenny asked if Ray would come back up north to their hometown of Carmel for the wake.

Going up there had been the greatest, wisest thing Ray had ever done in his life. Kenny was a normal guy, worked at a bank, had a wife, a kid, a house, a grill, a lawn. His friend had somehow managed to be happy without any strippers, hookers, criminals, coke, or hefty bags of dirty money anywhere in sight.

Hanging out for the weekend, Ray suddenly remembered that he, too, had once been a human being instead of a disgusting, self-absorbed, cruel, drug-pushing scumbag. When Kenny set him up with Denise, a teller at his bank who was the sweetest, most delicate, most innocent, most beautiful woman he'd ever met, that was all she wrote. He sold the clubs, his drug business. Got out, got clean, climbed right the hell out of hell.

Ray had hardly done a religious thing in his whole life—quite the opposite, in fact. But at that moment, as the Giants reliever threw his warm-up pitches, Ray Bowie looked up above the terraces of happy people to where the last silver burn of the sodium lights touched the black of the sky.

Thank you, he mouthed.

For all of it, he prayed, as a knock came at the glass at his back.

Chapter 61

RAY TURNED. BEHIND THE patio door was a heavyset Hispanic guy with a necklace of access passes over his Dodger-blue stadium-staff polo shirt.

"What's up?" Denise said.

"I don't know," Ray said. "You stay here. I'll figure it out."

Ray pushed through the door. There were three other Hispanic stadium guys with the pudgy one. They were all staring at him funny. They were tense, Ray noticed. Like him, they were big, meaty guys, and they were watching him closely, like they were bouncers and Ray was going to give them trouble. Something was wrong.

"What's up?" Ray said, squinting at them.

"Sorry to bother you, sir, but we were wondering

if we could start clearing the buffet," said the one who had knocked on the door.

Ray stared at the guy in pissed-off shock. He'd paid twelve grand to have some privacy for himself and his friends, not to have his chops busted by busboys while Dodger history was being made out there on the diamond.

"No," Ray said testily. "Come back when—I don't know, the game's actually over. Give me a goddamn break."

That's when the figure stepped out of the suite's private bathroom.

"Sorry, Ray," the man said, "but giving you a break is the one thing we can no longer do."

Ray, looking at the man's face, felt suddenly dizzy. Inside, at the center of himself, something slowly began to wobble like a coin spun on a tabletop.

It was Perrine. *Divine Mother of God*, Ray thought. It was Manuel Perrine.

Ray took a step back, raising his balled fists. One of the thugs pulled something out of the Dodger messenger bag he was holding. Ray saw oiled black metal. It was a Heckler and Koch submachine gun.

Manuel Perrine stepped over to him and put an arm over his shoulder.

"I'm sorry to interrupt the festivities, but it's been a while, my friend." Manuel grinned widely. There was a dreamy quality to his smile, a dreamy quality to everything.

"What the fuck is this?" Ray whispered.

"Come with us, Ray," Perrine said, lifting a hot wing from the buffet beside them. He sniffed it and tossed it back on the pile. "And we'll talk of many things. Of shoes and ships and sealing wax. Of cabbages and kings. Or we can take care of matters here, if you wish to involve your friends."

Ray swallowed.

"No, no, Manuel. I'll go with you. Whatever you want. Just let me say good-bye."

"Yes, of course," Manuel said. "But no monkey business now."

Ray went back out onto the patio. He stared at the flashing scoreboard. The crowd. His wife.

"What is it?" Denise said. "You look like you've seen a ghost."

"Something about my credit card. I'll be back in a second. I love you, OK?"

He kissed her hard, his lips burning, his fingers tracing her belly, and then somehow peeled himself away.

Chapter 62

THEY LED HIM OUT and into another suite down the hallway, which had its privacy blinds pulled down. Inside the door, one of the thugs slammed his head off the concrete wall hard enough to split the skin and began frisking him.

"Nothing," the thug said.

"That's quite unfortunate for you to go about unarmed, Raymond," Perrine said, sitting and swiveling around in a Dodger lounge chair. "Considering how vulnerable a man you are."

Ray stood there, blinking. He had met Perrine a few years back at one of his clubs. They quickly went into business and had become fast friends. He'd actually visited Perrine's villa in Mexico. Manuel had been like a mentor to him, taught him how to move drugs, how to keep an eye on the cops.

"I'm out of it, Manny," Ray said. "I don't know what you heard, but I'm out of it. The whole thing. I gave it to Roger."

"That's precisely the problem," Perrine said. "Roger is a DEA informant. What am I saying? That's wrong. What I meant to say is, Roger *was* a DEA informant. Your recommendation of Roger lost me at least fifteen million, Raymond. In fact, during the seizure, my brother-in-law was popped. To add insult to injury, my brother-in-law was then killed about six months into his sentence by one of my rivals. My sister, still to this day, continues to make my life unpleasant.

"Do you see my dilemma? You screwed me, Raymond, and the sad fact of the matter is that I have to unscrew myself. And, as you well know, there is only one way to do that."

"But I'm out of it."

Perrine peered at him.

"Look around you, Raymond. You are very much in it. Such a shame. You were so good at it, too. The looks, the street smarts, the LA charm, truly a natural. Believe it or not, I had big plans for you. But that was then. Any last words?"

Ray's face slackened with an almost catatonic

bewilderment. He was going to die now?! Just like that!?

"I, uh. I, uh," he said.

"Hmmm. Strange choice. I, uh, what? I, uh, therefore I am?" Manuel asked.

The thugs began giggling. A heavy blow to his kidney knocked him to his knees. There was a shriek, and then duct tape was smeared hard over his mouth and ears.

Ray stared down at the carpet, half unconscious with terror. He was unresisting as his shoes, socks, shirt, shorts, and finally his underwear were stripped from his body.

He had been adopted. That was why he'd been so excited about becoming a father. A lot of adopted people acted all forgiving about their biological parents, talked about how brave they were for abandoning their own flesh and blood, but not him. Once his kid was born, he'd been planning to show them. He was going to attach his kid to himself, hold the tiny, brand-new human in his arms and never ever let him go.

Only now he never would.

A hand grabbed his hair, pulled him up on his knees, yanked his head back, exposing his throat. Ray pinched his crying eyes shut as bright white camera light torched his face.

"This is what happens to those who stand in the way of Los Salvajes!" Manuel screamed as Ray felt something hard and cold bite under his right ear.

Chapter 63

PARKER AND I DECIDED to meet up for a late-night dinner when news of the Dodger Stadium murder dropped.

A little after one in the morning, we left the hotel and drove to a softly lit restaurant called Ammo, on Highland Avenue in Hollywood.

"I like the name," I said to Parker as we sat at a booth. "After what happened at the ball game tonight, we're probably going to need a case of double-aught buck and couple of boxes of fifty caliber to go."

Instead, we ordered some drinks. Jack and ginger ale for me, a pinot grigio for Emily. I'd actually had a couple of room service beers after I heard about the ball-game decapitation, but they hadn't worked at all. After seeing the now-national news coverage about the savagery committed in the midst of the Dodger home opener, I'd never felt more sober in my life.

On the ride over, Emily had told me that a team from our Perrine task force had been sent to the stadium, but we hadn't heard back from them yet.

"It's Perrine. We both know it," Parker said angrily as she placed her unringing phone down on the corner of the table. "He's marking his new US territory now and rubbing our noses in it in the process."

Emily sighed as she stared out the plate-glass window. She looked tired. Pale and drained, as if she'd just given blood. The hours she was putting in would have taxed anyone, not to mention the unrelenting pressure from above. And still we couldn't move the needle on what the cartels were doing. I shared her frustration. No doubt about it, we were getting our asses thoroughly kicked.

"I saw this video on the Internet recently," Emily said, "where these kids, these nice, normal-looking suburban kids, film themselves slowly, methodically, and mercilessly abusing a sixty-eight-year-old bus monitor. They call her fat, ugly, say that she should hang herself. And as she sits there, crying, these kids are laughing themselves silly. I mean, her tears are turning these kids on. It's like debasing this poor old woman is the greatest and funniest thing they've ever done in their life."

"I saw it, too," I said. "I wish I hadn't. It was like something out of *A Clockwork Orange*, only for real."

She lifted her wine and stared at it.

"You ever wonder if maybe Perrine is a symptom of a larger disease? As if things are . . . changing. As if people are changing. Their attitudes. The way we treat each other. Look at all this bath-salt stuff. People biting each other's faces off. The flash mobs where hundreds of punks go wilding in some store.

"Seems to me, the center is having some serious trouble holding these days, Mike. It's like Perrine is picking up on that and just going to town, trying to egg on complete collapse. Maybe it's time to head for the hills. Any room up in Northern Cali for one more in the Bennett militia?"

"Nah," I said, marking circles on the napkin with the bottom of my drink. "That's not the move, Emily. Trust me. The hills are a nice place to visit, but you don't want to live there. I know things are looking pretty bleak, but right here, right now, is the place to be. This latest crap from Perrine only proves it. He's trying to break our will, but he's out of his league. Bigger assholes than he have tried and failed. I told him before, when he was in custody, he has no idea who the hell he's messing with."

"How can you be so sure?"

I rattled the cubes in my glass.

"Think about Nine-Eleven, Emily. Three hundred Spartans stood up against a million invaders at Thermopylae, right? Well, down in the valley of Lower Manhattan on Nine-Eleven, four hundred and three firefighters, cops, paramedics, and service members stared up into the face of six hundred million cubic pounds of unmoored steel and glass and concrete that hovered, burning and groaning and swaying, above them. Six hundred million cubic pounds!

"And they didn't blink! They held the line, held their post. With burning debris and the bodies of the victims exploding around them, they stood there and stood there and stood there, saving life after life, pulling out person after person from the burning, bloody, hungry jaws of what can only be properly described as hell on earth. The victims in the towers and the Pentagon and on the planes didn't have a choice about being vaporized.

"Those four hundred and three on the ground had a choice, and they chose that others could live."

After a long moment, Emily nodded. "You're right," she said. "King Leonidas would have tipped his horsehair helmet."

"Of course, I'm right. That's our legacy, Emily. The terrorists think they won that day? Keep dreaming. The terrorists only proved what they feared the most about Americans. That among us live everyday superheroes, free men and women who at the drop of a hat, or in this case a skyline, will stand up and sacrifice their lives to save someone else. Who the hell on this earth is still ballsy and crazy enough to go down with the ship? Us! That's who!"

I clinked my glass to Emily's.

"Chin up, Agent Parker. Perrine thinks he's crazy? We'll show his ass the meaning of crazy before this thing is through."

Chapter 64

THE WAITRESS HAD JUST brought dessert when our phones went crazy. On the tabletop beside my untouched cheesecake, my iPhone started its almost subliminal hum a split second before Parker's mobile joined in.

"Oh, wait. Are you following Bieber on Twitter, too?" I joked as we both looked at the incoming texts.

"The task force is calling a meeting now? It's coming on two a.m.," Parker said, shaking her head at her BlackBerry.

"No rest for the semiconscious," I said, fishing out my wallet.

About half the task force was present and accounted for when Emily and I arrived upstairs at Olympic Station twenty minutes later. Instead of sitting at their workstations, the cops and agents were gathered together, standing in the very middle of the command center, in front of an overhead projector screen.

It was eerily quiet in the crowded room. Under the garish fluorescent lighting, pretty much everyone looked physically and mentally exhausted, not to mention frantic. Of course they were. The killing at Dodger Stadium was obviously an act of terrorism. Who knew what would happen next?

The lights dimmed after a moment, and the swirling circle of a loading digital video appeared on the white, sail-like screen.

"What's this?" I whispered as we stepped over beside Agent Rothkopf.

Rothkopf shook his head grimly.

"LAPD Detective Division just received an e-mail with an attached video. They think it's from Perrine."

The screen focused, and then Perrine was there. Sitting in a Dodger-blue leather chair, he was wearing disposable white Tyvek coveralls. From chest to knees, the coveralls were splattered in blood.

He must have been in one of the stadium's luxury suites. There were video game consoles behind him, video monitors, bar stools. Behind him on the wall were the framed Dodger jerseys of Don Drysdale, Sandy Koufax, Tommy Lasorda.

The camera zoomed back a little, and beyond the window of the suite, the packed stands could be seen. There was a sudden loud, swelling, sizzling sound as fans stood in succession, doing the wave. Perrine waited and then did it as well, rising out of his club chair with his hands raised before swiveling back for the camera.

"Hey, LAPD, FBI, and all my other fans out there tonight in La-La Land. How are you doing this fine evening? As you can see, I myself am having a blast here in your city."

Perrine smiled as he did a little drumroll on the arm of the chair. He seemed pumped, really enjoying himself.

From off screen, someone suddenly offered him something. It was a hot pretzel with mustard on it. He looked it over and then carefully took it by the napkin before he took a bite.

"I wanted to take this opportunity," Perrine said, chewing, "to communicate with this task force that has been set up to find me. Ask yourselves honestly, are you truly up for the job? You people have families, people who depend on you. How will you be able to look out for them? What if you come home from work tonight and they have some—what is the term—*assembly* required?"

He took another bite, thumbing mustard off the corner of his mouth.

"I always give people a chance to get out of my way," he said after licking his thumb. "That is why I am strongly advising you to relieve yourselves of your present duty. You should take this opportunity to transfer, retire, or, better yet, quit. In fact, if I were you, I would leave Southern California with your families as soon as possible."

The two dozen of us standing there looked from the screen to each other with the same question etched in every face. *Say what?*

"See, ladies and gentlemen, you think this is about drugs, but it isn't. Why do you think my men are so highly trained, so highly motivated to do whatever needs to be done? I am doing what the cowardly Mexican government will not. Piece by piece, inch by inch, gringo by gringo, I am taking and returning California back to its rightful owners, the Mexican people.

"What you took by force in 1848, I will now wrest back by force. The revolution has begun. I am formally declaring war on the United States of America."

"This bastard," I heard Rothkopf whisper through his gritted teeth when the video ended. "This goddamned barbaric bastard."

Every cop in the room made the same sound then, a kind of growl of shock tinged with rage. Emily had been right. Perrine was rubbing our noses in it. And loving every minute of it, apparently.

Chapter 65

SILVER DROPLETS EXPLODED VIOLENTLY in the morning sunlight as Lillian Mara pulled the immense black Ford Expedition up almost against the fence. On the other side of the chain-link, the water in the Olympic-sized public pool churned as the Van Nuys–Sherman Oaks under-twelve swim team did their laps.

As usual, the other swim moms and dads gave Lillian dirty looks from their poolside camp chairs. She knew what they were thinking. There she was again, the evil, blond new lady in the business suit and big, idling, earth-warming SUV who didn't even have the decency to get out of her car to watch her kid swim.

Sometimes she felt like getting out and explaining to them that the truck was actually her mobile office. As the newly transferred assistant special agent in charge of the FBI's LA office, she had to be available 24-7 to juggle case meetings with DAs and surveillance teams and undercover agents, and a secure, private communication link was a priority.

As if that matters to them, Lillian thought with a sigh. Everybody had an excuse, didn't they? Oh, well. She guessed she would just have to live with all the mommy-war scorn.

Lillian sat up and held her breath as a sopping, thin-shouldered ten-year-old blond boy dragged himself out of the opposite side of the pool and headed for the starting blocks.

"C'mon, kiddo, you can do this," Lillian whispered, cheering on her son Ian as he got into position. "Bend over more, just a little more. Chin against your chest. You have this, kid."

She let out a groan as Ian jumped weakly and, as usual, landed flat with a loud, belly-flopping slap in the water. Then she laughed to herself.

"Won't be the first time you fall on your face, little buddy," she told her baby boy as she watched him thrash intently across the pool. "Take it from personal experience."

Her phone, charging on the dashboard shelf in

front of the speedometer, began buzzing. She snatched it up when she saw it was her husband, and pressed the FaceTime option.

She smiled as her goofily handsome husband, Mitch, appeared. He was the head of mechanical engineering at Northrop Grumman and was on a business trip to Brazil.

She turned up the volume on the phone as a couple of landscapers beside the pool's parking lot fired up their air rakes.

"Hey, good-looking!" Lillian yelled. "Wearing your wedding ring still? Well, that's a relief."

"Just got the last of the carnival gals out of the room," Mitch said, nodding.

They both laughed.

As if. Mitch, a hulking former combat marine, had proposed to her the day they both graduated from Irvine. He once told her that he truly liked only three things in this world. Her, running, and beer. They had six kids now, two of them in college, and were still going strong. They were lucky people.

"How's Aquaman?" Mitch asked.

"I'm sorry to say I still don't see too many Olympic diving team invitations in Ian's near future," she said with a wince.

Mitch said something, but she couldn't hear

him at all as one of the landscapers came directly behind the SUV, the air rake screaming in the painful decibel range now, like a 747 taking off.

"Hold on a second, Mitch. I can't hear you," Lillian said. The side window suddenly smashed inward.

Staggered by the abrupt explosion, glass still spraying around her, Lillian turned to see the hard face of the Hispanic landscaper in the blown-open window, already half in the car. Her glance went to his hand. There was something black in it rising toward her face.

She was pulling the .40 caliber in the pancake holster on her right side when the pepper spray hit. Gagging on chemical fire, her face burning, her eyes blinded, Lillian still managed to draw her service automatic as the air rake shrieked in her ears.

Then the landscaper smashed her in the jaw with his huge fist, hard enough to make her teeth click. The last things Lillian heard were the thump of her gun dropping to the foot well and the sound of the truck door opening. The seat belt loosened then, and she was sliding and falling, tumbling into a wave of black that seemed to rise up to meet her halfway.

Chapter 66

WHEN SPECIAL AGENT MARA came to, she was being carried by someone large and strong up a slate walkway. The house they approached was a white stucco, Spanish mission–style structure with a clay tile roof. The man carrying her smelled strongly of tobacco and coffee. The door looked like something from a castle, with dark wood timbers banded in iron.

She opened her mouth but couldn't form words or even sounds. *Drugs*, she thought dully. She'd been drugged. The opulent door was creaking open when the black came back.

Music was playing when she woke up again. It was classical, a baroque cello concerto. Was it Bach? *No, it's Haydn*, Lillian thought dreamily. She even knew the piece, she realized. Concerto in D Major.

She wondered idly where she was, but something told her not to worry so much. She kept her eyes closed as she listened to the deep, warm tones of the cello playing melody, then harmony, then melody again.

Lillian opened her eyes when she realized someone was humming along to the music. A cute, perky-looking young Hispanic woman was standing alongside her.

A nurse? Lillian thought. But no. It couldn't be. The woman was wearing a shiny green- white- and- red Mexican-soccer shirt over yoga pants, with bright-pink-and-white Nikes. Her highlighted brown hair was pulled back in a tight, all-business ponytail.

Lillian blinked, quickly trying to wipe the last of the cobwebs from her foggy mind, assessing her situation.

She was in a dark, paneled room, some kind of office with wood blinds pulled down. There were bookshelves on one wall with no books in them. She was sitting, almost fully reclined, in a large leather office chair, her arms and legs strapped securely to the chair with thick, gray duct tape.

She remembered. Ian. The pool. The window crashing in.

Jesus, God, no, she thought as she began to shake hysterically, trying to break free. *No, no, no. Just no.*

"Relax," the athletic young woman said, stroking the back of the FBI agent's arm. "If you're not careful, you're going to hurt yourself. My name is Vida. I am going to help you, if you let me, Agent Mara. Or shall I call you Lillian?"

"What do you want?" Lillian sobbed. "Let me go. Why are you doing this to me?"

"There are many reasons. But for now, we'll concentrate on one," Vida said, lifting a stern finger. "Our organization is looking for a man who is in hiding. We believe that he may be in California. His name is Michael Bennett. Do you know him?"

"No," Lillian said, staring at the woman. "You have the wrong person. I am an FBI agent, but I run the white-collar division. I don't know anything."

"That truly is a shame," Vida said, turning on the heel of one of her pink-and-white Nikes and lifting something from the corner of the dark room. Lillian wheezed. It was a large, yellow-handled, heavy tool with an ax on one side and a sledgehammer on the other, known as a splitting maul.

The young woman hefted it neatly.

"No!" Lillian screamed as the young woman brought the sledgehammer side of the maul back and up and then down with authority onto Lillian's left elbow, pulverizing it into splinters.

Vida turned up the music as Lillian shook and screamed and howled in pain. When the white noise of Lillian's excruciation notched slightly back, Haydn was still playing merrily.

Vida lifted the sledge again.

"We're going to try this one more time. With the ax part this time. Where is Bennett?" she said.

"In Northern California . . . near Susanville," Lillian found herself saying between the sobs and the throbbing, center-of-the-sun agony that had become her left elbow. "I'm not . . . sure exactly where . . . I'd tell you his address if I could . . . but they wouldn't tell me . . . in a million years."

"How do you know this?" Vida said.

"An agent from the LA office," Lillian continued in her pain-induced, haiku-like rhythm, "was sent up there . . . to pick his brain . . . about capturing Perrine . . . I do the books for the office . . . I saw the destination on the manifest."

"An agent from the task force?"

"Yes."

"What was the agent's name?"

"Parker. Emily Parker," Lillian said without hesitation. She hated herself. She knew she was putting others in jeopardy. But she was in so much pain. And afraid. God, was she afraid.

Vida dropped the splitting maul and consulted a binder in the corner of the room. She flipped a page, then flipped it back. Then she lifted a phone.

"Bring the van around," she said into it.

Vida stepped back around to the rear of the office chair and pulled the gun from the waistband of her yoga pants.

"Just one more thing, Agent, and we'll get you right out of here," Vida said, raising the suppressed black-steel Smith & Wesson .22.

Chapter 67

A WAGON TRAIN OF FIRE trucks, ambulances, and cop cars was on the scene when we got to Venice.

There were beach cops everywhere, on four-wheelers and in 4x4s and pickups. Most of them were sporting M-16s. Crime-scene tape fluttered as aviation whipped past low overhead in a buzz of bright, shaking light.

There were dozens upon dozens of citizens pressed up against the crime tape. Most were shirtless. One interested observer seemed to be clad in nothing save a hotel towel. Coming out of the Vic, I looked over my shoulder as I heard a suspicious click-clack. But it was just some bushy-haired thirty-year-old skateboarder attracted to the bright, shiny flashing lights.

Getting out of the G-car, Emily and I stepped around someone's little dog, hitched to a public water fountain, and went under the crime-scene tape. Behind us, a squad-car siren was going off and going off and going off like a broken alarm clock.

There was reason to be alarmed, all right. We'd been scouring the city all day, chasing leads to try to find the fifteen-year-veteran agent who'd been snatched in broad daylight. Her husband, who was FaceTiming with her at the moment of abduction, had called it in from Brazil, of all places, where he was on a business trip. I didn't envy the man.

Especially now that we'd finally found his wife.

The crooked smile of a quarter moon shining above black water was the first thing to greet us as we walked down to the sand. There was the soft, distant boom-and-shush of waves crashing, the sound of the palm fronds rasping in the wind. We stepped under a second strip of crime tape and across a deserted bike path.

Beside the path, just in the sand and facing the water, Agent Mara sat in a wheelchair with two bullet holes in her head. A dirty blanket covered her loosely. There was blood on the right corner of her mouth. In her lap was a plain brown bag that, we had already heard from the first responders, contained her cut-out tongue.

She'd been strapped to a wheelchair with tie wraps, obviously killed somewhere else. This was just a dump site. Her left elbow had been demolished, I noticed in the glare of the five-hundred-watt halogen work light the crime-scene people had set up. It looked like it had almost been severed with some blunt-force trauma. She'd been tortured, no doubt.

We turned as Detective Bassman stepped out of the shadows, straight up to us.

"Hey," he said. "We looked for video in the stores along Ocean Front Walk, but it's not looking good. There's no evidence here. No prints any-where. No witnesses. No nothing. I got the coroner to red-ball the autopsy so we can get her back to her family as soon as possible. Did the husband get here yet?"

"Still in the air," Emily said.

"Probably for the best. He shouldn't see this. Unbelievable. I know I've given you feds some heat, and I'm sorry for that. I know how hard you guys work. I know how bad it feels when one of your family gets taken from you."

He quickly handed Emily a stack of bills.

"Passed the hat around. Get her poor kids some ice cream or something from us, OK? Tell them the LAPD isn't going to stop until we drop every last one of the people who hurt their mother."

"Thanks," Emily said. "I will."

"Hey, Bassman," I said as the big guy walked away.

"What is it, Bennett?"

"Maybe you're not such an asshole after all," I said.

He smiled, shrugged.

"Just don't let it get around," he said.

Chapter 68

IT WAS HOT WHEN they woke that morning, and even hotter now at eleven as they went across the scrubby, grass-filled field under the pitiless sun.

Brian Bennett slapped at a monster horsefly that stung at his sweating neck. Man, he was starting to hate the country. The biggest lie in the world was how nature was supposed to be so invigorating and healthy. If there was one thing that he had learned out here, it was that nature was nothing but hot, dirty, smelly, and boring beyond the realm of human tolerance.

"Shit!" Brian yelled as the horsefly stung him again.

"Cursin' now, Brian? Saints preserve us!" Eddie said, mimicking Seamus's Irish accent to a tee.

Brian turned around to catch Eddie smiling, a napkin sticking out of his nose from a nosebleed he'd gotten about a quarter mile from the house.

Brian laughed despite himself. You had to hand it to the kid. He just kept at it 24-7. Jabbering, doing funny voices, making fun of things—himself, mostly—like some clown or court jester or something. *A fool*, Brian thought. *That's what he is. My brother Eddie, the fool.* And he meant it in the best way possible.

"Quick question," Ricky said from behind Eddie. "Why are we wandering the earth like a band of post-apocalyptic nomads again? I hate to say this, big bro, but this Bataan death trek is quickly starting to teeter into the suck category."

"You can go back any time you want, wimp," Brian said angrily. "That goes for you, too, Eddie. I never asked you to follow me around. I couldn't care less what you guys do."

"Pardon me, but wasn't it you who woke us up at the crack of dawn, Brian?" Ricky said. "I distinctly remember someone who looked a heck of a lot like you saying, 'Get up, you idiot. It's time to go.'"

"It's OK," Brian heard Eddie say to Ricky. "Brian's just having one of his Brian moments. In other words, our big brother is going completely nuts."

You can say that again, Brian thought as he trudged across the not-so-fruited California plain. What fifteen-year-old wouldn't go nuts being exiled out here in the desert, like someone from the Bible?

And, just like a nut, he had woken that morning inspired to accomplish an important mission. He was going to walk until he found the river that Mr. Cody had driven them to a few weeks before. Not for any real reason. *Because it's there,* Brian thought as he paced over the seemingly endless plain of dry land.

He thought he knew the general direction, but they were three hours into the hike, with no water anywhere. *Has to be around here somewhere*, he thought, sheepishly squinting up at the sky.

He hadn't told Mary Catherine or Seamus about his plans. Hadn't asked permission. Hadn't even left a note. He knew it was slightly messed up to just get up and leave without saying anything, but that was pretty much the point. Dad was gone now. They were stuck out here, with no end in sight, and he was simply sick of it. The cows, the home-schooling lessons with the little twerps. Hell, he should just keep walking east until he made it back to Manhattan. Back to his friends. Back to his real life.

"*I don't know, but I've been told,*" sang Eddie after a while, "*this stupid walk is getting old! Sound off!*"

"*One, two,*" Ricky sang.

"Wait, wait," Brian said. "Shut up! Listen!"

They stopped in their tracks. There was a faint rushing sound coming from beyond the broken, distant tree line off to their right. They looked at each other for a beat, then started running. Brian in the lead, Ricky second, and Eddie dead last.

Brian stopped raising dust as he got to the ridge of the sandy riverbank. He just stood there, smiling. He stared at the sun twinkling silver off the fast-rushing water, stared at the green-brown surface of it, curving through the dry landscape like a ribbon of living glass. The slightly alkaline scent of the water was strong in the dry air. He'd never really smelled water before, at least not clean water.

I've done it, Brian thought. *Set a goal for myself and accomplished it.* A pointless one, maybe, but still. It felt pretty awesome.

"Hey, you did it! You actually found it, Pocahontas!" Eddie said, giving him a high five.

Gone

"Of course I found it," Brian said nonchalantly as he leaped off the berm and down the sand, toward the rushing water.

Chapter 69

THEY WERE SPLASHING AROUND and skipping rocks twenty minutes later, when they saw the kayak come around the bend upriver.

The aging hippie in it smiled as he expertly paddled over to the shore beside them. At first, Brian got a little scared because the guy sort of looked like the Unabomber. But when he stepped out of the Day-Glo-yellow kayak twenty feet away, he was wearing rubber fishing waders that went up to his chest.

Just some harmless old nut fishing, Brian told himself.

The hippie lifted a palm after he beached the kayak.

"How," he said like an Indian, then threw back his head and laughed. "Sorry. Always wanted to say that," he said with a twinkling, blue-eyed wink. "Name's McMurphy. Pleased to meet you, boys. You must be new around here. What brings you intrepid wanderers out this far into the great beyond? I don't see any fishing poles. Let me guess. Fame, fortune, and adventure?"

"Boredom, actually," Eddie said.

The man threw back his head again and cackled some more.

"Boredom," McMurphy said, tapping a finger against his forehead. "That's a good one, son. Boredom will work fine, too."

Wow, Brian thought, staring at the guy's wild eyes, his wild gray hair. This guy was pretty nutty. *Too many tabs of acid?* he wondered. He reminded him of someone. An old sixties actor. Dennis someone. He seemed harmless enough, at least.

Maybe this is what happens to you if you stay out here too long, Brian thought, glancing at the coot. He almost felt like asking him if he was once in the witness protection program, too.

"Holy cow! There you are!" came a shrill voice as they heard some rustling in the trees up the bank behind them.

They looked up to see Juliana at the top of the sandy berm. She was sitting atop one of Mr. Cody's

323

horses, Spike, wearing riding boots like she was the Queen of England. *Of course,* Brian thought. *They always let Miss Perfect do everything cool.* Juliana could do anything she wanted.

"Everybody is looking for you," Juliana said, staring at Brian. "What the heck are you doing?"

"Hello there, little lady. McMurphy's the name," the hippie said with a courtly little bow. "These boys with you?"

Juliana nodded.

"I was about to ask them if they wanted to learn how to fly-fish. Love to teach you, too. Why don't you tie up that noble steed there on a branch and come on down? What's his name?"

"Spike," Juliana said.

"Spike. Well, of course. Fine name for a fine horse. Speaking of which, what're your names?"

"We're the Warners," Juliana said immediately.

Brian sighed. Warner was the name they were supposed to use when coming into contact with strangers. *Juliana's just so responsible, isn't she?* he thought. *She should really get a medal or something.*

"How many of you Warners are there, anyway?" McMurphy asked. "You guys seem to keep popping out of the trees like squirrels."

Brian and Juliana exchanged a glance.

"Just the four of us," she said.

"Staying out at Mr. Cody's place, is that right?" the hippie wanted to know.

How'd he know that? Brian thought.

"I'm sorry, Mr. McMurphy, but my brothers need to get going. My, um, dad needs their help."

"Your dad? Wait, I think I've met you before. You came to church with that nice old Irish priest, right?"

"No," Juliana said. "You must be mistaken."

"Mysteries and wonders," McMurphy said, nodding. "Now, now. Listen to me jawing, chewing your ear off, prying into your business. Just ain't right neighborly, is it? I apologize. It's just nice to meet folks this far out in the yonder. I live by myself, and when I finally meet someone, all that bottled-up talk just shoots out of me like soda from a shaken can."

"Uh, OK, Mr. McMurphy. Nice to meet you," Juliana said, eyeing Brian, letting him know it was time to get moving.

"Pleasure was all mine, miss. All mine. Hey, wait. Before you go, let me give you a little something."

He fished something out of the creel in his

kayak. It was something green in a large ziplock bag. He offered it to Brian.

"Son, that right there is straight primo hybrid sinsemilla. You will not find its equal in all of North America. I grow it myself with love. Ask anyone in the valley, and they'll tell you McMurphy's is a cut above all others. Top shelf, drawer, and notch, as my daddy used to say."

Brian stared at him, stared at the bag, stared at Juliana.

"C'mon, it won't bite. Hell, I was a kid. You'll go crazy out here without having yourselves a little fun. Plus, it's a gift. You don't want to offend me none, right?"

"We can't, Mr. McMurphy," Juliana said, making up an excuse on the spot. "We're Mormon. We can't even drink soda. The use of marijuana would be completely against, um, our way."

"Mormons, huh?" McMurphy said, squinting up at her.

Juliana nodded.

"Well, isn't that nice," McMurphy said, putting the weed back into his creel. "I'll let you get back to your dad. Respecting your elders is always a good policy. Says that right in the Bible. So long, now."

Chapter 70

MARY CATHERINE HAD SWEAT on her brow and tears in her eyes as she rabidly zested another lemon in the scorching kitchen. Leo was coming over for dinner tonight, on his day off, and she'd learned that he liked lemons.

And what Leo wants, Mary Catherine thought, grinning to herself as she zestfully zested, *Leo gets.*

She already had three chickens in the oven, and a five-pound bag of potatoes boiling in a cauldron-sized pot on the stove. There were still the green beans and the salad to take care of, stuffing to make along with the gravy, but she wanted to get the lemon cake going or she'd be in the weeds.

Besides the lemons, pretty much everything was from Mr. Cody's farm, even—*Sorry, Chrissy*—the chickens. They were probably flouting some

FDA regulation to have the criminal gall to eat what they grew, but she had the feeling Deputy Marshal Leo would look the other way after he had a few bites.

Farm food this fresh just tasted different, Mary Catherine knew from happy experience. Eating it for the first time was like seeing high-definition TV after a lifetime of black-and-white. It was going to be nice having someone new at the dinner table after all this time.

The back screen door slammed, and Brian, Eddie, and Ricky stood in the mudroom, each one more sunburned and filthy and exhausted than the next.

She bit her lower lip to keep from bursting into laughter.

"Would you look at the state of ya! Were you wandering the earth or tunneling through it?"

"Ow," Ricky said, taking off a dusty sneaker. "Ow."

"Smells good. What's for dinner?" Brian asked, his filthy finger creeping toward the mixing bowl.

He howled as Mary Catherine whacked his hand loudly with the zester. Eddie and Ricky snickered.

"Get your butts upstairs and shower this instant

or I'll drag you out into the yard and hose you down. See if I won't, and don't think you're off the hook for going off by yourselves and skipping your lessons, getting us worried. As if I'm not busy enough."

"Why are you so busy?" Eddie said.

"I told you yesterday. We're having a guest tonight for dinner."

"A guest?" Ricky said. "Who?"

"Deputy Marshal Leo," Mary Catherine said.

"Deputy Marshal Leo?" Brian said. "How is he a guest? He works here."

"Mary Catherine, does Dad know about this?" Eddie said, raising his brow.

Mary Catherine stopped zesting. That was it. She knew the boys were having a hard time of late, especially Brian, but that was it. Like she hadn't been working her fingers to the bone for this lot. Was she not allowed to have something nice in her life? Something even a little bit hopeful?

Standing there in the kitchen, she remembered something from when she was a girl. One of her brothers would get cheeky, and her father, after coming in from haying all day or putting up fencing or some other extreme, fourteen-hour task of backbreaking cattle-farm manual labor, would let his fork fall from his callused fist with a clank. With the slow deliberation of a tank cannon acquiring a target, his weather-beaten face would slowly rise from his meal and shift until it was leveled at the offender.

He never said anything. He never had to. A judge about to deliver a death sentence couldn't approach the solemn, cold, carved-granite malevolence of his silence. There in his gray-blue gaze lay a guaranteed offer. With one more measly word, you would find yourself in the sudden possession of the entire universe of everything you didn't want.

Standing there in the sweltering kitchen, Mary Catherine suddenly gave that same look to the boys.

The boys glanced at each other, and slowly, one by one, silently, left the room.

Mary Catherine smiled to herself after they'd left. She'd always been her father's daughter.

Chapter 71

THE FOOD HAD COME out perfectly, even if Mary Catherine said so herself. The chicken wasn't dry, and the mashed potatoes and stuffing were seasoned to her exacting standards. Leo certainly seemed to enjoy it, from the way he cleaned his plate and reloaded. He especially seemed to enjoy the homemade pepper gravy, she noticed with delight.

It was the kids who were doing their level best to make the meal as unpleasant as possible. They ate with their heads down, slowly and all but silently, except for the harsh, scraping clicks of silverware off plates. Even Eddie and Ricky, who could eat their weight these days, were holding back, acting like they were at a funeral.

"Don't let these people fool you, Leo," Seamus

suddenly called out in the dead silence. "This fine bunch of formal young lads and lasses is usually quite lively come mealtime. You're having quite an effect on them."

"A positive one, I hope, Father Seamus," Leo said with a polite grin.

"Aye, without a doubt," Seamus said, chewing as he looked around the table. "Now tell me, Leo. I couldn't help but notice, that's quite some firepower you bring with you every evening. What kind of rifle is it?"

"Now, Seamus," Mary Catherine said, "is that polite dinner conversation?"

"Perhaps not," Seamus said with a shrug. "But I figure, even somewhat impolite dinner conversation is a tad better than none at all."

"It's an M-four," Leo said.

"An M-four?" Seamus said, nodding. "Is it not an M-sixteen?"

"Well, the M-four is sort of the latest version of the M-sixteen," Leo said. "The main difference is that it's smaller and lighter and has a shorter barrel, for close-quarter combat."

"Hmm," Seamus said, chewing. "What round does it shoot? A .223?"

The kids started to smile and giggle as they saw

Mary Catherine roll her eyes. At least the little ones. The older crew of boys looked like they were silently praying to disappear.

"No, a new 5.56 round, actually," Leo said.

"To account for the shorter barrel?" Seamus said.

"Exactly," Leo said, exchanging a smile with Mary Catherine. "Do you shoot, Father?"

Seamus's shoulders sagged as he sighed.

"Oh, no," he said. "They won't let me."

Chapter 72

IN THE SHADOWS, CATTY-CORNER from the farmhouse, laughter echoed in the earbud of a man dressed head to toe in black, crouching there, motionless.

The earbud was attached to a shotgun microphone he'd purchased in San Fran the day before, along with a zoom-lens camera. He would have gone in closer to get some shots through a window with the camera, but he'd spotted motion detectors along the property's perimeter coming in, so he didn't want to risk it. There seemed to be only one US marshal who was currently in the house, eating with the family, but you never knew.

He'd ridden in on horseback, careful to skirt the herds of cattle as well as Cody's farmhouse dogs. He'd tied up about a mile to the north and hoofed it the rest of the way. Care was required here, considering the marshal would probably shoot him on sight.

It's them, the man thought, listening to the tinny dinner chatter. They were everything his cartel contact had said to keep an eye out for: all those kids, the old man and the young woman with the Irish accents. It had to be the cop's family. Who else on the face of the earth could it be?

And to think that he had his drug-addict brother-in-law, Cristiano, to thank for this mother lode. He had gone by the house for his monthly sponge off his sister when Cristiano idly mentioned that a new Irish priest had been handing out cans at the food bank with three kids, one of them an Asian girl.

Right away, he put it together with the cartel APB. The Mexicans were looking for a large, strange family with adopted kids and an old Irish priest, hiding in or around Susanville. A half-million-dollar purse was being offered for information. Might even be some negotiating room there, too, he was told. The Mexicans wanted these people bad.

It didn't take too much asking around to hear that the priest had also been spotted filling in for

Father Walter, and that the family had driven to church in one of Aaron Cody's beaters. Now here they were. Thirty feet away. All five hundred Gs" worth of them.

He'd been one of the first to understand the wisdom of partnering up with the cartels when they started moving into the Central Valley, four years before. He was no brain surgeon, but he was smart enough to know what men who truly didn't give a shit about killing people looked like. Smart enough to know that getting on the wrong side of folks that serious was not an option if you didn't have a second set of eyeballs in the back of your head and liked waking up alive every day.

He'd become involved in the marijuana-growing business about a year after getting back to his hometown, Susanville, from an '05 stint in Iraq with the army. He'd traded in the M1 Abrams tank he'd been driving for a beer truck and had applied to the huge state prison nearby, like every other sucker in town, when he bumped into some old buddies who had a grow house going. He'd helped them expand and organize it, ramp up production and sales until they were the biggest outfit around. Heck, he hadn't even had to kill anyone. Just put a few guns to a few people's heads.

But now, squatting there in the dark like some Peeping Tom, he actually felt a little bad. He had a few rug rats of his own, and it was doubtful that the cartel wanted to find these people in order to deliver a Publishers Clearing House prize. But the problem was, half his crop had been seized by the state park rangers a month before. He owed a lot of dangerous people a lot of money he didn't have.

Here's an opportunity to make everybody happy and then some, the man in black thought. *Expand or, even better, quit altogether.* Get out while he was young and rich, with his head still connected to his neck.

It wasn't his idea, the man in black finally decided with a sigh as he sat there, listening and recording the family's laughter on his iPhone.

It wasn't his fault that God made the world so dog-eat-dog.

Chapter 73

SIX HUNDRED MILES TO the south, Vida Gomez was lighting a bath candle in the guest powder room when her cell rang.

She stepped out and opened a sliding door to take it on the balcony. They were in the Hollywood Hills now, the lights of Los Angeles spread out below in the huge bowl of the valley, white on black, like cocaine on black velvet. The new safe house was pretty much bereft of furniture, but it actually suited the place. It was nothing but sterile stone and glass, clean and cold, just the way she liked it.

"Vida, I have news," Estefan said excitedly. "I just received a call. We have a lead."

Vida blinked. She had sent Estefan up to Susanville to see what he could see immediately after they'd dumped the agent at Venice Beach two days before. Already he had made progress. This was good news.

"OK, slow down," she said. "Is it credible?"

"It can't be confirmed, but I've been speaking to our people up here, getting them to put out the word about the reward, just like you said. One of the locals just called me directly. He claims to know the exact location of the Bennetts. There's a problem, though."

"What is it?"

"The informant wants more money. He wants a million, and he wants half up front. What should I do?"

"Sit by the phone. I'll call you back," she said, hanging up.

She went back inside as Manuel came out of the bedroom in a short silk robe. Most crime lords got fat when they got rich, but not the Sun King. He worked out like a madman with weights for an hour every day and ran for another on the treadmill. He was a health-food nut. Though he was in his mid-forties, he could easily pass for thirty-five.

She couldn't help but stare at his broad shoulders as he went into the kitchen and took some pomegranate juice out of the fridge. Not for the first time, she felt herself get aroused. When he'd asked her to be his special personal assistant for the duration of his stay in Los Angeles, she thought he might make a move, but so far, unfortunately, he'd been the perfect gentleman.

He'd even informed her that he was having a guest over a little bit later. She knew what that meant. The two whores he'd had over the night before hadn't left until three a.m.

Then she remembered herself.

"I have news, Manuel. The FBI agent was right. The Bennetts seem to be in Susanville. We just heard from an informant who claims to know their exact location. But he wants a million, and he wants half up front."

"A million?" Perrine said, affronted. "That's thievery."

"Perhaps we could set up the informant? Force him to tell us?" Vida said, lifting her phone.

"No," said Manuel as he poured himself some juice. "I have another idea. Send that other one up there. The one who found the last two stinking rats for us. What's his name?"

"The Tailor?" Vida said.

"Yes, yes. The Tailor. He can easily find the

Bennetts *and* eliminate them, especially now that we know we're in the ballpark."

Perrine drank some juice and smiled, raising an eyebrow.

"And you know what happens when we get in the ballpark, Vida."

She had just forwarded Manuel's wishes when the front doorbell rang. She looked at the security camera. There was a tall, blond woman wearing a tube top and leather miniskirt and a raincoat. Just one hooker tonight.

Terrific, Vida thought, rolling her eyes. *Perhaps I'll get to sleep before two.*

Vida opened the door. The woman who stepped inside was even taller than she looked on the video screen, and very heavily made-up. Like a TSA agent, Vida put on blue rubber gloves before she went through the prostitute's bag. All cell phones and recording devices would be left in the living room, of course. The already-agreed-upon procedure was that the sex workers would be blindfolded throughout, so as to hide Manuel's identity. A detail the whores had no problem with, LA being a town where discretion was valued almost as much as debauchery.

As Vida was frisking the whore, she suddenly stopped and excused herself.

"Um, Manuel? A word, sir?" Vida said, knocking and entering his bedroom.

"Yes, Vida? Has my guest arrived?" Perrine said from where he lay back on the bed, smoking a cigar as he channel-surfed the seventy-inch flat screen.

"It's about your guest, sir," Vida said delicately. "I . . . I think she's an impostor."

"What do you mean? An impostor?"

"They sent a transvestite, Manuel," she said. "I just frisked her, him, whatever. *She* is a definite *he*."

The cartel king laughed as he shut off the TV. He shook his head at Vida affectionately as he stood and squeezed her cheek.

"Thank you, Vida, my innocent little country girl, but everything is completely in order," he said as he spanked her playfully on the rump. "Now, be a love and go blindfold that vision of loveliness and send her in with the champagne."

Chapter 74

IN THE AFTERMATH OF the horrific attack on Agent Mara, the entire task force began to work fourteen-hour days.

We interviewed every witness at the pool where she'd been grabbed that morning—the lifeguards, the parents of the other kids. We had spoken to her soul-broken husband, who simply told us that he had been talking to his wife when there was a loud machine sound and the screen blurred. Emily even interviewed her poor little son Ian, who was overwrought with grief.

But there was nothing. We hadn't even found her stolen truck yet. One second, the agent had been watching her kid in the SUV, and the next, the SUV was gone, with only a pile of broken glass in its place.

The following day, another two dozen new FBI agents were flown in to bolster our ranks. Also, the special agent in charge of the FBI's LA office, John Downey, was put at the helm of the task force.

It was obvious that the female agent's mutilation and murder had rung every bell and whistle at FBI HQ. As well it should have. Some were saying that the stakes for the bureau hadn't been this enormous since the unparalleled spree of bank robberies that had plagued the country during the Great Depression.

Put simply, Perrine was calling into question law enforcement's ability to deal with him. That could not be allowed to stand, especially on our own soil.

If I had any last doubts about the feds' commitment, they were thoroughly extinguished when FBI Director Joseph J. Rohr himself attended the task force's morning briefing via Skype. Instead of micromanaging the meeting, Rohr surprised me by listening intently and asking pointed but intelligent questions about logistics and manpower.

He seemed determined that we have every resource we needed. Moreover, instead of harping on ass-covering attention to protocol, the surprisingly witty former marine fighter pilot practically begged us to think as creatively as we could in tracking down Perrine.

After a few false starts, it was decided that the task force's new prime directive would be to laser-focus on the gangs in LA who were known to be closest to Perrine's Los Salvajes organization. That meant going with both barrels after MS-13.

So on the second morning after the murder, Emily and I were teamed up with a short, extremely intense bullnecked cop named John Diaz, who was a ten-year-veteran detective of the LAPD's Gangs and Narcotics Division. After the briefing, Diaz took us immediately from Olympic Station to a place called Langer's Deli, in the MacArthur Park area of Westlake. Though it was a pretty gritty inner-city neighborhood, as we sat at a window booth above the palm trees, I spotted a grand, white prewar building.

"Why does that look familiar?" I said to Diaz, pointing at it.

"That's the Bryson Apartment Hotel," Diaz said with a nod. "It's the building Fred MacMurray drives past in the beginning of *Double Indemnity*."

"Right," I said excitedly. "With a couple of slugs in his belly."

"Exactly," Diaz said, nodding again. "Actually,

MacArthur Park has a long history of gunshot wounds in real life, too. A lot of drugs, a lot of gangs. They drained the lake back in the seventies, and you wouldn't believe the number of guns they found. They say this is where MS-Thirteen was started in the eighties by Salvadoran immigrants.

"Speaking of which, I called a guy who might be able to help us on an MS-Thirteen lead. He's a friend, so I've been reluctant to ask him for any info. The worst insult you can make to these guys is to ask them to be a snitch. But after what happened to that lady agent, this shit is obviously not business as usual. He's on his way here now."

We were ordering pastrami sandwiches when a UPS truck pulled up outside. The brown-uniformed Hispanic driver who stepped out and lit a cigarette had a goatee and more than a few tats.

"And here he is now," Diaz said, standing.

"That's your source? The UPS guy?"

"Oh, yeah. Me and Pepe go way back to my old neighborhood. My uncle's a district manager at UPS, and I actually pulled some strings to get him the job when he got out of jail a few years ago."

"Is he MS-Thirteen?" I said.

"No, Pepe's Eighteenth Street, MS-Thirteen's rival. But don't let the uniform fool you. Pepe's in the game up to his tattooed neck. He knows everybody. You guys sit tight. I'll be right back."

Diaz went out and hopped into the truck, and we watched as it pulled out. The sandwiches had just hit the table when the truck hit the curb again. Diaz came back in, smiling. He clapped his hands and rubbed them as he sat back down.

"OK, the suspense is killing me," I said. "What can Brown do for us?"

Diaz spread a napkin on his lap.

"We need to speak to a guy named Tomás Neves. He's an MS-Thirteen shot caller who's done quite well for himself, apparently. In addition to moving a lot of weight, he's a partner in one of those custom car shops down in Manhattan Beach where the rich people live. Pepe said something this big would have to go through Neves. He usually rolls into his fancy car joint late in the afternoon."

"Excellent," I said, lifting my massive sandwich. "First lunch, then it's time for an episode of *Pimp My G-Car*."

Chapter 75

BEACH CITY CUSTOMS WAS south of LAX on the Pacific Coast Highway, in a commercial section of Manhattan Beach known as the Sepulveda Strip.

Diaz quickly tapped me on the shoulder as we were about to pull into its parking lot.

"What's up, John?" I said.

"Wait a sec. Drive around the block, would you?"

"OK," I said, continuing on and taking the corner past the body shop.

"How much do you want to find this guy Perrine?" Diaz said. "I mean, how much, really?"

"He put out a hit on my family, John," I said, looking at the LAPD cop in the rearview. "I want him as badly as humanly possible."

"I figured," Diaz said. "See, this guy Tomás is

348

going to be hard-core and definitely not stupid. If he's helping out Perrine, there's no way he's going to voluntarily come with us to be questioned. There's no way he's going to cooperate."

"I take it you have another idea?" Emily said.

Diaz nodded.

"Back in the late nineties, we had a scandal out here with a gang unit called CRASH. These CRASH cops went off the rails. They framed gang members, beat up on them. The sergeants used to give out awards if a gang member was shot."

"Your point being?"

"These gang guys remember CRASH. In fact, more often than not, during an arrest they and their defense lawyers claim we're up to our old tricks. I'm just thinking we might be able to use the rep of these crazy CRASH guys to put a little pressure on our friend Tomás."

"What do you mean? You want to frame him or something?" Emily said.

"No, of course not," Diaz said. "But what if we . . . I don't know . . . pretended to?"

"Yeah?" I said.

"I don't know," Emily said.

I smiled.

"I don't know, either, Emily. But the director

did tell us to get creative, to think outside the box. Besides, we need information, not evidence. It would never make it into court."

"Exactly," Diaz said. "It would be a bluff all the way, but at this point, that's all we got. We need to do something."

"Fine," Emily said. "You're right. This is beyond everything at this point. Count me in. I think."

"What do we have to do, Diaz?" I said.

Diaz pointed at a CVS pharmacy on the corner to our left.

"Pull in here," he said. "I need to pick up a few things."

Chapter 76

DEATH METAL WAS CHUGGING from one of the garage's four bays when we pulled into Beach City Customs' parking lot.

Inside, there was a man in coveralls down on one knee, tack welding at the tailgate of a Toyota pickup truck, blue electric sparks crackling in time to the head-banging blast beats. Through the window of the paint room behind him, a guy in a full filter-breathing mask was airbrushing flames onto the gas tank on a large Japanese motorcycle.

Parker and I exchanged a glance when we saw the bike. The shooters who had taken down the LA County cops had escaped on big-bore Japanese motorcycles.

Without any ado, Diaz stuck his head inside

the door of the Tacoma and killed the deafening devil tunes.

The welder stood and flipped up his mask, his pudgy brown face scrunched in wonder.

"You kidding me?" he said.

Diaz flipped his badge as he slammed the truck's door. There was a tire iron on the ground beside the vehicle. It made a musical bing-bong off the concrete as Diaz kicked it across the garage.

"Let me answer your question with a question. Does it look like I'm kidding you? Get Tomás now," Diaz said.

A broad-shouldered middleweight of a Hispanic man bounced out a door a split second later. He wore a tailored shirt and jacket over expensive jeans and had scar tissue over his eyes and cheekbones like ax cuts on a totem pole.

"Señor Neves, I presume?" Diaz said.

"Yeah? What?" he said with a stunned look on his malevolent face.

Tomás shrugged as we showed our tin.

"And?" he said.

"Señor Neves," Diaz said with a courtly little bow, "I know you're a busy man, but do you think it might be possible to speak with you for five minutes about a stolen car? If now's not good for you, we could always come back later with a search warrant and put you out of business."

"Why don't you come back to my office?" Tomás finally said.

"Señor Neves, I thought you'd never ask," Diaz said.

We followed him up the stairs, into a room with a spotless desk and a phone on it. There was a window in one wall and the cracked door to a bathroom in another.

"OK, here we are. Happy? So what the hell is this about? A stolen car?" Neves demanded.

"Jeez, dog. What is it with you? Could you be ruder?" Diaz cried. "This ain't the hood. This is Manhattan Beach. You're supposed to say shit like, *Would you like a seat, Officer? Can I get you a cold drink, Officer?* I mean, if you want to be a businessman, you should watch an episode of Martha Stewart or something."

"Fine. Would you like a seat?" Neves said.

"There you go. No seat, man, but do you mind if I use your facilities to freshen up a little?" Diaz said, holding up his palms like a magician about to do a trick.

"Whatever," Neves said.

"Thanks," Diaz said, heading into the can. "Cleanliness is next to godliness, you know."

Diaz wasn't two steps in when he stopped and turned.

Emily and I had to suppress our laughter.

"What the—?" Diaz said loudly.

There was a loud scraping sound, and a moment later, Diaz came out with a stunned look on his face and something dripping in his hand. It was the bar of soap he had wrapped in red cellophane in the parking lot of the CVS. A small package that had a strong resemblance to a kilo of cocaine.

"What have we here, Tomás?" Diaz said, shaking his head in dismay. "Little advice, señor. When you hide something from the cops in a toilet tank, you should really remember to put the lid all the way back on."

"Whoa," Tomás said, stunned. He blinked a few times, then shook his lean face vigorously. "This ain't happening. This is a joke, right? You're putting me on, yo?"

"Yep," said Diaz, throwing him up against the wall and ratcheting handcuffs around his wrists. "Wanna hear the punch line? You have the right to remain silent."

"You planted that shit there! You planted that shit!"

"Yes, I did, Tomás," Diaz whispered to him. "Want to know a little secret? Planting shit on scum like you is, like, my favorite hobby. Guess what? There ain't no stolen car, and the gloves are off, bitch. Just got the word from up top, and I couldn't be happier. CRASH times are here again!"

"You crazy, man. What the hell are you talking about?"

"Your buddy Manuel offed an FBI agent, and you think it's not going to come on you? What did you think was going to happen?"

"But I don't know any Manuel! What are you talking about? I want my lawyer. Yo, get Terrence! Go next door and get Terrence!" he started yelling.

Through the window, I saw the welder run out of the garage.

"John?" I said.

"It's OK. I got this," Diaz said.

Diaz grabbed the gangbanger and kicked out his legs as he body slammed him onto the desk.

"Listen to me, and listen to me good," he said. "Your lawyer isn't going to be able to help you when I toss you in MacArthur Park Lake with these cuffs on, *maricón*. Now start talking."

Tomás said something in Spanish then. Diaz said something back.

We all jumped when there was a sudden pounding on the door behind us.

Chapter 77

EMILY AND I IMMEDIATELY took out our guns.

"What is this? What's going on in there? Tomás, are you OK? What's going on in there? Open this door!"

"This is a police interview!" I yelled as I ripped the door open behind my gun. "Put your hands up now!"

I was surprised when I saw that the shocked-looking man standing in the doorway wasn't a Hispanic gangbanger but a petite Asian guy wearing golf clothes and Clark Kent glasses.

"How dare you point a gun at me! I'm Terrence Che, Mr. Neves's lawyer. Now, I demand that you tell me what's going on this instant!"

"They're framing me, is what's going on!" Neves yelled. "They're framing me, Terrence!"

Diaz rolled his eyes. "Shit," he mumbled as he reluctantly uncuffed Tomás.

"Who are you people? Why are you harassing my client?" Che said as I put my gun away.

"Well, it's kind of a long story," Diaz said, handing the lawyer the wet bar of cellophane-wrapped soap as he gently pushed him to the side.

"And wouldn't you know it? We're late for a meeting," Emily said as we exited the room.

"Wait, I'm not done with you. This is illegal," the feisty, pocket-sized lawyer said, following us down the stairs, into the garage. "You can't just go around assaulting people. What's your badge number?"

"Oh, my badge number," Diaz said, turning and giving him the finger. "LAPD Badge Number One. Got it? Super. Bye, now."

"Well, that went well," Emily said as we screeched out of the lot, hopefully before the lawyer could get the plates. "It did go well, actually," Diaz said, lazing in the back-seat.

"What do you mean? What did Tomás say to you?"

"He said, 'Please, man. Don't do this. He'll kill my family.' "

"So Tomás does know something," Parker said.

Diaz nodded.

"Apparently," he said.

Chapter 78

AFTER WE RETURNED TO HQ and relayed the info about Neves's connection to Perrine, the reaction up the chain of command was impressive and immediate.

FBI Assistant Director Dressler personally got on the phone to a senior intelligence analyst at none other than the NSA for a full Homeland Security Total Information Awareness workup on the gangbanger.

TIA was an NSA supercomputer-fueled data-mining tool that apparently could de-encrypt and scour each and every data source on the planet to find out about an individual. There were no warrants involved, not even any formal requests to phone or credit card companies that could be turned down. The NSA hackers just went in

wherever they needed to go and took what they
wanted.

It was supposed to have been shut down after a
hue and cry by the ACLU about privacy, but
apparently it wasn't as shut down as the ACLU
thought. Which was fine by me. At least in this
instance. Bending and even breaking rules was the
least we could do in stopping the utter savagery
that Perrine was waging on American citizens.

I admired the heck out of Dressler's get-her-
done attitude. He was even smart enough not to
ask us how we came across our info. All he wanted
was progress so he could nail Perrine's ass to the
floorboards. Perrine had made a bad mistake when
he had killed Agent Mara. The FBI was very, very
pissed.

I admired Diaz's attitude just as much. The
Charles Bronson look-alike had certainly stepped
up and taken charge of Neves back at the garage.
He was a throwback, one of those all-in all-the-
time cops who knew the cold, brutal truth that
sometimes the solution to a situation comes at the
business end of a billy club.

"Tell me something, John," I said as we put our
feet up with a cup of coffee at the back of the
command center. "This CRASH-unit scandal

thing. You didn't, perchance, have some personal experience concerning that situation, did you?"

Diaz squinted pensively at his coffee.

"You know, Mike, now that I think about it," Diaz said with a wink, "perchance I did."

Chapter 79

IT WAS NOON WHEN he left San Francisco and going on three by the time the Tailor saw the first sign for Susanville on 395.

He passed a thin cow, a dilapidated barn, some rusting machinery. The land beyond the open window, the washed-out sand and scrub grass, had a lunar quality to it, the awesome mountains in the distance like something from the cover of a cheap sci-fi paperback. The wind whistled in through the window as the sun glinted off the gold wire of his aviator sunglasses. He drove at a steady five miles over the limit and left the radio off.

The Tailor was average-sized, average-looking, a nondescript bald white man in his early thirties wearing a dark polo shirt and sharply creased stone-colored khakis. He'd been an FBI agent once back east, an army Ranger before that. Now he did things that had bought him a town house in San Fran, a marina apartment in San Diego, and almost a dozen bank accounts stuffed, at his latest tally, with nearly six million dollars in cash.

No one knew his real name. Among those who hired him, he was referred to simply as the Tailor because he dressed nicely and he always sewed everything up.

He got off 395 and passed the Walmart and drove into the town. He cruised past gas stations, beat-up pickup trucks in dirt driveways, some equally beat-up-looking folks on the sidewalks. There was supposed to be a prison, but he didn't see it. He checked his notes and parked on Main Street, across from a saloon. He dialed the number of the contact the cartel had set up.

"This Joe?" the Tailor said when the line was answered.

"Yep."

"I'm across the street, the white Chevy Cruze."

After a minute, a young bearded guy came out. He was broad shouldered and wearing cutoff denim shorts and a Nike T-shirt, the swoosh on it about as faded and washed out as the surrounding prison town. *Not even noon, and beer on his breath,* the Tailor noted as Joe climbed into the passenger seat.

"Could you put on your seat belt, please?" was the first thing the Tailor said.

"Come again?" Joe Six-Pack said.

"Your seat belt. Could you please put it on?"

The Tailor waited patiently for the contact to secure the belt before pulling out. California was click-it-or-ticket, and getting pulled over was not on the agenda. Not with what he had in the trunk.

"Where we headed?" Joe wanted to know.

"For a spin," the Tailor said. "Do you know this town?"

"I should. I've lived here all my unfortunate life. Can I smoke?"

"No," the Tailor said. "You work at the school?"

"Sorta. I'm the assistant football coach, and you can save the Sandusky jokes, thank you."

The Tailor handed him the file with the photos in it.

"You recognize any of these kids? They would have arrived within the last eight or nine months."

"Nope. Not even a little," Joe said after flicking through them. "An Asian kid around here? That, I would have remembered."

The Tailor nodded to himself. They were

homeschooling them. Witness Protection 101. The Tailor had expected that.

"Go through the pictures again, Joe, and think again slowly. You might have bumped into them at the Walmart, the local pizza place, on the sidewalk, church?"

"Wait," Joe said, holding up a finger. He fished through the folder again and took out the photo of the priest.

"This guy ain't Irish, is he? Has, like, an Irish accent?"

The Tailor was pretty sure he did, but he glanced at his notes anyway.

"Yes," he confirmed.

"My mom told me an Irish priest subbed for the local pastor a couple of weeks back."

The Tailor felt it then. A primordial tingling down his spine as warmth spread in his belly. He always thought of the sensation as how a shark must feel on detecting the first traces of blood in the water. Fresh meat this way. The happy fore-shadowing of victory.

The Bennett contract was a whale, all right. Three million. He knew what he was going to buy with it, too. A flat in Paris. Travel was one of his few passions.

"That right?" the Tailor said as he lawfully put on his clicker and made a perfect K-turn.

Joe nodded, pulling on his beard.

"The old biddies couldn't get over it. Imagine, that's what passes for news here in Susanville, USA."

"Where's the Catholic church?" the Tailor asked.

"Where's my money?" Joe said.

"In the glove box."

Joe took it out and gazed on it, smiling. *The Great Recession really must be hurting these hicks out here*, the Tailor thought. He'd never actually seen someone happy to be setting up a hit on a family for five hundred bucks in twenty-dollar bills.

"Make a left up ahead," Joe said. "The church is there on your right."

Chapter 80

MARY CATHERINE'S BEDROOM WAS on the third floor, in the quaint, rickety Victorian farmhouse's converted attic. It was little bigger than a closet, but its dormer window, with its clear, unbroken view of the flat grasslands and the grand Sierra Nevada beyond, actually made it her favorite spot in the entire house.

A bright moon was hanging just above the awe-inspiring peaks when Mary Catherine suddenly came awake a little after one a.m. She flipped her pillow over and lay there staring out the window, listening intently, wondering what had woken her.

After another minute, she decided that it was nothing, probably just the two glasses of the wine that Leo had brought over for dinner. She hardly drank at all these days, but Leo had seemed concerned about whether the wine he'd brought matched up properly with the roast chicken she'd served. Indulging in a couple of glasses of pinot grigio seemed the least she could do to assuage his fears.

Dinner with Leo is swiftly becoming part of the regular routine now, isn't it? she thought, smiling. Even the boys who had given her so much trouble had decided to stop the silent treatment when Leo quietly started talking baseball with them. Leo had that effect on people. There was something still inside him, an openness, a . . . gentleness. You couldn't help but like him.

She didn't know how Leo would fit into the picture once Mike came back, but she'd decided to cross that bridge when she came to it. She wasn't one for making people jealous, but she was actually looking forward to Mike's reaction. At least a little. It would be quite interesting to see how much Mike liked watching another man pay her some attention for a change.

She was looking out at the dark land, the mountains glowing in the starlight, and groggily thinking about Leo and Mike when she thought she heard something downstairs. Then she heard it again. A soft thumping, followed by the creak of weight on wood.

How now, brown cow? she thought, frowning, as she put her bare feet to the rough floorboards and found her slippers. Out her door and down the stairs, she stopped and looked over the banister of the second-floor landing. A suspicious, flickering glow of blue light was coming from what seemed to be the main level's family room.

She padded down the stairs and quietly around the corner of the kitchen. Just as she suspected, here they were. The things that go bump in the night, in the living flesh.

In the family room, with their backs to her, Eddie and Ricky were splayed out on the couch, thumbs and fingers clicking madly as they played the *NBA Street Homecourt* PlayStation game that Leo had brought them that evening.

"And one! Woop, woop! That's right. I'm good," Eddie said, raising his controller over his head as he did a little dance. "I'm gonna dunk on you like that all day long."

"Don't you mean all night long, you little sneak thieves?" Mary Catherine said, and watched the kids jump.

Eddie dropped his controller and lay facedown

in front of the TV, pretending to sleep, as Ricky turned around, smiling bravely.

"Mary Catherine. Hi. Um, you want to play winner?" he tried.

"Don't get cheeky with me. It's almost two in the God-loving morning. Heads on your pillows this instant, or I'll dunk the both of you in your rooms for a week. I've half a mind to talk to Mr. Cody and get you two night owls some milking work tomorrow. Maybe a week of watching the world go by from the underside of a cow will help you learn the meaning of a good night's sleep."

"Cow punishment? No! You can't! The horror!" Eddie yelled, jumping up and racing his brother out of the room, heading for the stairs.

She'd turned off the set and was going back through the kitchen when she saw the full coffee-pot. Leo, on duty now out on the porch, must have just made himself some. She primped in the mirror of the powder room and put her barn jacket over her pj's before she poured a cup.

She was going to kiss him, she decided with a smile as she went down the front hall with the mug. She'd been waiting for the right time for them to get closer, and tonight was the night.

"Hark, I go here," Mary Catherine said, smiling as she pushed through the screen door.

It took several long seconds for Mary Catherine to piece together what the lump down on the opposite side of the porch was. Then she suddenly understood. The coffee cup fell from her shaking hand and exploded between her feet.

Leo was down on the ground, on his back beside the toppled camp chair. Above him and above the porch's hand railing, there was a large, ink blot–like splatter on the clapboards. Mary Catherine covered her mouth as she scanned Leo's face. There was a hole over Leo's open left eye and a dark pool beneath his head!

Mary Catherine felt a shiver of cold shoot up her back as her breath left her. Leo was shot?! He was dead! No! How? What?

The first thought that came to her racing mind was that it was an accident. Had he dropped his gun?

But then she heard something. It came from somewhere off to the right, in the darkness by the main road. It was a whistle, the low double whistle of someone getting someone else's attention. It was followed after a moment by the distinct and brief, jagged crackle of a radio.

Gone

Mary Catherine stood there in the darkness and silence, not moving, not breathing, the spilled coffee staining her slippers.

They found us, she thought as she felt a sudden presence in the hallway behind her. As she turned toward it, she was grabbed in a bear hug and violently yanked back into the house, a callused hand pressing hard over her mouth before she could scream.

Part Four

FACE TIME

Chapter 81

THE NSA'S INTELLIGENCE PACKAGE on Tomás Neves and the members of his MS-13 set came in around eleven that night.

It was extensive. At the top were all ingoing and outgoing calls and texts to and from everyone's home and cell phones. Next came e-mails and Google searches. There were tax returns from the IRS, license plate numbers from the DMV.

"Big Brother's been working overtime, I see," Detective Diaz said, licking his thumb as he went through one of the stacks.

Diaz was right. There was almost too much info, if that were possible. Emily and Diaz and I ran out of desk space and had to actually lay out all the papers on the floor to try to get a handle on it.

Since our breakthrough the day before, three

more people had been added to our team to give us a hand. There was a hulking, fresh-out-of-the-academy FBI agent from Brooklyn named Ed Kelly and a couple of veteran LA-office Immigration and Customs Enforcement people, Agents Joe Irizarry and Steve Talerico.

The ICE agents were born-and-bred Angelenos and were especially helpful on logistics. Bonding over some Chinese takeout, we pored over street and Google maps of Neves's place in Reseda, trying to work out the angles, where best to place our vehicles for surveillance.

With our players picked out and our surveillance plan finalized, we geared up with night-vision and video cameras around two a.m. We'd only made it as far as the Olympic Station's garage when Emily's phone rang.

"OK," she said into it, then slammed the door of the G-car she'd just opened.

"That was the LA SAIC John Downey," she said as she pointed toward the elevator. "We need to go back up. Apparently something from Perrine just came in upstairs."

Rushing back up into the third-floor office space, I thought I was going to see the big smart screen pulled down again, with a crowd of agents and cops standing around it. There were a lot of cops standing around, but this time, the screen was still up and everyone seemed to be looking at me.

"In here, Mike," Downey said, waving to me from the door of the space's only private office. There were three techs in there with him, two of them tapping rapidly on laptops.

"What is this?" I said.

"It's Perrine. The maniac's just contacted the LAPD website. He says he wants a sit-down, to communicate with you face-to-face on Skype."

"Talk to me?" I said, squinting. "But I'm supposed to be in hiding. How does he even know I'm here in LA?"

Downey shrugged.

"I don't know. All I know is that it's an encrypted signal and we have NSA trying to trace it."

I have to admit, I got spooked then. Though I'd been at a few crime scenes, I'd kept a pretty low profile. Were the rumors right? Did Perrine really have a source in the task force? And what did it mean?

I passed a hand through my hair.

"I don't know," I said. "I'm not sure about this."

"I wouldn't even ask you, Mike, but he has a hostage. He says he's going to kill him in another five minutes if we don't get you."

"Of course he does," I said. "OK. I guess."

Downey took me over to the desk and sat me in front of a computer monitor. I took a deep breath when I saw the minimized Skype tab. I still didn't like this. I had a sick feeling that there was something seriously wrong. Something we'd overlooked.

A tech hit a button, and then Perrine was there. He was sitting in a beanbag chair next to a small, wide-eyed Mexican man who had tape over his wrists and ankles and mouth.

There was some kind of metal wall behind them. They were in a van, I realized. Perrine lifted a tennis ball and bounced it off the floor and wall of the van beside the camera and then caught it again.

When the hostage looked up, I saw his Roman collar. He was a priest! Perrine was holding a young priest hostage!

"Detective!" Perrine bellowed as he glanced at the screen. "Detective, there you are, at long last. I was wondering if you'd ever show up. You're looking tired. Having trouble sleeping, are we? Seriously, how have you been? How are the kids?"

I wanted to tell the arrogant scumbag to go screw himself, but I couldn't stop looking at the priest. The terror and pleading in his eyes. He was slight, in his early thirties. My heart went out to him. I needed to save this man's life.

"I'm here, Manuel," I said. "So you can let that poor man go now, OK?"

"Let him go? Good idea, Detective," Perrine said, standing.

The drug lord stepped offscreen. There was a sliding sound as the metal wall behind the priest moved sideways to reveal a blurring guardrail, the shoulder of a road, passing trees.

"No!" I yelled as Perrine, coming back into the frame, reared up his heel and booted the priest in the chest.

The man flew backward immediately out the van door, into the darkness. Without a cry. Without a sound. The man was just gone.

Chapter 82

DEAR GOD, I THOUGHT, feeling dizzy in the cramped, suddenly too-hot office. *Dear God.*

I watched as Perrine slid the door shut with a bang. He dusted off his hands as he plopped himself back down in the beanbag chair. He lifted the tennis ball and bounced it off the floor and wall of the van again.

"Now, where were we?" he said, catching the ball. "Oh, yes. Your kids. How is the law-enforcement version of the Duggar *familia?*"

"You bastard," I said.

"Mike, Mike. Please," Perrine said. "Do not mourn. That priest is in a better place now. He has gone to his God. You know, like your friend. What was his name? Hughie?"

He was taunting me now. Trying to get to me.

He was. I wanted to smash the screen with my fist, but I couldn't. I took a breath and refused to give him what he wanted.

"That's true," I said calmly. "Good point, Manuel. Hughie's gone to God."

I paused as I leaned in closer to the computer's camera.

"Just like your wife, Manuel. No, wait. I made a mistake. How could she be with God? I sent that bitch directly to hell."

Perrine hurled the ball against the wall and didn't bother catching it this time. He stood up and walked over to the camera until his face filled the screen.

"I have one more thing to show you, Bennett. My men are sending it to you right now. If you have any popcorn available, I advise you to get it popping and pull up a seat. You're going to like this, Mike. I know I will. We can talk after. Maybe when it's over, we'll trade notes. But if you don't feel like talking, that's OK, too. I'll understand. You probably won't be in the mood. *Au revoir.*"

The screen went blank.

"Wait," I said to Agent Downey. "What in the hell is he talking about? He's sending something else? What is it? Where is it?"

"Something's coming in now. It's another Skype request," a tech said, clicking a button.

The first thing I noticed about the footage on the screen that opened up was that it was from a night-vision camera. It was showing an empty field. The grainy image reminded me of a black-and-white TV image, only with dark green instead of black, and light green instead of white.

And it wasn't footage, I realized suddenly. Since this was Skype, it meant what I was looking at was something that was being filmed in real time.

The camera swung shakily to the left. A kneeling figure appeared. It was a soldier of some kind, wearing a dark hazmat suit with a full gas mask.

The fentanyl, I thought. Perrine was ordering another fentanyl attack and making me watch. Two more hazmat-suited soldiers appeared beside the first, and the camera started moving, shaking a little as the group moved across a field.

There was some kind of fence at the far end, which they climbed, and then they were standing in a dirt road. The soldiers started moving up the slightly curving, uphill road, covering each other. Then they went around a bend, and suddenly, there was a house.

Realizing what it was hit me not like an electric shock but like a sudden shot of anesthesia. I felt numb. Like I wasn't there anymore. Like I wasn't anywhere. Like the bottom of the world had just dropped out from underneath me.

"It's his safe house!" Emily yelled from somewhere behind me as the soldiers on the screen arrived at the porch.

"In Susanville! My God, his family!" Emily yelled as she burst into the office. "Contact the marshals! Where are the marshals? Perrine is attacking the Bennett family in Susanville as we speak!"

Chapter 83

THE SKYPE IMAGE WAS showing a dead marshal on the porch when I stood and walked out of Downey's office. I walked over to the corner desk Emily and I were sharing and just sat there rigidly, with my feet on a plastic file box, gazing steadily forward at a blank spot on the wall.

Emily rushed over to me.

"The image cut off, Mike. They kicked in the door of the house, and the image went blank. We're sending everybody there. Everybody."

I didn't reply, didn't look at her. I kept staring at the wall. I needed to be there for my family, and yet it was impossible for me to be there. This did not emotionally compute for me, apparently. It was like being tied to a chair and having to watch your two-year-old climb out and off the ledge of an open window. I felt beyond confused, beyond disoriented. I felt disintegrated inside.

I don't remember much about the next twenty minutes that went by. I vaguely remember a lot of activity around me, Emily making a lot of heated phone calls and Downey coming over to me a few times in order to assure me that every available unit was on its way to my family.

And what will they find when they get there? I kept thinking.

The next thing I knew, I was being guided by Emily up onto my feet. I followed along obediently as she took me out into the stairwell. But instead of heading downstairs, she led me up.

"What's going on?" I mumbled.

"They're bringing you up there to Susanville, Mike. A chopper is going to take you to a plane waiting for you back at the SoCal Logistics Airport. I'm going to be right beside you the whole time, OK?"

I suddenly stopped on one of the landings.

"What have you heard?" I said, breaking her hold on my elbow.

"Nothing yet."

"But it's been a while. Someone should have gotten there already," I said, grabbing her wrist. "They're all dead. Just say it now. Don't lie to me."

"I wouldn't lie to you, Mike. I'm not sure why no one has responded. All we know is that the US marshal on scene is not answering the radio or his phone, and neither is your family. I swear to you, the second I hear anything, I'll tell you, Mike. Let's just get up there and see what's going on, OK? You need to be up there," Emily said as we went out onto the roof.

Five minutes later, an MH-60 Black Hawk swooped down out of the night, and a burly young soldier guided me aboard and strapped me in. I would have said it felt unreal as we lifted off, out over the lights of Wilshire Boulevard, with the wind rushing in through the chopper's nonexistent doors, but it already felt unreal. I'd felt like I was outside my body ever since Perrine had shown me the video of my family's not-so-safe safe house.

At the airport, an air force jet was already gassed and waiting. A couple more unbelievably gracious and young, competent soldiers strapped me into this new aircraft, and we took off. Emily didn't tell me to sleep or calm down or talk to her or anything. After a while, I turned away from the window and found her hand in mine.

We touched down less than an hour later at Susanville Municipal Airport. When they dropped the jet door, I could see marked town-police and state-trooper cars parked alongside the tarmac, their lights wheeling. A trooper car rushed us to the state road where Cody's farm was. There was another clog of official vehicles just in front of the driveway turnoff. There had to be twenty cars, but why weren't they up at the house? My mind felt like it was exploding. Why were they just sitting there!?

A lanky, brown-haired FBI agent rushed out of the black Chevy Tahoe as we came to a skidding stop.

"What the hell is going on?" I said before he could get a word out.

"I know you're upset, Detective," the agent said. The young agent was handsome, square jawed. Instead of the MIB suit, he wore a tweed jacket and jeans, like a popular young college professor.

"My family is up there!" I screamed as I grabbed his tweed lapels.

He tried to shake me off. He wasn't trying hard enough. I swung him around into the road. "Four boys, six girls, my grandfather and nanny. Why aren't you helping them?"

The fed was finally able to dislodge one of my hands by punching down on it. I retaliated by punching the agent in his mouth. I was about to do it again when the state trooper who had brought me there linked his big arms around mine from behind.

"Is my family dead? Tell me!"

"Jeez," the young fed said, thumbing his lip. "We don't know, OK? We don't know yet. We can't get up there because of the fentanyl. We have a hazmat team on its way."

I went really nuts then. I elbowed the trooper in his ribs and started running for the driveway. Then I was tackled by two more troopers and another agent.

"Get off me now, or I swear to God, I will shoot all three of you!" I snarled as I writhed and fought them in the dirt alongside the driveway. I lost it then. Some wall inside me broke, and I was bawling. My face filled with tears and dust as I sobbed.

"Get off me. Get off me, you fucking cowards," I said as I wept.

"It's poison up there, Detective," said one of the troopers, with a Barney Fife twang. "I know you want to get to your family, but if you go up there unprotected, you're going to die."

"I know," I cried. "I want the poison. Give me the poison. I just want to be with my kids."

Chapter 84

I CALMED DOWN AFTER another few minutes of crying. Emily had taken me over to one of the fed SUVs and sat with me in the back. I'd melted down emotionally before, but never in front of so many people. And still I hadn't faced it yet. Hadn't faced the unfaceable.

The FBI hazmat squad showed up in a fire truck-like vehicle, already wearing their white hooded jumpsuits. After Emily spoke to them, they allowed me to gear up as well and follow them, as long as I stayed behind them and didn't hit anyone else.

Emily and I started up the road behind the eight-man contingent. The air filter of the full-face breathing mask had some sort of pine scent in it that made me want to throw up.

The agents halted suddenly as something moved in the distance ahead. One of the SWAT guys raised his rifle.

"Don't shoot!" I said through the interior mike when I saw what it was.

It was one of Cody's sheepdogs. He stopped in the road and started barking at us. *Good God. Aaron.* I hadn't even thought about him. Was he dead as well? For helping us? The dog barked some more and then ran back up the road from where it had come.

We went around a slight curve in the dirt road and saw the house for the first time, up the slope. There was no light on in the windows. Not a sound. In the dull, grainy moonlight, it was like I was seeing it for the first time. Its fish-scale shingles on the gabled roof, its gingerbread trim. The Queen Anne–style Victorian looked like it should be in the Pacific Heights neighborhood of San Francisco, not out here in the middle of the high desert.

I shook my head and stared at the dormer where Mary Catherine slept.

Mary Catherine.

I pictured her.

Mary Catherine sewing a vintage lampshade she'd bought on eBay. Mary Catherine down on her knees in the hallway with the girls around a bucket of joint compound, teaching them how to spackle and sand. How to fix something. How to make a house, even a safe house, into a home.

In my heart, I'd been planning on our being together someday, I realized as I stopped walking. Now, in a few minutes, I would be making a phone call and telling her family back in Ireland that she was dead. I squeezed my hands into fists when they started shaking.

"You OK, Mike?" Emily said. "You want to go back?"

I shook my head quickly. For a second I thought I was going to throw up, but then it passed.

"Let's keep going," I said.

I stepped on something when we got to the front yard. It was a Wiffle ball, or what was left of one. Brian hit them so hard, he caved them in. I thought about Brian then. Watching my oldest son play his first football game back in New York, the smile that creased his face on that rainy, freezing field when the coach sent him in off the bench.

I turned and looked at the open front door as the SWAT team went inside. There was a sudden bang of another door being flung open. "Clear!" someone called. I squatted down and stared at the dirt as I listened to more bangs and more shouts of "Clear!" as the SWAT guys swept the house.

Then one of the agents appeared at the front door. It was the preppy-looking one I'd hit. He waved us up.

"Mike, you really, really don't have to do this," Emily said.

I lifted the crushed Wiffle ball and stared at it as I gathered myself.

"Yes, I do," I said, standing and stepping toward the house.

"Mike," said the agent, holding up his palm. "I don't know what this means, but there's no one here."

"What do you mean?" I said, staring over his shoulder, into the foyer. "You mean they're dead? They're all dead?"

"No, Mike," the agent said. "There are no bodies. There's no anything. Your family isn't here, Detective. The house is completely empty. Everyone is gone."

Chapter 85

THE TEST FOR THE fentanyl powder actually turned up negative. I quickly shucked off the suffocating mask and frantically searched the house.

It was true. Everyone was gone. I looked through the rooms. The beds were unmade. Everyone's clothes seemed to be all there, including their sneakers. I even found Mary Catherine's cell phone charging on the bookshelf beside her bed. It was hard to say if there was any kind of struggle, but it was obvious that they had all left quickly and suddenly, in the middle of the night.

I stared out Mary Catherine's window at the dark mountains, going crazy. Perrine had my family. He'd taken them away.

Roadblocks were set up in the entire area.

Troopers and local police came with bloodhounds. The dogs kept running around in circles in the farmyard, indicating that it was unlikely that anyone in my family had left on foot.

I peeled off the hazmat suit in the kitchen and just sat there at the table, rubbing a hand through my hair over and over again as I stared at the worn pine floor, trying to think. Why would Perrine come to kill my family and just take them instead? The implications of it wouldn't stop coming, the possibilities of what he could do.

It was worse than finding them dead, I decided. I couldn't believe that this was happening. How could I?

I looked up to see Emily take a seat next to me. She began to cry.

"I caused this," she said. "You didn't even want to go to LA, and I came up like a good little soldier and put on the con job and the pressure. You didn't want to leave for exactly this reason. I caused this. I'm responsible."

I wanted to tell her she was wrong, but I was in no shape to comfort anyone. The lead jacket of what was happening was too heavy. I was surprised I had the strength to breathe.

That was when the dog came in through the

open back door. It was Cody's border collie. She rubbed against my shins, and I reached out and patted the sad-looking pooch on the head.

As I was doing it, I remembered what Cody had told me about border collies. How brave and smart they were. How they always kept moving, kept circling. How they never quit.

I suddenly stood and took out my phone.

"Emily, listen to me. Stop crying. There's still a shred of hope," I said quickly, thumbing through my contacts.

"There is?" Emily said.

I nodded.

"That my guys are not here, all dead, means that Perrine is going to want to use them somehow, right? We need to find Perrine before that happens. We still have one shot."

I finally found the LAPD detective John Diaz and pressed Dial.

"Emily, call the airport and tell them to get that plane ready to go," I said to her as Diaz's phone rang. "We need to get back to LA and pay Tomás Neves another visit, and he's going to tell me where Perrine is or he's going to die."

Chapter 86

THE PLAN I SKETCHED out with Diaz over the phone was hazy at first. But as Emily and I raced back to the airfield and the waiting air force jet, refinements were made and remade.

When we touched back down at Southern Cal Logistics Airport, Diaz texted to let me know that our course of action was irretrievably under way, for good or for ill. I no longer had the time or energy to care.

Following Diaz's directions, Emily and I drove thirty miles southwest, straight from the base to Wrightwood, California, a pine-covered valley north of LA in the San Gabriel Mountains. About a mile north of a ski resort shuttered for the summer, we pulled onto a narrow, winding road called Lone Pine Canyon Road. We followed it to its end and then turned onto a long and steep, thickly wooded driveway.

It was about ten in the morning as we pulled the car into the pine-needle-covered front yard of an old, faded forest-green cabin. Diaz's Mustang was already there, under a corrugated carport, along with a blue Jeep.

I rolled down the Crown Vic's window to a low hum of chittering crickets. You could see some hogbacked hills in the distance behind the cabin, but there wasn't another house to be seen. There weren't even any power lines. It was like we'd driven back in time.

For a few moments, I stared at the faded cabin, mulling things over. I wondered what I would find once I went in there. Nothing good in the slightest, I knew. But we were past that. Way past that.

"Stay here," I told Emily as I finally opened the passenger door.

"No. I'm going in," Emily said, opening her door. "I'm in this as deep as you, Mike. I don't care what happens next. I'm responsible."

"No, you're not," I said, reaching across her and slamming her door shut again. "I'm the one with nothing to lose, Emily. If you want to help me, I need you to stay and just sit here."

"But, Mike—" she was saying as I got out and shut the door.

Diaz had already told me that they were set up downstairs. Around back, I pulled open a rusty sliding door and entered a musty-smelling, pine-paneled room with a stone fireplace. Diaz looked up from where he was sitting on a folding chair in front of the fireplace, smoking a cigarette. He was dressed head to toe in black. Beside him, propped up against the hearth's river stone, were two AR-15s.

"What's the story?" I said, shaking his hand.

"He's in there," Diaz said, pointing his cigarette at the closed door behind him. "We Tasered the shit out of him as he was coming out his front door. Talk about not knowing what hit you."

"What does he know so far?"

Diaz blew a smoke ring up at the yellow water stains on the drop ceiling.

"We told him we work for Perrine's rival, the Ortega cartel, and I think he's fallen for it. He also thinks we have his family. He came on pretty hard at first, but right before you arrived, I got creative and convinced him that if he didn't start being helpful, I was going to make a call and turn his wife HIV positive. He started with the waterworks then, boy. Broke like a glass hammer. Funny, the things that can hit a nerve."

Diaz was putting the cigarette out on the sole of his boot when the door behind him opened and a large man wearing a ski mask stepped out. I stood there with a very puzzled look on my face as the man peeled off the mask. It was Detective Bassman.

"Wow! You're in on this, too?" I said as I shook his massive hand. "Risking your ass for me? I'm never going to be able to pay you back for what you're doing for me. Either of you."

"No problem, brother," Bassman said, flashing a smile. "My pleasure, believe me. I think he's ready to talk to us now."

Diaz handed me a ski mask.

"Let's do this," he said.

Chapter 87

NEVES WAS IN HIS underwear, lying on his back at the bottom of an empty, dated six-person hot tub. He had a puffy black eye and was gagged with tape. He was also handcuffed at the ankles and the wrists, and he was wearing a forty-pound weight vest that pinned him down flat onto the floor of the tub.

When I saw Neves lying there, scared and helpless in his underwear, I felt my resolve waver for a second. Gangbanger or not, Neves was a man. A man we'd kidnapped. A man we were about to extract information from by force, if necessary. Staring down at him where he lay shaking, I felt wrong, sick inside.

Then I remembered that somewhere right now, Perrine had my family, my kids, and I steeled myself with a long, deep breath.

Diaz lifted another vest from a corner and stepped into the tub. There was a ripping sound as he tightened up the Velcro straps of the second vest around Neves's lower legs.

Diaz plugged the drain before he stepped out of the tub and sat on its edge. Bassman flicked open a butterfly knife and slid the blade in between the tape and the man's mouth. When he cut the tape away, a thin string of blood flowed from a slit in Neves's lip.

"Dang. Nicked you there, Tomás. My bad," Bassman said as he violently tore the rest of the tape off Neves's face.

Neves's chest heaved as fresh tears sprouted in his light-brown eyes.

"Please," he said between hacked-off sobs. "Please. My wife, man. Please. She's pregnant, man. Two months. Don't hurt her like that. Don't give her the monster. The baby get it, too."

When I heard the amount of genuine pain and fear in Neves's voice for the second time, I felt something sway unsteadily inside me. I squeezed my hands into fists, willing myself to ignore him. I had no other choice.

"Hey, don't worry so much," Bassman said, pinching the gangbanger's raw, red cheek from the other side of the tub. "I hear they're doing amazing things on the AIDS front these days. Making some real medical breakthroughs."

Neves closed his eyes, his bloody lip quivering as he cried.

"OK, OK, OK!" he suddenly yelled. "You win! What do you want? Get me a cell phone. I'll give you everything I have. I got eighteen kilos at a safe house right now. Eighteen. You can have everything."

"We don't want everything. We want Perrine. Where is he?" I said.

Neves did some more flopping around and moaning.

"Shit, shit," he said.

"You in the shit, all right, Tomás," Bassman said, loudly palming Neves's head. He banged it back loudly against the floor of the hot tub. "You heard of quicksand? Well, you just stepped in quickshit."

"He's in Mexico, OK? He was here in LA. We set up some houses for him, but he's gone now. I swear to God. Perrine went back to Mexico early this morning. One of my guys got him over the border."

"To where?!" I said. "Where did he go?!"

"I don't know. You think he'd tell me? I don't know."

"Wrong answer," Diaz said, squealing open the tub's tap full blast.

"No! It's true! It's true!" Neves yelled out over the water splattering loudly off the side of his face.

We stood there as Neves screamed, lying flat on his back, and the water rose. In thirty seconds, it was up to his earlobes. After a minute, the water had reached his cheeks. He strained his neck, trying to raise himself up. Covered in the segmented weight vests, he looked like an overturned turtle trying to pull himself unsuccessfully out of his shell.

"He went to his summer place near Mexico City," Neves finally said, sputtering, the water now at his lips. "I'll tell you exactly where on the map. Just turn it off! Turn it—"

Diaz put a hand to my chest as I reached in to grab the criminal who was screaming bubbles now under the rushing water.

"Give him a second, Mike," Diaz said. "He needs to see how serious we are."

"Exactly," Bassman said, taking out a smartphone and thumbing it. "Let this guy soak his weary bones for a minute in peace, Mike. Can't you see he's had a hard day?"

Chapter 88

THOUGH HE HADN'T BEEN to it in over a year, the estate in the Sierra de Pachuca, fifteen miles outside the central-eastern Mexican town of Real del Monte, was by far Perrine's favorite.

Built around a once-flourishing silver mine, the twenty-plus square miles of his property had been part of one of the original haciendas given by the Spanish crown to one of Cortés's captains. The original grant was hung in a frame above the fireplace in Perrine's office. At parties, Perrine made a point to show his guests the section on the yellowed parchment that granted the landowner not only the acreage and natural resources, but full ownership of all the area's inhabitants as well.

The beauty of a good ranching hacienda like Perrine's was not just its plush main house and gardens, but its complete self-sufficiency and sustainability. On the twelve thousand rolling acres, they farmed massive herds of cattle and sheep, countless chickens. They even had corn and soybean fields and several freshwater resources, including a fish-filled mountain river. The staff who lived on the hacienda all year round was in excess of forty people. They were mostly vaqueros, whom Perrine took great pleasure riding with whenever he was in attendance.

In summers past, in exchange for the local governor's discretion and friendship, the hacienda often ran a children's camp for local charities. But the last two weeks of August were reserved for Perrine's expansive family's dozens of children. The last time he had attended, two years before, eleven of the children were Perrine's own. The children's eight different mothers also stayed.

Perrine fondly remembered eating dinner with them poolside, night after night, flirting with them as the endless courses and wines were brought by an army of waiters. After the fifth course, he would have trouble putting names to faces. After the seventh, he'd stop caring.

He smiled at the memories. Had he ever been happier than during those two weeks, playing with the bands of his happy, screaming children all day and with their mommies all night? Had anyone?

But as his plane touched down on his airstrip late that morning, the estate was empty of all guests. Though he had sold the hacienda to a dummy buyer years before, he knew that it was possible for the Americans to know his connection to it, so he very rarely and briefly visited it these days. He'd come now only after a trusted source high up in the local *policía* had assured him there were no special directives to watch the place, no suspicious gringos suddenly filling the local hotels.

Even if there had been any chatter, even with his current American project under way, Perrine would have been hard-pressed to cancel the affair that he was putting on tonight—it would have been unthinkable to shutter the event. He lived for the cartel's annual bonus party, a formal dinner for himself and his top one hundred captains, resplendent with speeches and toasts and culminating in waiters carrying valises filled with cash on silver trays.

Perrine sighed wistfully along with his Global Express's whining jet engines as the plane taxied down the runway behind his twenty-one-thousand-square-foot mansion.

Gone

What a life, he thought, taking off his sleeping mask and handing it to the new, blond American stewardess, Marcia, with a wink. He was truly a blessed man.

Chapter 89

OLD BETO, PERRINE'S HEAD vaquero, was standing beside his long-faced butler, Arthur, on the other side of the forty-five-million-dollar aircraft's drop-down stairs.

"Beto, what is it? You look excited," Perrine cried in Spanish as he handed his English butler his silk sport coat and began rolling up his sleeves. "Don't tell me she foaled?"

Bowlegged Beto nodded rapidly and smiled, the laugh lines around his bright eyes like cracks in brown glass.

"Show me immediately."

They walked along the front of his massive, marble-stepped mansion and around the pool to the air-conditioned barn. Though he had several Thoroughbred racehorses, Perrine's real passion was for the show horses. They walked past stalls filled with several million dollars' worth of them. He stopped to pat and pet his favorites, She-Wolf, and Blue, and Troubled Queen. The prize horses took their names from the Jackson Pollock paintings that hung in the mansion's front hallway.

Perrine peered into Troubled Queen's stall at the newborn foal. It was a filly, like he'd predicted. A pale-strawberry roan as pretty as her mother. The little horse peered back at him shyly before tucking itself back in, next to its mother.

"Look! She is afraid of me, Beto!" Perrine complained. "Can you believe this? Afraid of me?"

There was a troubled look on Beto's face.

"What is it?" Perrine asked.

"What are we to call her?"

Perrine stared at the baby horse, a finger pressed to his pursed lips. He finally raised his finger in the air like a maestro.

"We shall call her La Rose," Perrine announced.

"La Rose," Beto repeated reverently as Perrine patted the old man on his shoulder and turned.

What he didn't tell Beto was that "La Rose" came from the name of the captivating Paul Delvaux painting that he'd just picked up at Sotheby's. *Eighteen million was probably a tad pricey for the Belgian surrealist,* Perrine thought, rolling his sleeves back down, *but, hey, you can't take it with you.*

Arthur was waiting for him outside the front door of the barn, holding his cream-colored jacket. Perrine slipped back into it and shot the cuffs.

"Arthur," he said.

"Yes, Mr. Perrine?"

"A plane will be coming in about twenty minutes with quite a few, uh, lake-house guests aboard."

Arthur nodded without batting an eyelash. The lake house was where the men liked to blow off steam after the bonus-party festivities. Morning cleanup usually involved hoses and shovels, but boys will be boys.

"Are those new cameras that I ordered installed?"

"They went online yesterday with a closed-circuit feed into your bedroom, as you insisted," Arthur said. "Shall I have Hector and Junior waiting with the van at the airfield?"

"Yes, you shall, Arthur. Please remind them and the rest of the staff that these are special guests. Guests who will be treated with the utmost respect."

Perrine smiled proudly as he walked with his manservant toward his glittering pool, the tiers of manicured gardens, his magnificent mansion.

"That is, until I kill them, of course," he said.

Chapter 90

AFTER ANOTHER HALF HOUR, it looked like we'd gotten everything we were going to get out of Tomás Neves.

Between dunkings, he told us he had taken Perrine to a San Diego cartel house with a tunnel in its basement that went under the border. The tunnel exited in a tire shop, where a waiting car took Perrine to a plane at the Tijuana Airport.

He claimed that the plane had taken Perrine to an estate in Mexico near Real del Monte, where a party was going to take place. A chatty Salvajes cartel underling with whom he had coordinated Perrine's transfer had bragged to him that his older brother had been invited to a blacktie function there tonight for what was called a bonus ceremony.

Suitcases of money would be ceremoniously

handed out as hookers were brought in by the busload. Neves told us it was common knowledge that nothing made Perrine happier than drinking and carousing with his most efficient and most brutal soldiers.

At first, I thought, *What a load of bullshit*, but then I thought again. Perrine was amazingly cocky and arrogant. What better way to show how ballsy he was than to start a war with the US and then throw a party for his men.

As Neves was disseminating this information, I was in constant contact with Emily, who was outside, working her phone, firing off everything we learned to the LAPD task force so they could compare it with the flowchart we'd been building on Perrine's cartel. The cops and agents back at the shop were, in turn, collating everything through FBI, CIA, NSA, and DEA databases.

The first glimmer of hope came when she called into the basement.

"San Diego SWAT just hit the address Neves gave us, Mike. There really is a tunnel. And Mexican authorities confirm that a private plane did leave from the Tijuana Airport this morning at eight a.m."

We were passing around a box of Pop-Tarts

twenty minutes later, gearing up for some more tubby time with Neves, when there was a knock on the sliding-glass door.

"A DEA undercover in Cancún just drove up to a hacienda outside Real del Monte," Emily said breathlessly as I opened it. "He got a hit on one of the Salvajes cell numbers we have. Not only that, but the CIA just learned that the estate in question used to be owned by Perrine! Word is, they're taking this as actionable intelligence. We need to get rolling. JSOC is calling a meeting back at the base."

I left Neves with Diaz and Bassman and raced with Emily back to the SoCal Logistics Airport. After we badged our way through the guard booth, it was obvious some fires had been lit.

It was like someone had dropped a pinball into one of those kinetic mousetrap sculptures. Uniformed soldiers were pouring in and out of the dormitories and hangars. Dozens of bearded Navy SEALs and Delta Force operators clustered in small groups, loading guns and equipment kit bags as soldiers with clipboards did flight prep on the Black Hawk and Little Bird choppers out on the tarmac.

As we walked into the task force's war room, a

video teleconference with Washington and one of the JSOC generals was under way. Beside it in the split screen was a satellite image of a compound with a huge house, a pool, gardens.

Colonel D'Ambrose, sitting at the rear of the room, cracked the door and came out when he saw us.

"They sent up a drone," he said. "What your contact said is true. There's an enormous amount of activity going on at the estate. Not only that, CIA is still doing some forensic work on the imaging, but they think they spotted Perrine riding a horse on one of the mountain trails. The Defense Department is in conference right now with the president. We just got word that the president wants Perrine in a body bag. We're going in tonight under cover of darkness with everything we got."

"We did it, Mike? We found Perrine?" Emily said as she collapsed in an office chair, rubbing her eyes.

"I don't give a shit about him, Emily," I said. "We need to find my family."

Chapter 91

IT LOOKED LIKE THE set of a spaghetti Western, or maybe Wile E. Coyote's stomping grounds, rolling beneath my feet by midnight that night. Below was a wilderness of windswept desert, small buttes, and mesas. All of it was tinged green through the night-vision goggles I was wearing.

I shifted my weight to wake my numb butt, perched on the cold, hard vibrating metal floor of the Black Hawk chopper. It'd taken some favor calling and even more finagling by Emily, but in the end, we were able to go on the raid on one of the supporting Black Hawks with the FBI's hostage rescue team and some CIA personnel. Emily had emphasized my past personal contact with Perrine and my ability to ID him. I could ID him, all right, and was really looking forward to some more personal contact.

The dozen nap-of-the-earth airborne heli-copters in our armada included Black Hawks and Little Birds, two Cobra attack helicopters, and even a twin-bladed Chinook filled with a contingent of first-recon marines. Far above, somewhere among the glittering stars, there was even an AC-130 Spectre gunship bristling with machine guns and mortars and Hellfire missiles to back us up.

Not knowing what to expect, the Pentagon had broken out the entire toolbox. Which couldn't have made me happier. Perrine and his cartel were for all intents and purposes no different from an enemy army. It was finally time to deal with them as such.

It had been mostly flat desert, but as we flew, the terrain suddenly started to change. From the flat desert floor, low, corrugated hills with more vegetation began to rise. Soon the hills turned into majestic, rugged cliffs and sheer mountain-stream-filled valleys.

"We are coming in, in five," a voice called over the radio. A minute later, we went past a ridge, and Perrine's house was there. The Unabomber's cabin this was not. The satellite images hadn't done it justice. The dramatically lit, breathtaking French Second Empire mansion looked like a block someone had airlifted from the Champs-Élysées and plunked down in the middle of the Mexican mountains. Every one of its lights was blazing on its marble steps and columns like it was an opera house on opening night.

There were soccer fields, several barns, something that looked like a racetrack. At the rear of the house were illuminated gardens that tiered down and down to a massive, magnificent, softly lit tiled pool. Beyond the pool was a runway with three corporate jets parked at its end.

No wonder the US government hadn't told the Mexicans about the raid. How could this opulent palace so boldly exist out here in the middle of nowhere without their knowledge or consent?

The answer was, it couldn't. Staring down at the compound, I knew the rumor that Perrine was more powerful than the Mexican president was a hundred percent true.

Chapter 92

AS WE CAME CLOSER, I tightened my helmet's chin strap and checked the safety on my M4. I winked at Emily, across from me, to hide my mounting anxiety. Like me and the rest of the HR team, she was loaded for bear, dressed in black combat fatigues and strapped down with guns and gear. She winked back, then crossed herself and started praying.

As I was about to join her, an alarm suddenly went off in the forward cabin's glowing console. It sounded like a police whistle followed by a fire alarm.

There was a lot of excited chatter over the tactical line. Before you could say *surface-to-air missile*, a white streak whooshed up off the slope to left. As I watched in stark, helpless, gaping horror, the corkscrewing streak connected with the forward rotor of the Chinook, at the end of our column of aircraft. There was an air-cracking boom and a bright flash of light, and the Chinook was spinning and dropping, spiraling downward like a spinning leaf in October.

"Chalk three is hit!" came a voice over the mike. "Hard landing! Hard landing!"

Another sizzling corkscrewing missile flew up, just missing the Black Hawk across from us. Down through its wafting contrail, I could see men on the roof of a small cinder-block house perched on the edge of a ridge.

"Roof left! Roof left!" someone shouted over the line as one of the Cobra attack helicopters broke rank and dove toward the house.

I almost wet myself when its electric machine gun went off. It sounded like something caught in a shredder, or a massive industrial accident at a power plant. With an extended, sizzling, spine-tingling zap, a blinding white rope of bullets and tracers the size of Coke bottles beamed down out of the attack chopper, into the structure.

As the helicopter continued to rain lead, the second Cobra swiveled up and around on its axis like a record, and not one but two rockets sledded off from beneath its underbelly and downward in an exhilarating shower of sparks. A split second later, the guardhouse, or whatever it had been, disappeared in a blinding, three-story *pa-pow*ing blossom of white light. The concussion of the explosion that came a sliver of a second later whapped warm against my skin where I sat on the wobbling deck of the Black Hawk.

"We have small-arms fire!" someone said redundantly as from all around the well-lit house and compound, small flashes of light began to sprout. I clapped my hands over my ears when the gunner in the door of our chopper suddenly opened up with his .50 caliber. The sound of its empty brass shells pinging off the metal wall beside my head sounded like a hyped-up jazz drummer hitting the high hats.

I looked forward, behind the mansion, when I heard a tremendous thumping.

"It's the AC-One-Thirty," one of the FBI commandos said as the runway was chewed up by massive explosions.

"Hoo-rah!" someone yelled as one of the corporate jets was blown to smithereens.

It was quite satisfying for me to witness the awesome might of our military finally brought to bear and unleashed on Perrine and his inhumanly abhorrent organization. For a moment, listening to our guns, I forgot about everything. How mad I was. How afraid I was for my family.

Then the joy was gone as quickly as it had come as the Black Hawk descended toward the yard behind the compound's wall. I closed my eyes and prayed to God that we weren't too late.

Chapter 93

THE BLACK HAWK STAYED in a hover as the HRT guys started fast-roping down into a dusty yard alongside the compound's largest barn. The original plan was to land here with the marines in the Chinook, but obviously we were on to plan B.

With the advance team on the ground, the Black Hawk lowered and landed. I'd just noticed that barn's roof was on fire when someone came out of it. It was an old man with a blanket over his shoulders.

"Look out!" I yelled as the blanket exploded. Buckshot rattled off the side of the chopper and into the roof of the cabin beside me. One of the hostage rescue guys went down, clutching his thigh. There was a barrage of return M4 fire, and the old guy stiffened and dropped forward like the tailgate of a pickup truck.

Just as the old man hit the ground, the barn door burst open, and out came a bunch of horses. It happened so suddenly, I almost fell out of the helicopter. Two of the horses were actually on fire! Then I saw a lump on one of the horses on the far side of the galloping herd.

I looked through the sight of my rifle.

You've got to be kidding me.

The lump was a handsome, light-skinned black man in a tuxedo shirt and black pants.

I was just about to pull the trigger when Perrine disappeared on the horse, around the other side of the barn. I leaned to the side and slapped the pilot chopper on his back.

"Up! Up!" I screamed as I clicked the rifle's selector to full auto.

Up we went. Straight up like an express elevator. Perrine had broken away from the rest of the herd and was kicking his horse like a madman as he raced it toward the huge main house. He was just alongside the Olympic-sized pool when I braced myself against the wall of the heli and zeroed my sights. The M4 softly tapped my shoulder as I pulled the trigger and held it.

Through the Advanced Combat Optical Gunsight, I watched the horse go down and sideways onto the apron of the pool at full speed, sliding on the tile. There was a tremendous splash. Perrine and the horse were in the pool!

I backslapped the pilot again, but he was already ahead of me, swinging the bird over. He was still about twenty feet above the pool when I leaped from the chopper's side and dropped in a pencil dive.

It was a direct hit. From two stories up, my two hundred and ten pounds, plus the fifty pounds of gun and vest and tactical gear I was carrying, landed flush on Perrine's back like a bomb. The hard sole of my right combat boot connected with the back of his head as the left one crunched between his shoulder blades.

He was pulling himself out of the pool at the time, and the impact bashed the holy living shit out of his face against the metal railing. I found out later that I'd not only broken Perrine's nose again, I'd cracked open the orbital bone around his eye and fractured his cheekbone and knocked out half his teeth. He wasn't done, though. Of course he wasn't. This was Manuel "The Sun King" Perrine.

My gun went flying as the water rushed up.

Chapter 94

AS I PLUNGED INTO the pool, I clawed out my right hand and managed to hook Perrine's belt.

We went under the warm water. I remember thinking vaguely that I would have to get the heavy Kevlar vest off me. But that was for later. As we sank like a stone, the image off to my right was like something out of a Salvador Dalí painting. The horse was thrashing on the floor of the brightly lit pool's deep end, bubbles exploding from its flared nostrils, blood geysering from its bullet wounds like puffs of red smoke.

Perrine was thrashing, too, scratching back at my face, trying to kick me. But from where I was positioned, behind and beneath him, pulling him down like an anchor, he couldn't land anything solid. I grabbed his belt with my other hand and pulled with everything I had.

My boots hit the bottom of the pool when he finally caught me good with the heel of his shoe. Its sharp edge opened my face down the left side of my nose to my chin, adding my own spurting blood to the pool. By twisting around, he broke my grip somehow. As he swung toward me, I suddenly remembered from Perrine's bio that he had been some sort of French frogman commando.

Instead of trying to get to the surface, Perrine reached down and grabbed my head in his enormous hands and tried to snap my neck. Luckily, it didn't work. Was he too tired? The water pressure too strong? I don't know. It hurt like hell. He'd definitely pulled some muscles, but my neck stayed intact.

Still, he wasn't done. Perrine thumbed one of my eyes, and then his hands were wrapped around my throat. The half of his face that wasn't smashed up grinned at me as he throttled me. I kicked off the pool floor and lurched forward, head-butting him, but still he held on.

Struggling to break his grip, I finally spotted the tactical survival knife strapped to my leg. I ripped it out and stabbed upward at Perrine for all I was worth.

The knife was ripped from my hand as I hit something good. The pressure on my neck disappeared as Perrine let go of me and went up. Watching him go, I could see the handle of the knife buried to its hilt above his left knee.

There were cries of "Freeze! Freeze! Freeze!" when I exploded onto the surface. It was the FBI hostage rescue team I'd flown in with. Half of them were crouched in a defensive perimeter ten feet away from the pool's edge. The other half were facing the pool itself, the laser sights of their H&K MP7s dancing on the drenched chest of Perrine, who had somehow yanked himself out of the drink and now was lying on his back beside an overturned tray of hors d'oeuvres.

My strained neck started killing me as I doggy-paddled to the pool's edge and grabbed the ladder. In the distance by the house, there was still gunfire, but it was becoming sporadic.

I looked to my right as I heard a bomblike splash of water. It was the horse. It had somehow made its way to the surface. I watched as it splashed to the shallow end and leaped out, clicking over the tiles before it disappeared into the darkness.

Chapter 95

THE SPECIAL FORCES MEDIC assigned to our team patched me up as best as he could. He taped a ridiculously large bandage to my face and put me in a neck brace.

The entire fight had taken twenty minutes. We'd killed or captured forty-three cartel members, most of the drug-dealing assholes in attendance. We listened to the radio as the Special Forces secured the mansion and the rest of the compound. I waited breathlessly to be told that my family had been found, but it didn't happen.

Where the hell were they?

After a few minutes, Emily heard from Command that the local *federales* were now coming to join the party. It was to make up for the fact that we had flagrantly invaded Mexican airspace and conducted a covert raid without even so much as a phone call to the new Mexican president's office.

It pissed me off that the story would be that the Mexican government had helped. Forget the fact that Perrine had been hiding right out in the open, that very high-up people in the Mexican government were quite obviously on Perrine's payroll. *Back to political-bullshit business as usual*, I thought. *The same old lies, the same old situation.*

With the scene mostly secured, the hostage rescue team decided to move Perrine up to the main house. A few minutes after being pulled from the pool, he had fallen unconscious. He was still breathing, but his blood pressure was becoming a concern, and they thought, with his head trauma and blood loss, that he might be going into shock.

I insisted on helping with his stretcher. I desperately needed him to regain enough consciousness to tell me where my family was. We took Perrine up through his Hanging Gardens of Babylon, through the back of the mansion, and pigeonholed him in a ground-floor office.

As the medics worked on trying to get him awake, I decided to scour the house for any sign of my family. The inside was as opulent as the outside, if that were possible. Twenty-foot coffered ceilings, wedding-cake moldings. In the jaw-dropping, ballroom-like kitchen was an island slabbed with some kind of blue gemstone.

Some Delta Force guys were sitting on it, passing around a bottle of Dom Pérignon. Beside them was a long-faced guy handcuffed to a chair.

"Who's this?" I asked them.

"He says he's the butler," said one of the commandos, with a southern drawl. "He also claims he *no habla inglés*, but look at him. Look at those tombstone chompers on him. This guy's a Brit if I ever saw one."

"The butler, huh?" I said, immediately drawing my Glock. A round was already chambered in the pipe. I'd dealt with the fabulously rich before, back in Manhattan, and knew that butlers, like doormen, know everything.

"Whoa! Whoa! Whoa! Chill out!" the southern Delta Force guy said as I pressed the barrel under the guy's chin.

I ignored him as I stared into the butler's eyes.

"One question," I said. "One chance to get it right. A plane arrived after Perrine. There were prisoners in it. Where are they?"

"Up at the lake house," he said with an upper-crust British accent. "There's a road behind the runway."

Chapter 96

MINUTES LATER, I WAS roaring up the mountain road behind the runway on the back of one of the four-wheelers the Delta Force guys had wisely thought to bring with them.

As we were pulling into the front yard, AK-47 fire raked the dirt in front of us.

"Guess we didn't get all of them!" I screamed as I dove off the vehicle and rolled behind a low stone wall.

The Delta Force guys seemed much less fazed by the turn of events. Instead of retreating, they sped even faster forward on the four-wheelers, pouring deadly-accurate fire into the window as they went. Some big Delta Force psycho, who I learned later had played right tackle for Georgia Tech, actually drove his four-wheeler up onto the porch and put his size-fourteen boot to the door's lock.

Half of the door's frame was actually ripped off as he caved it in. Then one of his buddies threw in something I'd never heard of before. Not just one flash-bang grenade, but a whole firecracker pack of them suddenly went off.

They poured into the house behind the deafening banging. I rushed in behind them, eyes scanning the corners of the rooms I ran past. There was a bar, red couches, rococo mirrors. My family couldn't be here. This wasn't happening. I almost got sick. It looked like a brothel of some sort.

"Bennett! Back here! Back here!" one of the Delta Force guys cried.

I burst into a room.

How can men be so evil? I thought, looking around. *Just how?*

There were children.

Crouching fearfully on stained mattresses were about a dozen twelve- or thirteen-year-old girls. Relief flowed through me as I put my light on their tragic faces and realized that they weren't my kids.

Then the relief disappeared as my dread flooded back. If my guys weren't here, then where the hell were they?

Chapter 97

A FIVE-TRUCK CONTINGENT of Mexican *federales* and military had arrived by the time we raced back to the main house. Inside, six or seven Mexican soldiers were standing out in front of the door to the office where Perrine had been secured.

"What the hell is going on?" I said to Emily, who had her phone to her ear.

"The Mexicans are claiming they need to interrogate Perrine. Washington told us to back off. We had to let them."

"Is Perrine conscious?" I asked.

"I think so. Just barely," Emily said.

"I need to talk to him, Emily," I said as I walked toward the office. "My family wasn't up at that house. They didn't come in on that second plane. I need to know where they are."

"Calm down, Mike. You'll get your chance," Emily whispered. "Sit tight and let the honchos hash it out first. This is a delicate situation."

"Not gonna happen," I said, turning and marching past her, toward the guards. "No more hashing."

A crackerjack-looking, silver-haired Mexican soldier in a beret stepped in front of the door with his hands behind his back as I approached.

"May I help you?" he said with a smile.

"I'm United States law enforcement," I said, showing him my federal badge. "That man has been placed under arrest by me, and I need to speak with my prisoner."

His smile didn't waver.

"Impossible," he said as his men stepped up beside him menacingly. "This is Mexican soil and a Mexican matter. If you persist in annoying me, I shall be forced to place *you* under arrest."

I stared at him, trying to figure his angle. *Will they try to take Perrine?* I thought. *Is that it?*

I turned at a sound behind me to find my new Delta Force pals filling the hallway.

"Well, if you continue annoying my buddy," said the monster soldier who'd smashed in the lake house door, "me and my friends will be forced to place you fellas *underground, comprende?* Now open that door!"

That was when it happened.

From the other side of the door came a crisp, sudden POP!

I bulled my way in past the Mexican colonel and through the door.

Perrine was still sitting on the stretcher we'd brought him in on, with his hands cuffed behind his back. He was shot through the head, and his brains were blown out against the marble lintel of the fireplace.

Another colonel inside the office shrugged as he holstered his pistol.

"I had no choice. He was trying to escape."

I realized it then. They were cleaning up. Perrine knew too much. About the government, how far the corruption went. And still my family was missing. They'd killed the only man who knew where they were. Would this nightmare never end?

I lunged for the bastard who'd killed Perrine, but I didn't get a foot before someone grabbed me from behind. There was a lot of shoving, a lot of cursing in two languages, but it finally died down. I started shaking as I broke free and headed for the mansion's back door to the backyard, where they had just brought some of the Salvajes cartel guys they'd captured.

Someone is going to tell me where my family is, I thought as I reached for the handle of the French door.

I hadn't gotten it halfway open when Emily slammed into me. She was grinning as she shoved a phone into my hand. I put it to my ear.

"Mike? Mike? Is that you?" said a voice. It was an Irish voice, an Irish woman's voice.

I took the phone off my ear and stared at it. For a moment, I thought I was hallucinating. I slid to the floor. I put the phone back to my ear.

"Mary Catherine?" I said. "Mary Catherine?"

"Mike!" Mary Catherine said. "Oh, thank God, Mike."

"But how—? Where—?" I sputtered. "Are you OK? Are the kids OK?"

"We're all fine, Mike. The children, Seamus, me, and Mr. Cody are fine."

Chapter 98

"WHAT? HOW? WHERE?" CAME Mike's voice from the old CB receiver in front of Mary Catherine. She pressed the red key with her thumb.

"Don't worry, Mike. We're hiding out in a place not too far from Mr. Cody's, a safe place," she said, and let the button off.

"But the cartel sent a video of them kicking in the front door in the middle of the night," Mike said from the boxy unit's speaker. "I thought you were kidnapped. I don't understand."

"For the last day, we've been hiding out at Mr. McMurphy's house, up in the hills north of Mr. Cody's," Mary Catherine said. "We would have called you sooner, but there's no phone service up here. I'm actually talking to you over Mr. McMurphy's CB that he uses when he needs to contact someone."

"A CB?"

"Yes. Mr. McMurphy contacts his friend a few miles away on the radio band, and then his friend patches him through to a phone. But the friend was away for a few days and just got back. That's why we haven't been able to contact you."

"Wait. McMurphy?" I said. "Who the hell is he?"

"A nice man from town. He said he met you at church a few weeks ago when Seamus filled in to say Mass."

I shook my head in disbelief as I remembered the Nick Nolte-ish hippie with the gun.

"Him?" I said. "How did he get involved?"

"Up here in the hills, he's got a, um, unique farm, Mike. He keeps a low profile because of the business he's in. He also keeps his eyes and ears open. He heard through the grapevine in town about the cartel looking around for us. He was coming by to tell us that we were in danger right as the cartel was heading for the house.

"He came in the back door and woke us up and walked us down in the dark through one of the neighboring farms, to his truck. He drove us up to his place in the hills, and we're still here."

"So I'm not dreaming?" Mike said. "You're all alive and well?"

"You'll not get rid of us that easy," Mary Catherine said. "I'd put the kids on the phone, but they're exhausted, and I'd just as soon let them sleep. Now that the coast seems clear, Mr. McMurphy is going to drive us down to the Susanville PD in the morning. How does that sound?"

Chapter 99

ON AN OLD DIRT mining road in the rugged hills northeast of Susanville, in a place called the Tunnison Mountain Wilderness Study Area, a boxy Land Rover Defender with a whip antenna attached to its roof suddenly stopped as Vida Gomez put a hand to the driver's chest.

She adjusted away the static on the radio monitor she held just in time to hear Bennett answer the nanny loud and clear in her earbud.

"That sounds good. I'm on my way back. I'll meet you there."

"My God! It's him!" Vida said. "It's Bennett himself. Tell me you're getting this!"

In the seat behind her, Eduardo checked the frequency on her radio monitor, then rapidly clicked at a laptop that was attached to the antenna.

The screen showing their present GPS location locked for a moment, and then a pin appeared, showing the estimated position of the transmission.

The pin began to pulse strongly as the nanny said good night to Bennett.

Eduardo checked the screen against his compass and the geological survey map spread out on the seat beside him. He had worked in the signal corps of the Colombian government catching narcoterrorists before he had met Perrine and switched sides. There was no one better in the cartel at radio tracking than he.

He pointed to the juniper-covered hill beside them, toward a stand of trees.

"The nanny and Bennett's kids are less than a mile up there somewhere," he said.

Vida got on the radio, and after a minute, another 4x4, an FJ Cruiser, rolled down the steep incline of the mining road from the opposite direction.

"You have a hit?" Estefan said from behind the FJ's wheel.

"We just heard Bennett and the nanny," Vida said excitedly. "The software is saying we are within a mile, that they're up in those trees."

"Good," Estefan said. "About two hundred feet

back up the road, I saw a tire track going that way."

Vida smiled. She knew that the play after finding the Bennett safe house empty was to come up here to Northern California and conduct the search herself. Their contacts in town had put them onto an old, half-mad hippie doper who lived somewhere around here. His name was McMurphy, and not only had he given the cartel trouble in the past, but he'd actually been seen talking to the Bennetts at church.

She had tried to contact Perrine several times for running orders, but he wasn't answering. It was his party, she knew. She could picture him in his tux, presiding over the events.

She felt a tug of envy at not being invited. No matter. In the back of the Rover were twelve air-shipment boxes with dry ice. Twelve little boxes that would be packed with twelve Bennett heads and would be on their way to Real del Monte by morning. Manuel would know soon enough her devotion to him.

Around Vida's neck, on a gold chain, was the emerald ring Perrine had given her after she'd finally broken him down and they'd made love the last day of his stay. They didn't use protection, and it was the middle of her cycle. She hadn't taken a test, but she knew she was pregnant with his baby. It would be a boy, as handsome as his father.

Everyone had said what a charming man he was, but he was far better than just that. In their time together, he had been so kind to her, asked about her daughters, her life. He was like a father to her, or at least what she thought a father might be like, having never actually had one.

She sighed as a full-body tingle glowed all around her. Her, Vida. A simple farm girl. She'd always known she was special. That things would change for the better. And they would be getting better beyond her wildest dreams. For now, inside her, growing, was the Sun Prince.

"Vida!" said Estefan.

"Yes?" she said, shaking off the daydream.

"Shall we drive a little farther in or leave the cars here and walk?"

Vida grabbed her machine pistol and opened the door.

"Let's walk, but quickly," she said. "I want out of this shithole before the sun comes up."

Chapter 100

McMURPHY CAME IN AND placed a cup of tea in front of Mary Catherine as she hung up the CB.

"Did you get in contact with Mike?" he asked, plopping down in a camp chair.

"Yes, I did," Mary Catherine said, taking a sip. "Don't worry. I didn't tell him where we are. I wouldn't want you or your, eh, farm to get into trouble with the law or anyone else, after all you've done for us. Actually, I couldn't have told him if I'd wanted to. I don't know where we are."

McMurphy laughed.

"Heck, sometimes even I get lost out here," the burly sixty-year-old said. "But I figured remote is what the doctor ordered, with those bad old Mexican cowboys after you. This is the safest place I thought to bring you to."

The McMurphy Mountain Compound was actually pretty incredible. Instead of the run-down shack and marijuana fields she was expecting, his home was a sophisticated and elaborate underground bunker. Built almost directly into the side of a hill, his hobbit hole, as he called it, consisted of twenty old school-bus frames welded together in a long corridor with rooms T-ing off to the right and left.

Convinced of an impending nuclear attack, he'd built the complex in the eighties with some friends. Over a few months, they'd brought up the old buses one by one on a 4x4 flatbed, dug out the hill, welded them all together, and then buried them again.

He told her that when the nuclear winter didn't materialize, he slowly started to move his already flourishing marijuana farm underground, out of sight from the nosy feds. Most of the rooms were currently being used as hydroponic marijuana grow rooms, but there was also a kitchen, a gun room, a workshop, and several bedrooms stacked with bunk beds, where the kids now slept.

It had heat, ventilation, electricity run off propane, fresh water. Even two neat and clean bathrooms with showers and working toilets.

It wasn't just the compound that was surprising. McMurphy, despite his frazzled, nutty appearance, had been so nice and gentle with the children. Before he had brought the children in, he had closed and securely locked the doors to all the grow rooms. Like any gracious host, he made sure that everyone was comfortable and well fed. He didn't have any video games, but he had Monopoly and Scrabble and cards and a dartboard.

He'd shown the children the collections on the mantelpiece of rocks that he had found on his wanderings, pointing out the petrified sea creatures in them, put there millions of years in the past when the Sierra Madre had been the floor of an ancient sea.

The bus room in which they were now sitting McMurphy called the library. It was actually quite cozy. A mounted bull's head hung above a chess set. On the walls were shelves bursting with books, mechanical engineering tomes and leather-bound geology texts beside precarious columns of yellowed paperbacks.

There were also hundreds of framed photographs. McMurphy in wrestling tights, McMurphy in a Green Beret army uniform with his arm around a couple of other soldiers. A lot of them were of hippie people from the sixties. There was a shot of an absolutely beautiful blond woman in a top hat under a tree, playing the flute. One of a young, bearded McMurphy with some other long-haired and bearded blond men wearing Jesus shirts, sitting around a campfire. There was even a shot of some long-haired children in their bathing suits on the shore of a lake, playing with ponies and goats and dogs.

Mary Catherine gestured at the photographs.

"What's your story, Mr. McMurphy?" she said. "How'd you do all this?"

"Didn't I already tell you we dug out the side of the hill with a bulldozer and buried the buses one by one and welded them together like Legos?"

"I meant more like *why*," Mary Catherine said. "Why are you here in this place? How'd you get here, if you don't mind me prying?"

McMurphy sighed and leaned back as he crossed his legs.

"You want my story, huh? Hmmm. Let's see. I grew up outside San Fran. Five kids in the family. Dad was a plumber. My mom was a night-shift nurse at a mental hospital. I wrestled in high school and got good enough to get a scholarship to Berkeley. I was just about to get my mechanical engineering degree when a fit of conscience made me drop out and hitch up with the army.

"When I returned to the States, I somehow found myself hanging out in Berkeley with a group of writers and artists and drug addicts that would end up being called the Merry Pranksters. I actually stayed at Ken Kesey's house for a while. I really admired the wild and free, independent way he was living. The parties were a true goof."

"I can imagine," Mary Catherine said.

"Wanna bet?" McMurphy said, winking at her. "Anyway, one day in late 'sixty-eight, instead of relaxing and just having some innocent fun, these new people came to the house and started talking about the masses and the classes and starting a political movement, and I got straight right the heck out of there. I eventually ended up here with some friends, living off the grid, off the land."

"Who's the pretty lady with the flute?"

"She was my woman for a while. We had three kids. They're gone now, obviously. Took off in the early eighties, when I started building this bomb shelter. Everybody's gone. Just me now. The last of the Mohicans. Bilbo McMurphy, the last hobbit, at your service."

He looked around the room, wincing.

"I know how I must look to you. Like some weird old hippie survivalist, right? You're thinking this mole-like freak is off his rocker to be living in a hole in the ground."

"You saved all our lives, Mr. McMurphy," Mary Catherine said. "What I think of you is that your home is incredible, and that you're a very good man."

McMurphy smiled, genuinely surprised.

"You do? Really?"

"Yes, of course," Mary Catherine said.

"In that case," McMurphy said, retrieving a Zippo and a pot pipe from his pocket, "do you want to smoke some dope with me?"

Mary Catherine shook her head, disappointed.

"No, Mr. McMurphy," she said. "Remember our deal with the children here. Unfortunately, your home will have to remain a dope-free zone until we leave."

McMurphy sighed as he put the pipe away.

"Oh, well. Different strokes and all that," he said, standing and yawning. "Good night, now. Get the kiddies up early, and we'll leave at first light."

Chapter 101

MARY CATHERINE HAD JUST laid her head down on one of the bomb shelter's bunk beds when the beeping sound started.

She went out into the hall area to find McMurphy running like mad toward the front of the compound.

"What is it?"

"Motion detector!" he yelled, more animated than Mary Catherine had ever seen him. "Outside perimeter's been breached! I knew it. Sector B. It was the CB. They must have picked it up. Dammit! Just like the damn cops. These freaks must have ways of scanning for radio signals."

She followed him as he ran into the gun room and spun the combo on the green locker's Master lock. Inside, shining with gun oil, was an arsenal.

Tactical shotguns, scoped hunting rifles, several M-16s. McMurphy pulled out one of the automatic rifles and slipped in a magazine with a loud clacking sound. He threw ten or so other magazines into a bag and tossed the bag and rifle over his shoulder.

"What are you doing?" Mary Catherine asked.

"If they find one of the ventilation shafts, they could do anything. Plug it up, smoke us out. Didn't I see on the news that they're using some sort of poison-gas chemical weapon? They'll kill us in a heartbeat. I'm going outside to make sure that doesn't happen."

McMurphy started going toward the back of the bus complex.

"Isn't the front door the other way?" Mary Catherine said.

"I can't go out the front. Are you crazy? I need to go out through the tunnels."

"The tunnels?"

"I forgot to tell you about them," he said as he pulled up the handle of a door at the rear of the main corridor. On its other side was a dirt tunnel about four feet tall, strung with lightbulbs.

"I've been digging tunnels for years and years. Out the back of the complex, all through this hill.

It's actually what I did in Vietnam. Cleared the tunnels. They called us tunnel rats. The ones I built are just like the ones I saw in Cu Chi. Hell, better. Just shut the back door behind me. No, wait. Dammit, almost forgot."

He suddenly ran back toward the gun room, where he began flipping through a CD-filled shoe box.

"Give me five," he said, suddenly handing Mary Catherine a disk, "and then put this on the CD setup there and crank it!"

"What? Why?"

"I got speakers strung up in the trees all along the slope, strobe lights. We used to use it for parties, drop a couple of tabs and go on nature walks. We were really into mind expansion for a few years. Anyway, we can use it now. It'll wake these murdering bastards right up! Ha, damn right this'll teach them!

"Remember, lock the door behind me, now," the merry prankster called as he ran off and disappeared around a corner of the tunnel.

Mary Catherine closed the bus door behind him before she looked at the CD case.

AC/DC.

Highway to Hell.

Chapter 102

IT TOOK THEM TWENTY minutes to find the clearing with the double-wide trailer. Looking down at it from the rim of a ridge, Vida found the pale, low structure, sitting there all by itself in the center of the flattened hillside clearing, strangely iconic. Like a temple. Like a tomb.

It's a tomb, all right, she thought, going down the pitch-black slope on the rocky, narrow trail behind Eduardo, Estefan, and Jorge. *The Bennett Tomb.*

It was when they neared the bottom of the trail that she felt it. There was something subtle and subliminal, like a kind of ground hum in the air. *Or is it me?* she thought. Some kind of pressure change on her eardrum from the altitude?

When the sound came a moment later out of

the dead silence, she fell immediately to her knees, thinking she'd literally been hit with something, a rocket or a bolt of lightning. Then, from all around her, the buzz-saw electric guitar chord repeated again, speeding faster as drums kicked in.

Living easy, living free, season ticket on a one-way ride, shrieked a rough, joyously unhinged voice.

Rock music? But from where? she wondered, trying to think. She scanned around. Were there speakers in the trees? In the ground?

The first "Highway to Hell" refrain had just started when the lights came on. Floodlighting from the trees beside the trailer suddenly bathed the entire slope they were standing on, completely exposing them. Then the lights started to strobe. It was like the whole desert hill had suddenly been moved to the middle of a dance-hall club. What the hell was this?

She was flipping up the now-useless night-vision goggles when the gunfire erupted. Estefan, in a crouch at the front of the line, suddenly dropped forward and slid down the trail face-first. Eduardo, behind him, starting to backpedal, suddenly sat down and began rolling after him.

"Back! Back!" Vida screamed, pushing Jorge behind her.

She could feel heavy slugs slam into the dirt at her heels and off the rocks beside where she'd just been standing as she retreated back up the hill. As gunfire popped up dust on the trail, she looked around for muzzle flashes to return fire at, but she couldn't make out a damn thing because of the strobing lights.

She dove over some rocks at the top of the trail and lay flat, gasping, her heart trembling. The hard-rock music chomped on like a chain saw carving at the night. She knew it was just a tactic, but it put a chill through her just the same. This was no pushover they were going up against!

She cursed herself as she crawled through dirt toward the grass berm where her last man was hugging the ground. She'd gotten sloppy, and two of her best soldiers had paid for it with their lives. It was just her now, and Jorge, the young up-and-comer in the group. Just great.

She had to think. The trailer sitting there in the middle of the clearing with only one way down to it had obviously been a decoy, some kind of trap. There would be others.

She scanned the ridge above the clearing for the next logical point at which to take up a firing position on the trailer. She found it thirty seconds later. Off the trail to the left, about twenty-five yards through the brush, was an outcropping of rock that one could lie on and from which one could fire down on the trailer with pretty good cover.

She grabbed Jorge and pointed at the flat rock.

"Crawl over to that ledge and lay fire on that trailer and keep position until I tell you otherwise!" she screamed over the music.

Vida watched him go over the sights of her machine pistol. Jorge had emptied a magazine out of his AK-47 and was putting in another when it happened.

A clump of grass on the hill behind him suddenly, incredibly disappeared. From where the grass had been, a silhouetted figure rose up. He bobbed straight up out of the ground, silently, like a carnival-game Whac-A-Mole.

Only this mole was holding a rifle.

Chapter 103

THE SHADOWED FIGURE AND Vida fired simultaneously. Jorge pitched forward and off the outcropping as the figure disappeared.

Vida arrived out of breath at the spot where she'd seen the figure and looked down and stood there, gaping. She clicked on her flashlight. There was a hole in the ground with some kind of trapdoor attached to a chimneylike passageway with a ladder. At the bottom of the ladder lay a squat, gray-haired man, staring up at her with the side of his head shot open.

Vida laughed. *The hippie! How do you like that?* She'd done it! She'd truly whacked the mole!

Vida let out a breath as "Highway to Hell" ended. So that was where they were. The hippie had hidden the Bennetts literally underground.

No matter. She'd grabbed victory from the jaws of defeat. Even with her two friends dead, she could still pull this off and get back to Mexico with her twelve little boxed presents.

Vida changed the magazine in her pistol and slung it over her shoulder as she grabbed the ladder's first rung and lowered herself. Slowly, ever so slowly, Vida made her way along the low-ceilinged corridor. It was strung with lights and had wooden loading skids for a floor. It looked just like the tunnel under the border at San Diego that had brought her into the country.

She turned a hard right-hand, ninety-degree corner, and there was a door. *What the hell?* The door was yellow and had rounded edges, like the door of a school bus.

Before Vida could take another step, the bus door opened inward.

Vida gasped at the young woman standing there. Her pale face, her blond hair. It was the nanny! The nanny, with a black gun in her hands.

Vida raised the machine pistol. She had brought it as far as her waist when the deafening shotgun blast sounded, taking off most of her left shoulder and the left side of her face.

Suddenly, Vida was sitting on the tunnel's floor,

still gripping the pistol. But, try as she might, she was unable to lift it. It was too heavy.

It was kicked out of her hand.

"Why?" said a voice.

Vida looked up with her good eye. The blond woman, Mary Catherine, was above her. So pretty, so American looking. Like a girl in a Coca-Cola ad.

Blood from the open artery in Vida's neck sprayed softly against the dirt wall in a pinkish mist. She could actually feel the life going out of her, her heart slowly losing whatever magic it was that made it beat. Her soul was slowly losing its grip on her body, like a man hanging off the edge of a cliff. She was dwindling now, winding down.

"For money?" Mary Catherine said sadly.

Vida could see that she was crying.

"They're just kids, you know. Kids. Don't you remember being a kid? Don't you have kids where you come from?"

Vida put her good hand to her belly, cupping it. Her baby. Her prince. The bright, searing pain of it all spiked through her. What would be, what would not.

The last thing she felt was a single tear running down the intact side of her face as the tunnel lights dimmed.

Epilogue

Chapter 104

IT WAS A LITTLE before noon when I got out of the state-police car in the crowded yard out in front of Cody's house. It looked like the entire Susanville police force was there, along with agents from the US Marshals and local FBI.

It also looked like a party. Out back, Cody had his huge, smoking barbecue going as some country-western song blasted from a radio in the window. Something about God being great and beer being good and people being crazy.

Count me in, I thought as I hit the stairs for the deck.

Cody actually handed me a beer after I shook his hand, despite the fact that it wasn't even noon. I immediately cracked open the can of Coors and tapped it to the one Cody was working on before I took a swig.

"Sorry for all the trouble I brought down on you, Aaron. I almost got you killed."

The old cowboy grinned.

"Many have tried, Mike. My two brothers, my drill instructor, the Vietcong. Hell, even my first wife. But luckily, none of them seemed to figure it out."

He pointed his beer toward the field beside the horse barn.

"Now, go see your family. They been missing you, I hear."

I walked over slowly, watching my kids play Frisbee with Cody's dogs. In the immaculate blue sky above them, a bunch of hawks were playing, swooping and circling as if they wanted to join in.

Beside the field, Mary Catherine and Seamus were sitting at a picnic table. Seamus saw me as I stepped up, but I put a finger to my lips as I stood behind Mary Catherine. I looked down at her, her blond hair, the self-possessed way she carried herself. If this was a dream, then I simply wasn't going to wake up.

I leaned forward and put my hands over her eyes.

"Guess who?" I said in her ear.

She stood, squealing, and hugged me, clung to me unabashedly. I clung back just as hard. At that moment, I felt it leave us. The animosity that had been between us for the last few months. All hatchets were buried, all fouls erased. Because we still had each other. We still had everything that counted.

Life and love and time.

Without hesitating, we also started kissing. When we broke it up, we were both crying. We looked over at Seamus, who was sitting there blinking up at us, flummoxed, speechless. I leaned over and loudly kissed Seamus on the top of his bald head.

"Have ye gone mad, Mike?" Seamus said, pushing me away as he rubbed his head. "You haven't gone Hollyweird on us down there in LA?"

Before I could answer, I turned around to the sound of screaming kids. They were still sweaty and dirty from their time in the hippie bomb shelter, and now they were covered in the soda and ice cream that Cody insisted they have for lunch. They looked like ragamuffins, like chimney sweeps, like the Little Rascals. In a word, beautiful.

I started crying again a little as I embraced

them one by one. I had thought they were dead, and now they were alive. It was like they'd been resurrected.

"Look at you," I said, wiping my eyes after I hugged Fiona. "You're filthy."

"I don't mean to be rude, Dad, but you don't look so hot yourself," Fiona said, pointing at my face bandage.

"Well, it's been a long day, hasn't it?" I said. "A long couple of days and nights for you."

"Face it, Pop. It's been a long nine months!" said Brian, fingering the Frisbee. "So what's the story?"

"What do you mean?" I said, feigning ignorance.

"He means, did you catch that Perrine guy?" Ricky said.

"Exactly," said Trent. "Do we have to move again?"

I pictured Perrine once more, on the stretcher with his head blown open. I'd been so pissed at the Mexicans, but that feeling was gone now. They'd done me a favor. Done the world a favor.

"Yes, Trent," I said. "I hate to break it to you, but unfortunately, we're going to have to move again."

I waited for the collective groan.

"Where this time?" asked Eddie, who sounded like he was about to cry.

"I don't know. I was thinking of this place—what's it called again?" I said, scratching my head.

"Nooo! It's so nowhere Dad doesn't even know what it's called!" Bridget cried out.

"No, wait," I said. "I remember now. It's Man . . . something. Manhattan? That's it. Manhattan. I hear West End Avenue is nice this time of year."

All around, little eyes and mouths opened in shock. There were more O's than in a box of Cheerios. The kids started cheering then. The cops and Cody looked over as my kids screamed and leaped up and down. The dogs started barking. Even Seamus got up and did a little jig before he threw an arm over my shoulder.

"God love ya, Michael Bennett!" he said.

When Alex Cross becomes the obsession of a murderous genius, no one's safe...especially not his family.

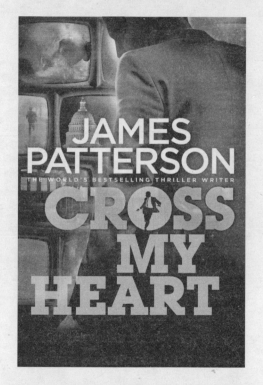

For an excerpt, turn the page.

'Twas The Night Before Easter

I TRUDGED AIMLESSLY through the dark empty streets of Washington, haunted by the memory of my son, Ali, telling me that the only way to kill a zombie was to destroy its brain.

It was three a.m. Storms punished the city.

I'd been walking like that for hours by then, but didn't feel hungry, or thirsty, or tired in any way. When lightning bolts ripped the sky and thunder clapped right over my head, I barely flinched. Not even the pouring rain could slow me or soothe the agony that burned through every inch of my body because of what had been done to my family. With every step I kept seeing Ali, Bree, Damon, Jannie, and Nana Mama in my mind. With every step the horror of what had happened to them ignited inside me all over again, and loneliness and grief and anger.

Is this what Thierry Mulch wanted? I kept asking myself.

Thierry Mulch had destroyed everything that I loved, everything I believed in. He'd gutted me and left a dead, soulless man doomed to endless, meaningless movement.

As I walked, I kept hoping Mulch or some anonymous street predator would appear and blow my head off with a shotgun, or crush it with an ax.

There was nothing more I wanted than that.

Sixteen Days Before

SITTING IN A parked work van on Fifth Street on a beautiful April morning, Marcus Sunday used high-definition Leica binoculars to monitor Alex Cross's house and felt a genuine thrill thinking that the great detective was sure to make some sort of appearance in the next half an hour.

After all, it was a Thursday and seven-thirty in the morning. Cross had to work. So did his wife. And his children had school to attend.

Sunday had no sooner had that thought when Regina Hope, Cross's ninety-one-year-old grandmother, came up the sidewalk from the direction of St. Anthony's Catholic Church. The old bird was tough and she was moving at a surprising clip despite the cane. She walked right by his van, barely giving it a glance.

Then again, why would she?

Sunday had attached magnetic signs to the van that advertised "Over the Moon Vacuum Cleaner Company." And behind the tinted glass he was wearing the uniform of said company, a real find at the Salvation Army. Fit perfectly.

The used vacuums in the back of the van were purchased at a secondhand store out in Potomac for sixty bucks apiece. The phony magnetic signs had been ordered online through Kinko's. So had the phony badge on his left shirt pocket. It read "Thierry Mulch."

A lithe, fit man in his late thirties with close-cropped, salt-and-pepper hair and slate gray eyes, Sunday checked his watch as Cross's grandmother disappeared inside the house. Then he took up a black binder stowed between the driver's seat and the center console.

Flipping it open, he noted the tabs on the first five section dividers, each marked with a name: Bree Stone, Ali Cross, Jannie Cross, Damon Cross, and Regina Hope, otherwise known as "Nana Mama."

Sunday went straight to the Regina Hope/Nana Mama section and filled in the exact time the old woman had entered the house and from what direction. Then, waiting for more sightings, he flipped to the back of the binder and found a four-page copy of the house's floor plan, which had conveniently been filed with the city planning board last month as part of Cross's application for permits to redo his kitchen and bathrooms.

Alternately studying the plan and the house itself, Sunday made notes on the diagrams regarding entries and exits, position of windows, landscaping, and the like. When Cross's wife, Bree Stone, also a detective with the D.C. Metro Police, came out on the porch to fill a bird feeder at 7:40, he recorded that act as well, and the fact that her backside looked glorious in a tight pair of jeans.

At 7:52, a truck bearing the logo "Dear Old House" pulled up in front of Cross's house, followed by a waste disposal company hauling a construction Dumpster. Out came the great detective onto the porch to greet the contractors and watch the unloading of the Dumpster. So did his grandmother, his wife, and two of his three children: fifteen-year-old Jannie and seven-year-old Ali.

Nice happy family, Sunday thought, studying them through the binoculars in turn. *The future for them seems bright. Looks full of promise. Doesn't it?*

Sunday allowed himself a smile, thinking that a

good deal of the fun in any adventure was the planning, the preparation, and the anticipation. Maybe more than half, he decided, enjoying the way his ever-fertile brain conjured up various dark ways to destroy the dream scenario unfolding before his eyes.

Then Dr. Alex left with his kids. The three of them walked past Sunday on the other side of Fifth, but the detective had barely looked at the work van.

Then again, why would he?

Sunday felt deflated after Cross and his children disappeared. It just wasn't as enjoyable scouting the house with the detective absent, almost like looking at a maze in desperate need of a rodent.

Sunday checked his watch, shut the binder, and put it away, feeling that he was a free, authentic man with a purpose that would not waver no matter the consequences. He started the van, thinking that wavering in any way was almost an insult to one's opponent. You had to want to destroy your enemy as much as he wanted to destroy you.

As Sunday drove off, he believed that he was up to his task. He also believed that Cross's family deserved the wickedness to come.

Each and every one of them.

Especially Dr. Alex.

MUCH LATER THAT same day, Kevin Olmstead, a soft-featured man in his late twenties, spotted the neon sign of Superior Spa, a massage parlor on Connecticut Avenue reputed to offer "happy endings."

Happy endings, Olmstead thought, running his fingers delicately over his smooth skin. Despite all the craziness in his head, he still knew the enduring value of a happy ending. He had enough money in his pocket, didn't he? He seemed to remember withdrawing cash from an ATM sometime that day.

Was that real? Do I still have the money?

Olmstead stopped, blinking, trying to get his thoughts to track again, a common problem recently. Then he dug in the right front pocket of his jeans, pulled out a wad of cash. He smiled again. He wasn't losing the old noodle when it came to sex *or* money.

Excited now, he hurried toward the massage parlor.

A man in a business suit, no tie, darted out the front door, looked furtively at Olmstead, and then scurried past him. Something about the man's demeanor activated searing memories of another massage parlor and another night.

Olmstead remembered most vividly the smell of citrus cleaner. And he vaguely recalled five bodies: three women in bathrobes, a Cuban in a striped bowling shirt and pork-pie hat, and a white guy in a cheap business suit, no tie, all shot at close range, all bleeding from head wounds.

Pain ripped through Olmstead's own skull, almost making him buckle to the ground. Was that real? Had that happened? Were there five people dead in a massage parlor in . . . where? Florida?

Or was that all a hallucination? Some blip in his meds?

Olmstead's mind surfed to another memory: a hand putting a Glock 21 pistol into a knapsack. Was it the knapsack on his shoulder? Was that his hand?

He looked at his hands and was surprised to see that he wore flesh-colored latex gloves. He was about to check the knapsack when the front door to the Superior Spa opened.

A young Asian woman looked out at him and smiled. She was dressed luridly in red hot pants, stiletto heels, and a T-shirt with "Goddess" spelled out in glitter.

"It okay," she said in halting English. "We no bite. You want come inside?"

Happy endings, Olmstead thought, and went toward her, feeling an overwhelming sense of gratitude for the invitation.

Everything about the Superior Spa was a marvel to Olmstead, even the thumping rap music. But what entranced him most was the smell of citrus disinfectant. As one might do with a freshly baked pie, he sniffed long and deep, flashing on the image of those corpses in Florida. Were they real? Was this?

He looked at the little thing in the red hot pants and said, "Any other girls working tonight?"

She pouted, poked him in the ribs. "What, you no like for me?"

"Oh, I like you fine, Little Thing. Just looking at options."

A big, hard-looking man in a black T-shirt came out from behind the maroon curtain. A second Asian woman followed him. Scrawnier than Little

483

Thing, she gazed at Olmstead with pink, watery, vacant eyes.

"See anything you like, bro?" the big guy asked.

"I like *them* both," Olmstead said.

"You think this is Bangkok or something? Make a choice."

"Cost?"

"Shower, soapy table, massage, seventy-five to me," the bouncer replied. "Anything extra, you talk to the girl. Anything extra, you pay the girl."

Olmstead nodded, pointed at Little Thing, who looked overjoyed.

The bouncer said, "Seventy-five and you gotta check your pack, bro."

Olmstead went soft-lidded, nodded. "Lemme get my wallet."

He swung the pack off his shoulder, set it on one of the plastic chairs, and unstrapped the top flap. He drew back the toggle that held shut the main compartment and tugged the pouch open. There was his wallet deep inside. And a beautiful Glock 21.

Was that a suppressor on the barrel? Was the weapon real? Was any of this?

Olmstead sure hoped so as he drew out the pistol. When it came to happy endings, a wet dream was rarely as satisfying as the real thing.

JUST AFTER EIGHT that night, I was getting ready to pack it in, head home, have a beer, see my wife and kids, and watch the last half of the game. So was John Sampson. It had been a long, grinding day for both of us, and we'd made little progress on the cases we were working. We both groaned when Captain Murphy appeared, blocking the doorway.

"Another one?" I said.

"You've got to be kidding," Sampson said.

"Not in the least," Murphy replied grimly. "We've got at least three dead at a massage parlor over on Connecticut. Patrolmen on the scene said it's a bloodbath just based on what they've seen in the front room. They're waiting for you and Sampson to go through the rest of the place.

Forensics is swamped, backed up. They'll be there as soon as they can."

I sighed, tossed the Kimmel file on my desk, and grabbed my blue "Homicide" windbreaker. Sampson did the same and drove us in an unmarked sedan over to Connecticut Avenue just south of Dupont Circle. Metro patrol officers had already set up a generous perimeter around the massage parlor. The first television-news camera crews were arriving. We hustled behind the yellow tape before they could spot us.

Officer K. D. Carney, a young patrolman and the initial responder, filled us in. At 7:55 p.m., dispatch took a 911 report from an anonymous male caller who said someone had "gone psycho inside the Superior Spa on Connecticut Ave."

"I was on my way home from work, and close by, so I was first on the scene," said Carney, a baby-faced guy with no eyebrows or lashes, and no hair on his face or forearms. I pegged him as a sufferer of alopecia areata universalis, a disorder that causes a total loss of body hair.

"Contamination?" I asked.

"None from me, sir," the young officer replied. "Took one look, saw three deceased, backed out, sealed the place. Front and back. There's an alley exit."

"Let's button up that alley too for the time being," I said.

"You want me to search it?"

"Wait for the crime-scene unit."

You could tell Carney was disappointed in the way only someone who desperately wants to be a detective could be disappointed. But that's the way it had to be. The fewer people with access to the crime scene the better.

"You know the history of this place, right?" Carney said as Sampson and I donned blue surgical booties and latex gloves.

"Remind us," Sampson said.

"Used to be called the Cherry Blossom Spa," Carney said. "It was shut down for involvement in sexual slavery a few years back."

I remembered now. I'd heard about it when I was still out working at Quantico for the FBI. The girls were underage, lured by the promise of easy entry into the United States, and enslaved here by Asian organized crime syndicates.

"How in God's name did this place ever reopen?" I asked.

Carney shrugged. "New ownership, I'd guess."

"Thanks, Officer," I said, heading toward the massage parlor. "Good work."

I opened the door, and we took three steps into a scene straight out of an Alfred Hitchcock movie.

The place reeked of some kind of citrus-based cleanser, and stereo speakers hummed with feedback. Sprawled in every ounce of her blood, an Asian female in red hot pants, heels, and a white T-shirt was sprawled on the floor. One round had hit her through the neck, taking out the carotid.

A second victim, also Asian female, dressed in a threadbare robe, lay on her side next to a maroon curtain. She was curled almost into a fetal position, but her shoulders were twisted slightly toward the ceiling. Her right eye was open and her fingers splayed. Blood stained her face and matted her hair, draining from the socket that used to hold her left eye.

The third victim, the massage parlor's night manager, was sprawled against a blood-spattered wall behind the counter. There was a look of surprise on his face and a bullet hole dead center of his forehead.

I counted four nine-millimeter shells around the bodies. It appeared that the killer had sprayed disinfectant all over the room. Streams of it stained the bodies, the furniture, and the floor. There was an empty five-gallon container of Citrus II Hospital

Germicidal Deodorizing Cleanser concentrate by the manager's corpse. We discovered a second empty container of it beyond the maroon curtain in the L-shaped hallway, as depressing a place as I've ever been, with exposed stud walls and grimy, unpainted plaster boards.

In the back right room, we found the fourth victim.

I'm a big man, and Sampson stands six foot five, but the bruiser facedown on the mattress was physically in a whole other league. I judged him at six foot eight and close to three hundred pounds, most of it muscle. He had longish brown hair that hung over his face, which was matted in blood.

I took several pictures with my phone, squatted down, and with my gloved fingers pushed back the hair to get a better look at the wound. When I did, his face was revealed and I stopped short.

"Sonofabitch," said Sampson, who was standing behind me. "Is that—?"

"Pete Francones," I said, nodding in disbelief. "The Mad Man himself."

Also by James Patterson

ALEX CROSS NOVELS

Along Came a Spider • Kiss the Girls • Jack and Jill •
Cat and Mouse • Pop Goes the Weasel • Roses are Red •
Violets are Blue • Four Blind Mice • The Big Bad Wolf •
London Bridges • Mary, Mary • Cross • Double Cross •
Cross Country • Alex Cross's Trial (*with Richard DiLallo*) •
I, Alex Cross • Cross Fire • Kill Alex Cross • Merry Christmas,
Alex Cross • Alex Cross, Run • Cross My Heart

THE WOMEN'S MURDER CLUB SERIES

1st to Die • 2nd Chance (*with Andrew Gross*) • 3rd Degree (*with
Andrew Gross*) • 4th of July (*with Maxine Paetro*) • The 5th
Horseman (*with Maxine Paetro*) • The 6th Target (*with Maxine
Paetro*) • 7th Heaven (*with Maxine Paetro*) • 8th Confession
(*with Maxine Paetro*) • 9th Judgement (*with Maxine Paetro*) •
10th Anniversary (*with Maxine Paetro*) • 11th Hour (*with Maxine
Paetro*) • 12th of Never (*with Maxine Paetro*) • Unlucky 13 (*with
Maxine Paetro*)

PRIVATE NOVELS

Private (*with Maxine Paetro*) • Private London (*with Mark
Pearson*) • Private Games (*with Mark Sullivan*) • Private: No. 1
Suspect (*with Maxine Paetro*) • Private Berlin (*with Mark Sullivan*) •
Private Down Under (*with Michael White*) •
Private L.A. (*with Mark Sullivan*)

NYPD RED

NYPD Red (*with Marshall Karp*) •
NYPD Red 2 (*with Marshall Karp, to be published June 2014*)

STAND-ALONE THRILLERS

Sail (*with Howard Roughan*) • Swimsuit (*with Maxine Paetro*) •
Don't Blink (*with Howard Roughan*) • Postcard Killers (*with Liza Marklund*) • Toys (*with Neil McMahon*) • Now You See Her (*with Michael Ledwidge*) • Kill Me If You Can (*with Marshall Karp*) •
Guilty Wives (*with David Ellis*) • Zoo (*with Michael Ledwidge*) •
Second Honeymoon (*with Howard Roughan*) • Mistress
(*with David Ellis*)

NON-FICTION

Torn Apart (*with Hal and Cory Friedman*) •
The Murder of King Tut (*with Martin Dugard*)

ROMANCE

Sundays at Tiffany's (*with Gabrielle Charbonnet*) •
The Christmas Wedding (*with Richard DiLallo*) •
First Love (*with Emily Raymond*)

FAMILY OF PAGE-TURNERS

MAXIMUM RIDE SERIES

The Angel Experiment • School's Out Forever •
Saving the World and Other Extreme Sports •
The Final Warning • Max • Fang • Angel •
Nevermore

DANIEL X SERIES

The Dangerous Days of Daniel X (*with Michael Ledwidge*) •
Watch the Skies (*with Ned Rust*) • Demons and Druids
(*with Adam Sadler*) • Game Over (*with Ned Rust*) •
Armageddon (*with Chris Grabenstein*)

For more information about James Patterson's novels, visit
www.jamespatterson.co.uk

Or become a fan on Facebook